Secrets
of the
Conclave

to David
for always believing

CHAPTER 1

NYONA

A BRANCH SNAPPED. Nyona dropped into a squat, her heart in her throat. She pivoted slowly on the game trail, her fingers trailing along the ground. Shadows from the trees prevented her from seeing too far into the distance as she scanned the forest around her. *There it is again.* She focused on a spot to her left, slightly down the hill. Nothing. Just when she started to fear the worst, a young deer emerged from a cluster of vegetation, breaking another branch.

A sigh of relief escaped Nyona's lips. *I knew it*, she exulted. Those who might be following her would never make so much noise. She breathed in and out slowly to calm her pounding heart. After the animal continued on its way, she brushed the dirt from her hands and resumed her walk up the hill.

Soon, the muted clanging of bells reached her ears. The familiar sound meant she didn't have much farther to go. Brien probably was worried by now, though what she'd found—that his source, cultivated over many months, was correct—would make up for it.

Nyona slid her thumbs under the straps of her pack, shifting the weight of the books. A smile twitched at the corners of her lips. Her aching shoulders were worth it: she finally had what she needed to truly protect Tovi.

Thinking of her daughter made her quicken her pace, and soon Nyona crested the hill and emerged from the forest. The clearing contained two humble structures: a wooden barn with a line of windows up high and a squat, stone house with hardly any windows at all. *Home.* She ducked under a perimeter of red and yellow flags, which kept even healers away. Brien's idea had worked wonders. If no one visited, no one could unravel their ruse.

One head turned her way, then others, and a cacophony of bells and bleats followed. A trip of goats ran toward her, the animals bumping and jostling for position. Six months ago, they'd been skinny, starved beasts. Now they provided a steady supply of milk, and feed grain was cheap.

"I know, I know," Nyona told the goats that bunched around her. "Just a moment." She swatted away a doe that was nibbling at the cloth of her leggings, then shrugged out of her pack and slung it onto a hook attached to the outside of the barn. When she opened the barn door, the goats rushed around her to get inside. Late-afternoon sun filtering through the windows above dimly lit her surroundings.

"There you are!" Brien stepped out of the front stall, grinning broadly with relief. He'd wanted to make the daylong trip to Aldham, Nyona knew, but an itinerant scholar was a role that a man simply could not play. He kneed his way past the goats and leaned down to give her a quick kiss. "Is everything okay?"

Nyona didn't hesitate to respond. "Yes," she said, her mouth curving up into an answering smile. "I found it! I'm sorry it took so long, but the shop wasn't open when I arrived. The bookseller was ill, apparently, so I had to wait for her assistant. She accepted the research credentials you got for me without question, but it took forever to dig through everything they had." It would probably take days to get rid of all the dust in her lungs.

"Wait—my source never mentioned an assistant. What was her

name? How long has she been there?" Brien's dark eyes grew darker still in suspicion.

"I don't remember. She said she'd only started recently." Nyona patted his arm. "I'm sure your information was just a little out of date." Brien's source—whomever it was—certainly wasn't omniscient. Information traveled slowly in the absence of Adepts.

"You may be right. I don't think he'd been to Aldham in some time." He scratched at the short, black hair on his chin. "But did she see what you found? We could count on the bookseller keeping quiet, but…"

Nyona shook her head. "No, no, don't worry. The shop was busy by the time I left, so it was easy to keep the book hidden away from the ones I actually bought. To her, I'm sure I was just another scholar looking for new additions to my collection." Though for all the attention the bookseller's assistant had given her, Nyona probably could have stolen all of the books in her pack rather than just the one.

Brien nodded, then asked, "You're certain?"

"Absolutely. Even if she'd seen it, she wouldn't have realized what it was. The book appears to be a history of Corinas—a boring subject not worthy of much notice." Nyona turned and leaned backward against him, then took hold of his arms and wrapped them around her. "And just in case, I came home through the marsh. That's also why I'm back so late. No one would have followed me through there; it's too risky if you don't know where to put your feet." The line of green film coating her boots revealed her own missteps, but she'd keep that—and the fact that she'd been frightened by a silly deer—to herself.

Brien kissed the top of her head. "I suppose you're right," he murmured into her hair.

"Of course I am, love." She squeezed his arms, then disengaged from his embrace. "Is Tovi still inside the house?"

"She came out for a bit earlier, before lunch, but I haven't seen her since then. I think she might be asleep." Brien pushed an errant goat aside to clear their path, and his brow creased anew as they walked outside. "Should we be worried?"

"I don't know. I don't know what to expect from her at this point; it's all new for me."

"Not as new as it is for me." He raised an eyebrow, a hint of his usual easy smile at the corners of his lips. A dimple dotted one cheek. "The book should help us both, yes?"

"I certainly hope so." Nyona pulled her pack from the hook and slung one strap over her shoulder. Shadows extended over the clearing as the sun dipped behind the hill. "You're not still planning to head back to Travum tonight, are you?" It would take him half the night. Brien made sure to travel far for employment and supplies, to places no one would ever care to follow him home from.

"They're expecting me, but I'd rather spend the night here. If I leave right before dawn, I should be fine. I'll come up with some excuse."

"All right. I'll go start supper, then, and check on Tovi. You're finishing up out here?"

Brien nodded, then headed back into the barn to attend to the goats.

Nyona walked along the broken cobbles to the house, musing. While she had tried to appear hopeful for Brien, she was not at all confident the book would help. Her brief review in the shop had revealed that the book did contain what she sought, which made the risk in obtaining it worthwhile. Yet whether she could apply that information was an open question. It had become clear long ago that she didn't know what she was doing when it came to Tovi's training. But she had to try *something*. If Tovi didn't learn some control soon, then...no. Best not to think of that.

Nyona leaned against the wall of the house with one hand, her palm finding a rare spot devoid of moss, and pulled off her boots with the other. She unlatched the door and entered the front room but left the door open to circulate the stale mustiness inside with fresh evening air. She dropped her pack on a chair. Her shoulders ached. It wasn't common for her to carry a pack filled with books all day.

This late in the day, little light came through the windows and door. Nyona reached for the lantern beside the chair, intending to adjust the flame, then jerked her hand back as bright light surged through the glass to illuminate the room. She straightened and glanced up. "Tovi. We've talked about this," she said in a neutral tone. *Getting angry never helped.*

Her daughter peeked over the railing of the sleeping loft. "I wanted to help," the child said in a soft voice. "You seem tired."

"I know, love. But you mustn't practice without my instruction. You know we have to be very careful."

Tovi's green eyes blinked underneath her mop of dark, disheveled curls. "Then why teach me at all?"

Nyona sighed and beckoned for Tovi to come down to her. *If only she were older. Then I could tell her everything.* Yet her five-year-old child already perceived so much. Would it really be so hard to explain?

Tovi climbed down the loft's ladder and hopped the last few rungs to the floor. Nyona squatted and took the girl's hands in her own. Their eyes met. "I'm teaching you so you know how to control your Ability until you're old enough to not have to worry about it anymore. And I'm teaching you so you know how to resist using your Ability unless it is absolutely necessary," she said, pushing the end of Tovi's nose with her finger on the syllables of the last two words. Tovi dissolved into giggles, and Nyona couldn't help but grin at her daughter's mirth. "Now, go outside and help Brien feed the goats."

Tovi ran out of the house, forgetting her shoes. Nyona walked to the door as Brien caught Tovi by the waist and swung her up into the air. Tovi's breathless laughter carried across the clearing. Nyona's smile disappeared as she thought about what would happen to her family—and what they might be forced to do—if she failed to teach Tovi how to resist doing what came naturally.

She glanced at the lantern and its flickering light. Tovi had been experimenting far too much lately. It was hard to fault the child. When she was Tovi's age, she had used her Ability every day under the Masters' careful supervision. They certainly never allowed any child to proceed until they deemed her ready. *Masters control Ability,* they always said, and punishment was swift for any Adept who dared to disobey. Maybe she should try some of that iron-fisted discipline on Tovi.

Nyona laughed quietly to herself as she moved into the kitchen. As if she could act a Master! She filled a pot with water from the cistern and placed it on the stove. Rummaging through the cupboard, she pulled out some onions, potatoes, and salted beef. She could have purchased more food supplies in Aldham, but she hadn't wanted to linger. It had been only six years since she'd left the Conclave, and someone might suspect she wasn't who she pretended to be.

Once the soup began to simmer, Nyona sliced days-old bread and some hard cheese. She had almost finished when Tovi bounded back into the house. "Can I help?" Tovi asked, balancing on her toes against the table.

"Why don't you set out the cups and bowls?" Nyona sprinkled pepper into the pot and stirred the mix with a spoon. Pottery clanked behind her.

"Mother, will I learn something new soon?" Tovi asked, as if their earlier conversation had not ended but merely paused. "I'm tired of practicing what I already know."

"No. Especially given that you keep practicing when you shouldn't be. I'll let you know when you're ready for the next step." *Once I know what the next step is.* Nyona hoped beyond hope that the book would have the answers she sought. But the point was to teach Tovi how to resist using her Ability—would the book speak to this? Doubt gnawed at her insides.

Even if she wanted to teach Tovi in truth, she wouldn't know what to do. Allowing an Adept to do too much, too soon only ever resulted in harm—both to the Adept and to those around her. At the Conclave, a young Adept of Tovi's age would be surrounded by older Adepts and Masters to guide her path. Truth be told, a normal five-year-old Adept already would be well versed in advanced techniques.

Of course, Tovi wasn't a "normal" Adept. Nyona still wasn't sure how the girl was an Adept at all.

Outside, Brien whistled a random tune as he washed his hands and forearms using water from the rain barrel at the corner of the house. He came inside, closing the door behind him, and sniffed loudly. "Smells like I'm just in time!" Grinning, he tousled Tovi's hair, then picked up the breadboard and set it on the table.

Nyona lifted the mixing spoon to her lips and slurped. "Go ahead and sit down. I'll dish this up."

Tovi climbed into one of the chairs. Her impatience with her mother seemingly forgotten, she chatted amiably with Brien and Nyona about the goats, the flowers she'd picked that morning, and the squirrel she'd chased up a tree. Once Nyona brought over the bowls of soup, they continued their conversation while they ate.

It felt almost as if they were a normal family.

Once the meal was complete, Tovi slid from her chair and scampered up the ladder to the sleeping loft. She greeted her toys and began acting out a nonsensical story involving horses and singing flowers. Nyona and Brien exchanged fond smiles as they carried dishes back to the kitchen's worktable. It was good to hear Tovi be a child.

"How's she doing?" Brien asked in a hushed voice.

Nyona shook her head. Up in the loft, singing flowers laid siege to a city. "She's so impatient, and she's not even trying to hide it anymore. She used her Ability to increase the lamp's flame right in front of me, and who knows what she was doing before I got home. If she keeps this up, someone will notice."

"Have you considered that—maybe—it might be time to—"

"No!" Nyona took a calming breath, then lowered her voice to a whisper. "I will not do that to her. I will not."

"Even if the alternative is the Conclave finding her?"

"It's not either-or," she argued. "I'll do what I must to avoid that choice. I've seen what can happen after an implant, Brien. I told you. Tovi could go mad, or worse. I will not risk that. I'll find a way. The *book* will show me the way."

"It'll take you time to read and apply it, though, even if it contains what you seek." He sighed, then wrapped his arms around her waist, pulling her back against his chest. "I don't want anything bad to happen to her, either. I promised you that I'd protect you both.

And I have and will. But we can't go on like this forever. We have to stop running sometime."

Resentment flared, but she immediately quenched its flames. It wasn't fair to expect Brien to understand—truly understand. And he *had* given up a lot to be with them. She grasped his arms. "Please—I don't want to argue about this now. We just need to get through each day as it comes. I'll start reading the book tonight; maybe by the morning, we'll have an answer."

"Sure," he said, doubt clear in his voice and deep creases of worry between his brows. "But if we don't find help soon, we may reach the point where an implant is the only option if we want to keep her." He pulled away. "Well, in any case, I'm going to try to get some sleep. I've an early start tomorrow." With that, he retreated to their bedroom and closed the door.

Nyona bit at her lip. How long had he felt this way?

The night outside had grown quiet, and Tovi's floral machinations seemed to be ending. Nyona crossed the room and picked up her pack from the chair. Sitting in the vacated space, she rummaged inside the pack, removing several packages wrapped in brown paper and twine. Most were unimportant. The small one with the extra package knot, though—that was the one she'd traveled to find.

She picked at the complicated knots with a fingernail. It was Brien who had first learned about the possibility of the book. Nyona still wasn't sure exactly how he'd found out about it—he kept his sources secret, even from her. Once he found out that copies still existed, he made discrete inquiries at her urging, until he found the bookseller in Oldham. She carried a special collection of old and rare books, including those the Conclave wished didn't exist. While such books were not meant for the general population, scholars were allowed greater access. It had taken two months' worth of Brien's wages as a day laborer to get a forged set of research credentials, but oh, the doors that had opened to her as a result...

The twine slipped away. She slid her fingers under the edge of the paper and carefully flipped the package over and over until she exposed its contents. It didn't look like much from its plain, brown cover. *A History of Corinas*. A boring, innocuous title. And indeed, it began much as any other history book.

Yet after about fifty pages, in what seemed to be random intervals, lines describing the use and control of Ability began to appear. Nyona rubbed her temple absently while she turned the pages of the book, searching. Somewhere within this jumbled mess of words was a solution for Tovi.

Ah, my love. How can I help you?

Nothing was how it should have been. Tovi's mere conception had been a surprise, let alone when she displayed hints of Ability as an infant. Nyona had refused to accept it at first, but as Tovi grew and started using her Ability unconsciously, willful blindness was no longer an option. Nyona had tried training her using the techniques she remembered from the Masters, but she'd been so young then. And it wasn't as if she'd ever become a Master herself. She didn't really know what to do to guide Tovi's path.

Nyona shook her head. How much time had been lost to her own stubbornness and refusal to accept what was happening before her eyes? There was no reason to delay any longer. She began reading this puzzle of a book anew, but her mind and body soon succumbed to the efforts of the day, and she slipped into sleep.

A sound jarred Nyona awake. Moonlight illuminated the room in a milky glow, and a breath of air stirred against her cheek. The front door was ajar. A quick glance up to the sleeping loft revealed Tovi's absence. *Not again.* More annoyed than worried, Nyona slipped her feet into her shoes.

A muffled shriek brought Nyona to her feet. Anger instantly forgotten, she raced for the door. It flew inward, smacking her full in the face. Reeling, she found herself prone with a great weight on her back. A filthy hand shoved a rag into her mouth, and someone wrenched her arms behind her back, roughly binding her hands behind her buttocks. She turned her head to the side, but she could hardly breathe due to the hammering of her heart and the pain from connecting with the door.

Suddenly, Brien appeared in his nightshirt, armed with the short sword he kept under the bed. He charged a figure in black near the door, never pausing even when the first dagger drove into his chest. Then a second one embedded in his throat, dropping him to his knees. He choked and flailed at the knife's hilt for what seemed an eternity before he toppled sideways, lifeless.

Nyona tried to scream, but couldn't do much more than gurgle past the gag. Tears burned in her eyes. *I brought this upon him.* She'd been the one pushing him to make more inquiries, to take on more risk—and now, her worst fears had come to pass.

Despite all their efforts to hide, the Conclave had finally found them.

"Fires, Sonya, what did you do that for?" said the man who sat on top of Nyona. "Captain's not going to be happy."

"What was I supposed to do? The lunatic came right at me. Besides, you're the one who said he wouldn't be here, so be glad I'm always prepared. This could have ended badly." The lamp flickered on, and a woman dressed in close-fitting leathers reached down to retrieve her blades from Brien's corpse. Nyona's eyes widened in recognition. The bookseller's assistant glanced her way and sighed with impatience. "Why aren't you finished with her?"

"Sorry. I got distracted."

"Well, get on with it. It's not like she'll cooperate at this point." The woman surveyed the books scattered on the ground. "Once you're done, throw all of these in the pack. We'll sort them out later."

"Fine," the man replied sourly. He shifted suddenly and lifted Nyona's head from the floor. *This is it,* she thought, struggling and kicking. The man pulled the rag from her mouth and dumped the contents of a vial down her throat before she could put voice to a scream. She sputtered and choked on the acrid fluid, and the room started to spin. Her struggles soon ceased and her senses dulled. The man got off her back. As Nyona lay on the floor, unable to move and with her vision constricting down into darkness, she thought she heard the woman say something about taking the girl.

Chapter 2

Alia

Alia opened her eyes and squinted at the light streaming through the window. With a groan, she threw her arm over her eyes. Morning had come too soon, as it always did. For a few moments, she tried to convince herself that she could return to sleep, but the incessant chirping of birds dashed that dream. She breathed in, filling her lungs, and exhaled in a rush.

A rustle drew her attention to the bed on the other side of the room. Sarabie still slept with the edge of her blanket scrunched under her neck. Measured breaths from between her lips periodically puffed a wisp of hair away from her face. Sarabie's eye mask blocked out light, but even so, she normally was the first to wake. Yet the last few weeks, she had been sleeping more and more.

Extended sleep was one of the last signs before Ascension. They both knew it, but as her best friend, Sarabie had spared Alia's feelings and pretended like it wasn't so. It wasn't as if talking about it could change the way things were.

Alia stopped that train of thought before it caused her to burrow under the covers anew. It was well past time to be up, and she could not be late again for Ritual. Being late meant that they'd deny her entry to the Ritual Hall, and the punishments for missing the weekly ceremony were becoming rather tedious.

Just last week, they'd made her monitor the area around Travum for the entire night. Such a pointless task—Travum was a small mining town with no Adept in residence nor even one on temporary assignment. There simply had been no reason, other than punishment, why the Masters would force her to monitor an area with no Adepts for unauthorized use of Ability. Given that the assignment was an obvious farce, she'd risked a well-needed nap. It wasn't the first time she'd disobeyed the Masters without detection, and she was certain it wouldn't be the last.

That said, it wouldn't do to purposely attract even more of the Masters' ire. Not that they would do much more than keep her from a full night's sleep. Some of the Masters liked to make noises about a more *permanent* solution to what they viewed as intolerable behavior, but those were empty threats. The last time the Masters had implanted an Adept as punishment, Alia hadn't been much older than a child. They wouldn't dare implant an Adept now; they needed every one they had left.

Alia stretched her arms into the air over her head, clasping her hands together to pull her shoulders away from her body. Her jaw popped as she yawned. Resigned, she kicked the blankets away from her legs. Outside in the courtyard, tall, thin trees swayed in a gentle breeze, their leaves fluttering against one another. Perfectly groomed rose bushes dotted the perimeter. Walls of yellow and amber stone, punctuated by windows, rose up nearly to the tops of the trees. It all presented a graceful, albeit boring, picture. In all of her nineteen years—or at least as far back as she could remember— there'd never been a flower out of place or a broken branch on the ground. Never changing. Dull.

She crossed the room and gently rocked Sarabie's shoulder. "Wake up," she said. When her friend did not respond, Alia shook harder. "Come on, wake up. Ritual's about to begin."

Sarabie woke with a start. She flipped her eye mask over her forehead and raised herself up on her elbows. Her long, black hair twisted around the mask in snarled tufts. "What?" she asked, rubbing at an eye.

"Ritual. It starts soon."

"Already? It seems like we just had Ritual."

"Yes. Last week." Alia snorted at her own joke. "Seriously, I can't be late again. I'm exhausted from all these off-hour duties. And you don't want to end up like me—so get up."

Sarabie pulled off the eye mask and discarded it on her nightstand. "It would be one thing if you only had to work at night, but you have morning duty one day, night the next, and who knows what the day after that!" She shoved herself off the edge of her bed and walked to the lavatory, continuing the conversation as she went. "They must have a good reason, though. The Masters wouldn't waste your Ability, even if the duty is meant to be unpleasant for you."

Wouldn't they? Alia thought. *Sarabie the eternal optimist.* Sarabie never questioned their purpose or the Masters who ruled them, and she even looked forward to what came after Ascension, believing with all her heart that an Adept's destiny was her duty. To be fair, most Adepts shared Sarabie's beliefs. It was what they'd all been taught, after all. At least she didn't seem to care that Alia held unorthodox views, and despite her blind faith, Alia was still glad to have Sarabie as a friend. It wasn't as if she had many of those to spare.

Alia shook her head as she poked around inside her wardrobe. Perhaps all those years of wishing and hoping to avoid the inevitable had resulted in her current predicament. The Masters certainly hadn't yet determined why only she out of all her Initiate showed no signs of progressing toward Ascension. While Alia was unenthusiastic about what would come *after*, she didn't want to be left behind.

"Why so quiet?" Sarabie asked as she returned to the room clad in a white robe.

Alia shrugged. "No reason." She retrieved her own white robe from a jumbled pile at the bottom of her wardrobe and pulled it over her head. "Ready? If we're late, you'll get in trouble, too."

Sarabie laughed. "Oh, don't worry. I'm good, remember?" She spun in a circle and her robe billowed out around her ankles. "Fine," she said as Alia glared in only half-jest, "I will hurry for your sake."

Alia rolled her eyes. "Thanks." She glanced at the clock.

"Just one more minute, I promise," Sarabie said. Standing before the mirror, she brushed the tangles from her hair with quick strokes, then secured it along her temples with hairpins she plucked from the dressing table. "You're lucky you don't have to deal with hair. It wastes so much time."

Alia's bare scalp reflected in the mirror in sharp contrast to Sarabie's long, dark locks. Pale green eyes stared back at her above a small nose and a pair of thin lips. She scratched at her forehead, keenly aware of her missing eyebrows. From what she'd been told, she'd had hair when she was very young, but it fell out when she was only a few years old. The medics never determined the cause, but upon confirming the affliction didn't negatively affect her Ability, the Masters had left it alone as an unexplained oddity.

An apt description of me as a whole, it seems.

"Done!" Sarabie patted a few flyaway strands into place.

"Finally." Alia rolled her eyes and opened their door. "Let's go." A smattering of girls in white robes rushed past them. She beckoned to Sarabie. "Quickly. Really, we'll be late if we don't leave this second!"

Sarabie hastened out the door, and Alia latched it behind them. Halfway down the wide hallway, Alia realized she'd left her bed in disarray. If the Masters inspected their room that morning, she'd be in for another unpleasant assignment tonight.

It didn't help to dwell on what she couldn't do anything about, so instead she focused on walking as quickly as she could toward the Ritual Hall so as not to compound her problems. Fortunately, they didn't have far to go. Their room was one of the last residences in this wing of the Conclave, and its location had saved Alia many times from being late even more frequently.

Their path turned sharply to the right, and they hurried under an ornate archway to enter a narrow, stark corridor. Bronzed sconces held lamps, and in the distance, more girls in white robes dropped away from view.

The stairs at the end of the hall were ancient and steep. Alia and Sarabie slowed their pace as they approached to avoid missing the first step. The intricately carved doors at the bottom of the stairs were still open, and the sound of conversation drifted up toward them. Alia sighed in relief, then laughed when she realized Sarabie had done the same thing at the exact same time. Sarabie grinned and took her hand. Together, they carefully navigated the steps—all fifty-three of them—to the bottom.

The Ritual Hall was awash in a sea of white. Plenty of space remained near the platform below, but as the oldest Adepts, Alia and Sarabie sat in the back. Craning her neck, Alia spotted an open space far along the last row of curved benches on the left side of the room. She tugged at Sarabie's sleeve and pointed. "Over there."

Sarabie nodded, then led them past those already seated, giving greetings to some and apologies to others as they squeezed and bumped their way through the crowd. Everyone she spoke to acknowledged her with a smile, and once seated, she chatted amiably with the Adept seated next to her. Unlike Alia, Sarabie possessed an easy social grace that seemed as natural to her as smiling.

Alia folded her hands in her lap and waited for Ritual to begin. As the moments passed, her eyes wandered around the large, semicircular room. Curved beams of dark, polished wood supported the high ceiling, while the benches they sat on—made of the same wood—mimicked the ceiling's concentric pattern. A wide, straight aisle cut the benches' pattern in half from the entry doors down to a raised platform. A second door, lacking any carving at all, was set in the stone wall behind the platform. To the door's right, a gorgeous red-and-silver-patterned tapestry hung against the wall.

Sarabie nudged Alia's side with an elbow. "Do you see Marta?" she whispered.

Alia leaned forward to look down the curve of Adepts to her left and right, then surveyed the top row on the other side of the room as well. "No. Do you think she's still in the Ward? It's been six days, though. I hope everything's okay." A horrible thought suddenly washed over her. "Wait a minute, what if it's over for her, and it's time for her to—"

"Oh my goodness!" Sarabie interrupted, her face lighting up in a broad smile. "It must be so! If she'd simply been ill, we would've heard something by now." She clapped the tips of her fingers together in a quick spurt of solo applause. "Oh, if this is true—can you believe it? How exciting for her to be the first!" Sarabie immediately turned back to the Adept next to her and shared their suspicions.

Alia looked down and picked at her fingernails. She should be happy for Marta; after all, Seclusion was supposed to be a wonderful, restful place after so many years of service. Yet she couldn't help but think that if Marta were the first of their Initiate to enter Seclusion, then others—like Sarabie, who was showing all the signs—would soon follow. It was bad enough to lose Marta, one of only a handful of Adepts still friendly to Alia, but to lose Sarabie...

The doors to the Ritual Hall closed with a thud, returning Alia to the present. All conversation amongst the Adepts ceased as six women in gray robes walked down the aisle. Unlike the Adepts' plain, white robes, silver decorations of rank adorned the Masters' garb. Alia started when she realized that one of the women, who bore only a single silver stripe on her left sleeve, was someone who had entered Seclusion almost two years ago. If the last Initiate was starting to come out, then Alia's Initiate would definitely be on its way in—including Sarabie.

Once the six Masters reached the platform, they fanned out to stand along its base. Alia stood with everyone else. She grasped Sarabie's hand, then reached for the hand of the Adept several feet to her left and closed her eyes. Within the space of two slow breaths, she connected with the Adepts around her. In her mind, members of her own Initiate were strong and sure, while the youngest Adepts, still new to their training, were like butterflies skittering from one flower to the next.

Three deep notes thrummed through their collective consciousness. They inhaled and exhaled as one. "Who dares to intrude upon Adepts?" they asked.

"Those who were once as you," came the answer.

"What is your purpose?"

"We seek only to guide your way."

"You may enter."

As if we had a choice. Keeping a thread of connection to the bond, Alia opened her eyelids halfway. Masters wearing robes emblazoned with varying amounts of silver stripes and whorls entered the Ritual Hall through the door in the back. It was a large group—much larger than usual. They almost filled the platform.

Alia's eyes opened wide when Master Gersemi emerged from the crowd. Her robe was so covered in silver markings that hardly any gray cloth showed. Even her brown hair, which she had gathered and pinned to one side of her head in a long cascade, had strands of silver. *It must be true, then.* The Conclave's Headmaster would not be at Ritual unless something important was going to happen. At the edge of the platform, Master Gersemi surveyed the room. Alia snapped her eyes shut—the last thing she needed was for the older woman to notice her distraction—and immersed herself in the bond.

After several more minutes, the low tonal bell sounded again. On its third beat, the warmth of her fellow Adepts drifted away from her mind. Alia freed her hands and sat. Although she found Ritual mostly a waste of time—she and the rest of the senior Adepts had heard the histories so often they could recite them by heart—she did like the beginning. It made her feel as if she were a welcome part of the community of Adepts, even if only for a few minutes each week.

Silent anticipation thrummed within the Hall as they waited for Master Gersemi to begin. After what seemed an inordinate amount of time, she spoke, her deep voice resonating through the Hall. "Welcome, Adepts. Today is a good day." She paused again before she continued. "First Initiate, please stand."

Alia stood once again, as did Sarabie and the other girls who comprised their Initiate. The twenty-one remaining Adepts of the

First Initiate were all around nineteen years old, though none of them knew their ages for certain. They'd originally had thirty members, but two had died during some sort of training mishap in their very early years, and six others during the plague that had ripped through Corinas seven years ago. Then, of course, there was Marta.

Master Gersemi looked up at them with a smile, though it seemed to flicker when her eyes passed over Alia. She thought it might be her imagination, but then Sarabie squeezed her hand. *She noticed it, too.* Wonderful—the attention of the Conclave's Headmaster wasn't exactly something she craved.

After her perusal of the First Initiate, Master Gersemi continued. "Today, we bring to you one who was once as you." She gestured behind her, and a path opened up to the back door through which they had just entered. A Master opened the door.

Marta entered the Hall wearing a black robe devoid of any decoration. The cloth stood in sharp contrast to the blonde hair that flowed in loose ringlets around her shoulders. She passed the gathering of Masters to the front of the platform. As she came to stand next to Master Gersemi, a smile threatened at the corners of her lips.

Master Gersemi took Marta's hand. "This is Marta, of the First Initiate. Today is her Ascension." A murmur of excitement passed through the Hall. "Do not be saddened by her loss, for she is our future," she said, reciting the traditional words. "Let us celebrate and give thanks for her loyal service."

Two Masters approached Marta. She held her arms above her head as they removed her black robe. Intricate designs of red dye covered her pale, bare skin. One Master shook out a bundle of deep red cloth and pulled it over Marta's nakedness. The second placed a band of silver set with red jewels over her forehead. Master Gersemi kissed Marta lightly on each cheek and embraced the young woman close.

And just like that, it was done.

The Hall erupted with cheers and applause. Alia clapped along with everyone else, composing her face into what she hoped was an acceptable smile. Even though she'd expected this, actually seeing it happen caused a sinking sensation to swoop into her stomach. There was no way she could mimic Sarabie's ridiculously wide grin.

Sarabie's eyes glistened. "I'm so happy for her! I never thought she would be the first of us. Did you?"

"No. I thought maybe Kati—or you."

"What? Me? I'm nowhere near Ascension." She laughed. "You're being silly."

"You sleep more and more each week."

"Well, that doesn't mean anything, really. I've just been tired." She brushed away streaks of tears on her cheeks with the back of her hand. "Anyway. Today is about Marta. Let's go before it's too difficult to reach her."

Alia followed Sarabie down to the platform. Chaos surrounded Marta as Adepts and Masters tried to congratulate her good fortune all at once. Sarabie passed Kati, Marta's roommate, whose smile seemed nearly as forced as Alia's. To be the first of an Initiate to enter Seclusion was a distinct honor. Marta would receive many unique gifts now and a prime placement once she became a Master. Kati had to be bursting with envy.

Alia paused next to her. "How are you doing?" she asked, speaking just loud enough to overcome the commotion surrounding them.

Kati started. "Alia! Don't sneak up on me like that." She fanned at her face with her hands. "I am well! I'm so pleased Marta is entering Seclusion. She is such a wonderful gir—um, woman, I mean, and I just know she will bring us a new Adept soon."

"Oh, I'm sure she will. But aren't you a little disappointed you weren't the first?"

Kati shot her a sharp look. "Of course not! Why would you ask such a thing? It would be horrible and selfish for anyone to be disappointed in Marta's success." She tossed her hair over a shoulder and turned her back to Alia.

Liar, Alia thought as she sidled through the crowd. Then again, what had she expected? It's not as if Kati would have admitted her true feelings to Alia, even if they had been by themselves.

By the time Alia had worked her way to Marta, Sarabie was already there, yammering on to the soon-to-be Secluded. The wait gave Alia time to admire Marta's crown. The silver-and-ruby band lay across her forehead, with the largest jewel at the center of her brow. Only the first of an Initiate to cross into Seclusion received a Crown of Ascension set with rubies. The rest would receive crowns set with garnets—except for the last person. Red-colored glass would adorn that Adept's crown.

Sarabie finally stepped away. Mustering everything she had to keep a warm smile fixed on her face, Alia took Sarabie's place and reached up to embrace Marta. "Congratulations," she said. "I wish you all the best."

Marta smiled back, seemingly genuine in her pleasure to see Alia. "Thank you. I know you all wondered if anything was wrong with me, but they wouldn't let me leave the Ward until they were sure. I thought they'd at least let me tell Kati beforehand, but they didn't."

"How do you feel?"

"Wonderful! I'm so excited and honored to be the first to enter Seclusion! I can't wait to see what it's like."

"Actually, I was wondering how you felt—you know…"

"Oh. That." Marta's smile faded. "They tell us what happens, of course, but I don't think you really can prepare. I felt it leaving me all week." Her voice dropped to a near-whisper. "And when you all did the bonding Ritual today? I was just on the other side of the door. I shouldn't have, but I tried to participate. I felt, well—*something*—but it was just residue. In a few days, I imagine even that will be gone."

Alia suddenly felt ashamed for asking. It was known that the transition from Adept to Secluded could be a difficult one. The rumor was that the Masters created the Ascension ceremony and related fanfare to make the loss easier to bear. She shouldn't have reminded Marta of this on what was meant to be a happy day.

"But just think," Alia said, hoping to change the subject. "No more duties for you! You'll spend at least a year getting pampered—you'll get to sleep when you want, eat what you want, and be showered with gifts! How wondrous is that?"

Marta gave a delicate shrug. "I won't miss our duties, that's true —especially night duties—though I'll still be occupied with lessons. But I will miss all of you," she said quietly. "It will be strange to spend the next few months without seeing any of the people I've lived my entire life with."

"By the time you see me again, you'll probably be a Master," Alia joked. Marta rewarded her attempt to lighten the mood with a laugh. Everyone knew she'd be the last of their Initiate to reach Seclusion. *At least I'll get a special crown, too, even if it is made of glass.*

She hugged Marta one last time, and as she stepped away from the platform, another Adept took her place. Returning to the top of the Hall, she passed the youths of the Eighth and newest Initiate. Which of them would be the first to Ascend? There weren't that many of them. They were all so small. *So young. And so naive.* They did not yet know how the Masters used them.

Soon, the congratulations ended. All of the Adepts returned to their seats and remained quiet while they waited for what would come next. A bell sounded, deeper than the usual tones that signaled the beginning and end of the bonding Ritual. The Masters cleared a path to the red-and-silver tapestry that hung against the back wall. Four women carefully removed the tapestry from the wall, revealing a small, carved door.

The bell continued to sound while Marta proceeded toward the now-exposed door. She waited before it as the bell's tones slowly faded away. Her shoulders rose and fell, as if she had taken a deep breath and exhaled. She opened the door and crossed the threshold into darkness.

CHAPTER 3

MATHIS

THE FIRE CRACKLED and spat. Mathis stared at the pulsating glow of the embers, enjoying the calm. The Captain had finally ordered a proper camp after a week of running. It was about time; they all needed a full night's sleep, and the dried meat and oat bars they'd been eating had long passed palatability. The tents were already set up and the horses staked and groomed, so he had nothing to do now but wait for the hunters to return.

His eyes wandered around the small camp. A few people had gone down to the creek to wash, but most either sat by the fire or reclined in their tents. Some were in the Captain's tent, which was tall enough to stand in, unlike the rest. Mathis imagined they were discussing with her whatever it was that needed to be figured out following the events of the past week.

What a mess. The mission was supposed to be simple and straightforward: retrieve some banned book from the woman who had purchased it in Aldham. She lived on a farm affected by disease, so the Captain had assigned Sonya and Owen to the job, who'd both survived the plague in their youth. Maybe if she'd known the warning flags were subterfuge, she would've sent someone with more sense.

Sure, they'd managed to get the book, but they were supposed to do it quietly, without killing anyone. And the Captain certainly hadn't authorized them to take anyone captive. Sonya claimed she'd killed the bodyguard because he attacked her first, but Owen said Sonya had provoked an attack by running headlong into the farmhouse without caution.

And all of that had come after they'd stumbled upon the girl.

Mathis accepted a flask from a fellow Guardsman sitting next to him. He took a long swallow, and warmth coursed down his throat. The liquor wasn't the best quality, but it would serve. He drank again.

He still couldn't believe Sonya and Owen had managed to capture an Adept. If it had just been Sonya's word, he wouldn't have believed it, but Owen didn't lie. They must have surprised her; the girl's efforts to fight them off hadn't slowed them one bit, and before she could use her Ability on them again, they'd rendered her unconscious with something they'd gotten from Hasso.

At first, the Captain was skeptical of the girl's identity as well. It was unheard of for a young Adept to be so far outside the Conclave without an entire team of handlers. But something soon changed her mind, and the next thing he knew, she'd ordered their twenty-person unit to pack up and start running back to base. She didn't want them to be anywhere near that farm when the Conclave showed up to investigate.

Mathis looked up from the fire as the hunters approached the camp. Anova shrugged out of her backpack and handed it to the cook, then grabbed a bucket and headed back out toward the creek. Jekros rested two sets of bows and quivers against a tree, then walked over to where Mathis sat.

"Any luck?" Mathis asked, offering the tall man the flask.

Jekros squatted next to the fire. He took a sip and grimaced as he swallowed. "Yeah. Plenty of small game out there. We saw a few deer, but didn't bother since we're only here for one night. We gathered up some fresh greens, too, and Anova found some of those brown mushrooms you like so much. After the last week, it will be damn near a feast!"

Mathis groaned. "Fires, only one night? I was hoping we'd get a few days of rest here. It's not a bad spot."

"Take it up with the Captain. She's still hell-bent on getting back to Morell, even though Hasso implanted the girl." Jekros gestured with the flask to a small tent next to the Captain's. Mathis's eyes followed his motion.

The tent flap was open. Ysitra, seemingly bored, guarded the Adept. The child stared into nothingness, oblivious of the Guardswoman and even of the bandages wrapped around her own neck. She'd been that way since she'd woken up after Hasso's surgery. Whatever else Mathis thought of Hasso, it was clear the medic knew his work. The girl was no Adept now.

"It seems to me that the implant means we *don't* have to rush anymore," Mathis said. "With that thing stuck in her neck, she can't use her Ability or communicate with the Conclave." The maypop extract they'd been using to keep her unconscious had done the same thing, but the Captain had wanted to be able to question her. Not that the girl had obliged the Captain in that regard.

Jekros shrugged. "Don't want to be caught out here, though. We're too small a force. And now we have even more baggage, thanks to Hasso."

Mathis grunted in agreement. A few days ago, Hasso had gone ahead by himself to meet with someone about getting an implant. Knowledge from his earlier life, no doubt. Yet he'd returned not only with an implant, but with the strange woman, Renai. Hasso claimed it was part of the deal for getting the implant, which were near impossible to find, and the Captain had agreed to take Renai to Morell.

Mathis thought that this was a bad idea. Renai was clearly crazy. Plus, all afternoon, he'd caught her watching him with a sly smile on her face. He'd ignored her for the most part. But it was hard not to pay heed to the curves of her hips and breasts, especially when the clothes she wore barely covered the latter. Nor could he look past the large red scar that traveled from her left shoulder up to the top of the back of her neck.

Mathis didn't want to think about Renai right now. Nothing good would come of it. He pushed his hands against his knees and stood. "Is the boy out prepping what you shot?" he asked Jekros.

"He better be. It'll be full dark soon," the hunter replied.

"I'll check on him on my way to the creek. If we're going to be back on the road tomorrow, I want a wash," Mathis said.

"Tell him to hurry it up."

"Will do."

Ysitra glanced at Mathis as he approached his tent, which was next to hers. "No change," she said, though he hadn't asked. The child didn't respond or even look in his direction, as usual.

"So? Makes it easier to guard her."

"Mathis," Ysitra reproached. "She won't do us any good if she remains like this forever."

"As if she could do us any good in the first place," he muttered. He ducked inside his tent.

Once inside, he rummaged through his pack and pulled out a thin camp towel and a chunk of soap. For all he cared, the Adept could remain incapacitated for the rest of her life. He resented that the Captain had ordered him to guard her until they reached Morell—a duty that should have gone to Owen or even Sonya, given that they were the ones who'd caused all the commotion by taking her. Admittedly, Owen was busy watching over the woman they'd found with the child, ensuring she remained unconscious. And giving the girl to Sonya would only lead to a damned disaster.

Nonetheless, why the Captain would choose him, of all people, to help watch over and protect an *Adept* was beyond him. She knew his distaste for Adepts ran strong. Besides, the whole point of the rebellion was to destroy the Conclave, and in his opinion, eliminating Adepts was a surefire way to accomplish that goal. Without them, the Conclave was nothing.

He scooted back out of his tent, then passed between his and

Ysitra's toward the forest beyond. As he walked away from the circle of tents, he spied Avrey in the distance. The boy appeared to be skinning large rabbits. The carcasses of animals that had already gone through the process hung from a nearby tree branch.

At only twelve years of age, Avrey was one of their youngest recent recruits. He'd only been around for about a year, but he'd made himself useful as the cook's assistant. His attitude often left much to be desired, something common in boys his age, but Mathis couldn't fault his commitment. The kid was motivated to do whatever he could to help their cause succeed.

That tends to happen when you watch the Conclave execute your parents, Mathis thought.

Avrey looked up from his work when Mathis reached him. "Heya! Do you see how nice and fat these are? We'll be eating well tonight." The boy wiped at his forehead with the back of his arm, avoiding the gore on his hand. His red, stringy hair fell back into his face, and he blew upward in frustration.

"Looks like it's time again for you to cut back that hair of yours."

Avrey continued his work. "Yeah, yeah; no time. It grows too damn fast, anyway. I should let it grow and braid it back like Hasso."

"As long as that's the only thing about Hasso you want to copy," Mathis said, shooing away some bugs from the meat.

Finished with skinning the last rabbit, Avrey picked up a small knife. "Hasso's not that bad. He's a little strange, sure, but I don't know what you have against him."

Mathis didn't want to talk about the spy-turned-medic. The boy had his own demons; he didn't need to know about Mathis's.

Avrey sliced open the animal along its lower abdomen, then reached inside to remove the entrails. He set aside the liver, then dropped the rest into a hole in the ground that already contained feet, skin, heads, and undesired organs. Oblivious to Mathis's silence, the boy continued his conversation. "It's a good thing Hasso was with us this time, though. Can't deny that."

"I know," Mathis said. "But that doesn't mean that I have to like him."

Avrey smirked as he kicked dirt over the hole and tamped it down with his feet. "Yeah, well, maybe we wouldn't have needed his help so bad if that sweet sister of yours hadn't killed someone."

Mathis cuffed Avrey on the side of his head. *Damned boy.*

"Hey!" Avrey yelled. "What in fires was that for?"

"She's not sweet. And don't call her my sister."

"By the laws, she *is* your sister. I'm just speaking truth." He picked up the knife again, glistening with blood, and pointed it toward Mathis in a playfully threatening manner. "Don't you know you shouldn't hit someone when they have a knife and you don't?"

"That's the perfect time to hit someone, because then you can take it for yourself." Mathis plucked the knife easily from Avrey's outstretched hand, ignoring the boy's protests. "Here, even though you don't deserve it, I'll go clean your gear for you. You'd better take that meat back up to the camp. The Captain will expect those to be cooked soon."

"Yeah, yeah," Avrey grumbled, but he moved a little more quickly at the reminder. He rinsed his hands in a pan of water and dried them on a rag tucked into the back of his belt, then reached up to collect the carcasses strung from the branch.

Mathis smiled as the boy walked away. He reminded Mathis of himself at that age—he had the kind of focus, drive, and loyalty to their cause that only came from losing everything you had ever loved. At least Avrey didn't have to associate with the person responsible for his loss and pretend that everything was okay, just because the man had later switched sides.

With his towel slung over his shoulder and Avrey's pan and knives in his hands, Mathis wound his way through the trees toward the creek. The Captain understood the importance of camping near a source of fresh running water whenever possible, and the creek was not too far away.

In the distance, Owen crested the hill that sloped down to the creek. His friend must have had the same idea about bathing, as his medium-length hair was slick against his head and neck. With summer still in force, it'd dry in no time. Mathis hated the feel of wet strands clinging to his neck, so he kept his own hair short.

"How's the water?" Mathis asked when they met on the trail.

Owen squeezed some water from a portion of his hair. "Clear and not too cold. Nothing you'd want to spend much time in, but fine for a quick wash."

"Good. I heard we were moving out tomorrow, so I figured I'd try to get some of this stink off me first."

"What's with the gear? You cooking tonight?"

"Nah. I passed Avrey on the way out and figured I could clean his stuff since I was going to the creek anyway."

"Mighty efficient of you," Owen said, wiping away a bead of water from his temple. "Is the Captain still conferencing with Sonya and Hasso?"

"She was when I left. Say—who's watching the woman while you're out here?"

"No one, but Hasso said she won't wake up until tomorrow. Since she's not an Adept, it'll take longer for the maypop extract to wear off." He patted Mathis's back. "I suppose I should get back, though. Enjoy your bath," he said, then continued in the direction from which Mathis had come.

A sudden gust of wind rustled the leaves in the trees. The forest was full of oak, aspen, and maple, and the trees' heavy canopy blocked much of the day's remaining light. Mathis picked up his pace. He wanted to finish bathing and get back to camp before it became too dark to see where he was going.

Mathis wondered what kind of information they would get out of the woman once she woke. They needed to find out why the Adept had been at that farmhouse. Their unit had been recruiting heavily in the area well before they'd heard about the banned book. Was the Adept there to monitor their activity? The Conclave had to know the Guard was riddled with people sympathetic to the rebellion, but as far as he knew, they didn't know how far up in the ranks that sympathy went. *Maybe they do now.* It was a disquieting thought.

At the bottom of the slope, the dirt and detritus beneath Mathis's feet grew damp, and a few steps more brought him to the creek. Dark green water flowed around large boulders along the edges, and there likely were more hidden beneath the surface in the middle. Mathis squatted and washed Avrey's gear, using a few fallen maple leaves to scrub at some stubborn tissue stuck on one of the blades. His task complete, he walked a few feet upstream and set the knives and pan on one of the boulders next to his camp towel.

He peeled off his shirt and grimaced at the sour smell embedded in the cloth. It was too late to do anything about that tonight; washing his body would have to suffice. He pulled the chunk of soap from this pocket, stripped off the rest of his clothes, and stepped into the water.

True to Owen's word, the water was cold, but bearable. Mathis waded farther into the creek, then held his breath and ducked under the surface. He stood quickly, lathered up his body and hair with soap, and submerged once more to rinse. Shivering, he quickly sloshed back to the creek's edge and grabbed his towel. Within minutes he was dry and dressed.

"Now wasn't that a pretty sight," a woman's voice purred from above.

Mathis jerked his head toward the voice. A slim figure with short, dark-blonde hair slid partway down the trunk of the tree nearest to him. She sat on a thick branch hanging low to the ground, her legs dangling.

"Dammit, Renai," Mathis said brusquely, angry that she'd scared him near to death. "Get down and go back to camp before Hasso finds out you wandered off."

"Oh Mathis," she said, grinning and swinging her legs back and forth. "I didn't *wander*. I had a very specific destination in mind."

Mathis didn't have time for her eccentricities. "Get down," he repeated. "I'll take you back to camp."

Surprisingly, she did as he commanded. As she hopped to the ground and unfolded to stand, he couldn't help but notice the large scar again. It stood red and angry against the pale skin of her neck.

"The tree was calling to me," she whispered, leaning closer to him. "I needed to climb. It promised me I would see again if I did."

He frowned. "There's nothing to see here but trees and water, and you can see that from the ground."

Renai pouted, hugging her arms around her body. "Mathis. If I didn't climb, I wouldn't see anything at all." She smiled wickedly, catching a bit of her lower lip with her teeth. "And I certainly wouldn't have seen you. Maybe I could see you again, up close?" She reached for the front of his pants, then giggled and skittered away when he batted at her hand. "I'm only teasing, Mathis. But come, let's go. We don't want anyone to think that you *wandered* off." She turned and walked up the slope without waiting to see if he followed.

Mathis shook his head. He grabbed Avrey's gear and then jogged to catch up with her. He kept a few feet behind her, though, so as not to encourage any more of her antics. She'd been staring at him all day, and now this? Normally, he'd be flattered to have the attention of an attractive woman, but this one wasn't right in the head; he knew it. Then there was her history as well; he wanted no part of that.

When Renai had shown up with Hasso that morning, Mathis had thought she was just another recruit. Then she opened her mouth and the crazy started to come out. Yet the Captain was allowing her to accompany them to Morell—a plan even his sister thought was senseless, and he and Sonya agreed on very little.

He'd overhead Sonya arguing with the Captain about it earlier while they were in the Captain's tent. They'd kept their voices low, but not low enough to escape Mathis's keen hearing as he stood nearby.

"Why are you allowing her to remain with us?" Sonya had asked.

"It is no great burden for us to travel with one more person," the Captain had responded.

"She's insane. Don't we have enough to worry about with the others? Why take this on as well? Hasso should have left her where he found her."

"He did not have a choice in the matter. If we wanted the implant—and thanks to you, we needed one immediately—taking her on was part of the price we had to pay."

"Look, Jana, you know as well as I do that capturing that Adept is a boon for us, especially since we have the book now, too. Don't pretend otherwise. And just because Hasso had to take Renai to get the implant, that doesn't mean we have to keep her now."

"It was agreed that we would take her to Morell, not leave her in the middle of the forest where the Conclave could find her."

Sonya had laughed—a sharp, curt sound. "I doubt the Conclave is looking to add a madwoman to their ranks."

"No, but they certainly would have an interest in finding out what happened to her implant. Do you think she would be able to resist their methods?"

"*Her* implant?" Sonya had asked, sounding incredulous. "How is that even possible? They wouldn't have implanted it temporarily, like Hasso did with the girl."

"You are correct. It was not temporary. But somehow, she managed to tear it out herself."

"Fires. Was that before or after she went mad?"

"I do not know. It could have been either. It is a wonder she is still alive." The Captain's voice had faded as they moved farther into the tent. "There is much you need to learn, Sonya, if you want to move up in our ranks..."

Mathis had not spoken to anyone about what he had overheard. The Captain would tell the unit that Renai had once been an Adept if it served them to know, and only when she was good and ready to do so.

Once they returned to the camp, Renai ducked into her tent, fastening the flaps shut behind her. Owen, who sat outside the tent where their older captive remained unconscious, raised his eyebrows. Mathis shrugged and laid his towel over the top of his tent to dry. There was no point in trying to understand Renai.

Tiny, momentary sparks from fireflies began to appear in the deepening shadow of evening. In the middle of the camp, Avrey monitored spits of rabbit over the fire while the cook stirred what was probably a concoction of greens and mushrooms. The smell was delicious.

Movement in his peripheral vision drew Mathis's attention. Hasso and the Captain exited her tent, both dressed in standard Guard uniforms, and walked toward Ysitra and the Adept. The

Captain, who wasn't a particularly tall woman, still towered over the small, slender medic. Her cropped brown hair also contrasted with Hasso's long, jet-black braid that drifted nearly to his waist.

Mathis moved out of the way as they approached. Without a word, Hasso squatted in front of the Adept and moved a finger back and forth in front of her face. She didn't respond. He tapped her elbow. Still no response.

As Hasso fiddled with the bandage at the Adept's neck, Mathis realized he'd seen no sign of his sister since he'd returned from the creek. "Captain, where's Sonya?" he asked.

"I sent her out to follow up on some information Hasso obtained. She will return to Morell when she is finished with her mission."

Mathis almost smiled. It was the best bit of news he'd had in some time, even though it meant that the Captain continued to put misplaced trust in Sonya's abilities. But with Sonya gone, he'd get a little peace now, and once they got back to Morell, he could relinquish his duty as an Adept-Guard without her harassment. Things were looking up.

Suddenly, Owen leaped up, yelling. The captive woman's head poked out from inside the tent. Her curly hair was plastered to the sides of her head where she had slept.

She's not supposed to be awake until tomorrow—

The woman scurried on her hands and knees from the tent as Owen charged toward her. She eluded his grasp and chaos erupted in the camp as she dashed toward the Adept, who continued to stare straight ahead, unfazed by the commotion. Several Guards moved to block the woman's way, and in her attempt to get around them, she smacked right into Mathis. He restrained her arms behind her back and held her close. She may have been surprisingly quick after nearly a week of unconsciousness, but it took no strength at all to resist her struggles.

"Let me go! LET ME GO!" she cried.

Hasso came to them in an instant, vial in hand, but the Captain restrained him with a touch. "Let us see how cooperative she is first," the Captain murmured. She fixed her gaze on the woman.

"Easy question," she announced in her officer's voice. "What were you doing in that farmhouse?"

"You already know why I was there," the woman spat, jerking her arms periodically as if she could break from Mathis's hold. "The •Masters always send Guards to do their dirty work."

A look passed between the Captain and Hasso. "You believe we are here on the Conclave's business," the Captain said carefully.

The woman ignored them as she twisted her neck to look down at the Adept. "Tovi, Tovi, it's me. Love, look at me, what's wrong —" She gasped. "You *implanted* her? Why would the Masters order such a thing? My daughter's Ability has harmed no one! I've made sure of that!" She collapsed against Mathis's chest with a small cry.

Her daughter? The situation had become entirely confusing to Mathis, but he kept his grip on the woman to prevent her from falling to the ground. *How could the child be her daughter?* Impossible. The girl was an Adept, and besides—

Renai launched at the woman, beating at her with fists. "YOU! You stupid bitch, I hate you, I hate you!" Renai screamed.

Mathis tried to push away Renai while still keeping hold of his captive. "Get her off me!" he roared.

Hasso jerked Renai backward and forced the vial he had intended for the other woman between her lips. Within seconds, Renai slumped to the ground. The woman in Mathis's arms was quiet.

"What in fires was that all about?" the Captain asked. "Hasso, if you cannot control Renai, then I will need to reconsider my decision to keep her with us."

Mathis's captive answered. "She was my roommate when we were Adepts," she said in a low, barely audible voice. "And I betrayed her."

CHAPTER 4

ALIA

THE PERCUSSIVE SOUND of rain pelting against the windows echoed through the lofty reception hall. Alia stood in an alcove behind the Masters, her hands clasped in front of her within the bell sleeves of her formal robe. She stifled a yawn. Two hours had passed already, yet the line of petitioners seemed no shorter.

Since her arrival in the city of Aldham three weeks ago, Alia had done nothing of import other than hear petitions, and she tired of the tediousness of it all. Someone would claim the theft of an animal, a book, a son, or merely one's dignity. The accused would deny the charge with vigor, and both sides would voice their positions with dramatic embellishment. But in the end, it didn't matter who acted the most sincere. Alia always learned the truth—and the truth was that Aldham had more than its fair share of liars. How the Masters here had managed to control this depraved city for over two years without the assistance of an Adept was a mystery.

Not that they particularly wanted her help. The Conclave

claimed this far-flung post was one of honor, yet the Masters here barely tolerated her presence. They certainly hadn't asked her to help them root out pockets of rebellion, the supposed reason for her assignment.

She suspected the real reason the Conclave had sent her so far away was because, at home, she served as a constant reminder of a potential flaw in their perfect, controlled world. Adepts enabled the Masters of the Conclave to rule all of Corinas, but if an Adept's Ability lasted through to when she was of a Master's age...

While Alia had always expected to be the last of her Initiate to enter Seclusion, she'd never anticipated this kind of delay. Adepts in the same Initiate always lost their Ability around the same time. Sarabie had lost hers only a few weeks after Marta, and everyone else in their Initiate—except Alia—had entered Seclusion within a month of Sarabie.

That had been four months ago. And now, here she was in this horrible city two weeks away from Corval. The Masters wouldn't have shipped her so far away if they expected her situation to change any time soon.

A young page interrupted her self-pity. "What is your determination, Honored One?" he whispered, head bowed.

"One moment," Alia said, stalling. A woman, poorly dressed for the occasion in a threadbare brown dress, stood at the podium behind the ornate balustrade that separated the Masters' raised table from the rest of the hall. Alia had missed what the petitioner had said, but it didn't matter. No one had told the truth all day, and this woman would be no different.

The woman gripped the top of the podium. "I know you do not believe me," she said, unprompted. "But I am telling you truthfully, good Masters. The rebels attacked us at night, destroyed our harvest stores, and killed anyone who got in the way. You must help us!"

Clashing weapons and pounding hooves filled Alia's mind. She pulled the corner of the curtain away from the window with a shaking hand and peered out into the night. A group of riders galloped down the dirt road threading the village, throwing their torches on the thatched roof of the storehouse as they rode by.

Flames engulfed the structure, and the sudden blossom of light revealed a curly-haired, barefoot child standing in the middle of the road. She cried out to the child, warning her to run away. The girl turned and *saw* her, shaking her head...

Alia stumbled forward, the vision broken.

What was that?

The page caught her arm, steadying her for a brief moment before backing away as if she were made of thorns. "I apologize, but you were falling and...I-I apologize, I meant no harm, p-please know this!" Abject panic tinged his babbled plea.

"No, it's all right, it's all right," Alia said, waving him away. The law forbade males from touching an Adept without permission, but the boy could hardly be blamed for ensuring that she did not fall. Besides, he was only a child. "I will not report you."

Relief washed over his face. "Thank you, Honored One!" Crisis averted, he recalled his duties. "May I bring your determination to the Masters?"

"Yes. The petitioner is telling the truth," she pronounced.

The boy scurried back to the table where the three Masters sat. The one in the middle, her blonde hair piled high atop her head, leaned back to hear the boy's report. The Master raised her eyebrows as the boy whispered in her ear, then turned to consult with the other two Masters. An Adept could provide the truth, but what to do with that truth was left to the Masters.

The petitioner stood at the podium, nervously picking at the hem of her sleeve while she waited. Alia frowned. The woman's words had sparked such vivid images! But that child—an Adept, surely, though Alia didn't recognize her—had not been part of the woman's recollection. It had felt like a warning, yet she had no idea what it might mean, nor who might have authorized the transmission. No one besides Sarabie and Marta cared one bit about her.

Master Ciara knocked twice on the tabletop. "We find that your petition is...valid," she said, and a murmur of surprise emanated from the crowd. "We will need time to determine a proper response. Return to your village and tell your people that the Conclave will conduct an inquiry and will take appropriate action."

"Thank you, thank you!" the woman said over and over as an attendant escorted her out through a side door.

Master Ciara knocked once again against the table. "We are done hearing petitions for today. We will reconvene in three days at the usual time." The Masters shoved their chairs away from the table and stood, and the disappointed crowd started to disperse.

While the other two passed through a back door, Master Ciara paused. "Adept Alia," she said, inclining her head in Alia's direction. "No report to the Conclave is necessary at this time. You may return to your chambers."

"Yes, Master Ciara," Alia said, somewhat confused. She'd assumed they'd cut short the time for petitions so they could consult with the Masters in Corval right away. To be sure, the rebels would not win much support by attacking innocent villages. And perhaps the Aldhamian Masters planned to send a unit of the Guard to deal with it once one returned to the city, and they wanted to postpone a report to Corval until a solution was underway. It wouldn't be the first time Alia had observed political maneuvering while on an assignment.

Reprieve granted, Alia escaped into a small passageway behind the alcove. She walked at an angle to avoid brushing her shoulders against both the outer stone wall and the inner wooden one. She hadn't taken very many steps before indistinct voices began to filter through the inner wall. She paused. While it was anathema to use Ability against Masters, nothing prevented her from eavesdropping like any other person. Before she could decide against it, she tiptoed several more paces and pressed her ear up against the wood.

"Listen here, Ciara...we all agreed...would not do anything to jeopardize..."

"It can't be true that...we would have known." Master Ciara's deep voice carried farther than the first Master's, but Alia still couldn't make out all her words. "This seems to me the work...the Conclave...must get in contact...a warning."

"Sonya knows...out of Aldham now...plans have changed."

Alia leaned back, her neck aching slightly. *Interesting.* So Master Ciara *did* want to tell the Conclave about the rebels, while the others did not. Alia repositioned her ear against the wall, hoping for a less distorted sound this time.

A door slammed. Startled, Alia jumped back from the wall, hitting her head on the stone on the other side of the narrow passage. She winced as she felt through the silk scarf she wore to protect her bare scalp. A lump was likely. *That's what you get for eavesdropping.*

With a headache looming, Alia abandoned her efforts and hurried to the door that led to the residential courtyard. Outside, a stone portico that ran alongside a formal garden protected her from the weather. Ahead of her, a door burst open, and two young girls ran into the garden. One jumped into a large puddle, splashing the other. Laughing, the doused child chased the first girl back through the door from which they had appeared. Alia smiled briefly at their frolicking. What must it be like to live such a carefree life?

She reached the end of the portico and entered the residential portion of the government's building. Thick, multicolored rugs ran down the middle of the hallway, and small tables holding elegant lamps stood along the wall between doors. The children were nowhere in sight, and all was quiet.

At the far end of the hall, her guards stood silent at her door. They weren't really necessary; no one would be mad enough to attempt breaking into an Adept's chambers. Alia nodded to them as she approached, and one of them pulled a key from his belt and turned to unlock the door for her.

Once inside, she kicked off her shoes and wriggled her toes in the thick shag rug. These accommodations were far finer than anything she'd experienced. A chaise in a deep green color rested before a marble hearth where the remains from the morning fire smoldered. The servants had placed a bouquet of white flowers in her room yesterday, and they continued to fill the air with a delicate, fresh fragrance that reminded her of spring.

There was even a shelf full of books, which she'd flipped through out of idle curiosity on the off chance there were some interesting pictures. Yet as usual, they were full of nothing but words she couldn't read. Her rooms clearly weren't intended for an Adept.

Alia crossed the room and entered the bedroom to the right. She flopped onto the bed, luxuriating in the billowy feather mattress. In Corval, her bed consisted of a simple wooden frame and a hard mattress not much wider than her body. In contrast, this bed had a massive, canopied frame and could fit at least six people if they squished together.

She rolled over and gazed at the canopy—another sign that this room was not meant for Adepts. Despite having looked at it for the last three weeks, a flush grew in her cheeks as her eyes traveled over the embroidery depicting a lovers' scene. Would Generation be like that? Would her partner hold her that tenderly, and would she be that eager for his touch? Generation was supposed to be the high point of Seclusion, and after, she would give birth to another Adept. It wasn't something she particularly desired, but it was inevitable.

At least, it was supposed to be inevitable—assuming one got to Seclusion in the first place.

A knock at the front door broke through her musings. Alia scooted off the bed and walked through the sitting room to open it. A servant wearing the uniform of the Aldhamian service waited outside, carrying a covered tray. Alia's guards were gone. Their officer must have come to her senses and given them something more useful to do than stand in the hallway, bored.

"Greetings, Honored One," the servant said, her eyes downcast. "I have your afternoon meal."

It wasn't quite the usual time, but Alia imagined the kitchen knew the Masters had ended petitioning early. "Please, enter," she said, pulling the door open wide. "You may put it over there." She gestured toward the table near the windows.

The young woman bobbed her head and came inside, her eyes never leaving her tray. Alia was used to it. Most citizens were nervous around Adepts; they often believed Adepts always knew their thoughts. They didn't realize an Adept only used her Ability in that manner when permitted to by the Masters, and that sort of unauthorized use of Ability certainly would be noticed.

Alia lounged on the chaise, then accepted a small cup of wine from the servant. She sipped, and robust flavors of minerals and spice lingered on her tongue. The varietal was unfamiliar, but it was most appropriate for a dreary winter day. She drank more deeply.

After a few moments, the sounds of table-setting subsided, and Alia looked behind her to see if the servant was finished. The woman stood near the table, staring at Alia with intense blue eyes. Alia frowned, intending to ask the servant what she was doing, when the room suddenly started to spin.

"How pathetic," the woman sneered, dropping all pretense of servile obedience. "I expected it would take longer, though I'm happy to be wrong. Still—I expected more from a full-grown Adept; truly, I did."

Alia's limbs tangled as she stood up. She clung to the chaise for support and fumbled for her Ability. It was becoming increasingly difficult to breathe, and a haze threatened her vision. "Guards!" she tried to shout, but the word came out as a mere grunt.

"Fires, I don't have time for this," the woman said. She picked up the metal serving tray from the table and swung the flat side of it directly toward Alia's face.

CHAPTER 5

NYONA

TOVI OPENED HER eyes.

Nyona exhaled in relief. Her daughter had been in a trance for hours, but she hadn't dared to interrupt. All she could do was watch, wait, and worry, for what Tovi was trying to do with her Ability went far beyond anything Nyona had thought possible.

"Did it work?" she asked, her voice tight. "Did you see anything?"

Tovi turned away from the bright light shining through the window. A cream-colored ribbon gathered back her dark curls, revealing the small scar along the base of her neck. It was fading, but Nyona hated that she might forever bear a reminder of what had been a terrible mistake. If only she had known more about the rebellion before, she could have sought them out instead of running and hiding. Tovi would never have been implanted—and Brien would still be alive.

Part of her knew his death wasn't her fault. How could she have possibly known the rebellion included the Conclave's own Guard? That didn't assuage her guilt, however. Brien had given up so much to be with her, and at the end, she had failed to protect him. And now, here she was, consorting with those who had ended his life.

He would understand why, she thought. He would have done the same had their fates been reversed. He'd known that keeping Tovi away from the Conclave was more important than anything else.

"Tovi," she repeated, attempting to draw her daughter's attention. "Tell me what you saw, love."

Tovi returned her gaze with eyes the color of budding leaves in spring. The coloring of her irises grew more prominent as her pupils slowly returned to normal size. "There was a fight in a village," the girl said in a soft voice, containing none of the childish exuberance that had been her wont a mere six months ago. "There were horses and fire, and people screaming, dying."

Nyona took Tovi's hands in her own. It was too much for a five-year-old child to see. At least, it was too much for the child Nyona wanted her daughter to be. Nyona herself had seen far worse by the time she was Tovi's age, but that didn't mean she wanted the same experience for her child.

Focus, Nyona thought. The time for all that had passed. She'd acquiesced to Captain Jana's plans, had she not? Thinking on what might have been served no purpose. "Was the Adept there?" she asked, rubbing her thumbs back and forth over Tovi's hands.

"Yes. Well, she was not there, but I saw her watching me."

It worked! Nyona felt excitement surge through her. "Were you able to tell her what we practiced?"

"I tried, but I couldn't. It was too hard; all I could do was shake my head." Tovi's lower lip trembled. "I'm sorry, mama."

Nyona gathered Tovi into her lap, hugging her close. "It's okay, love. You did well! I'm so proud of you, and Captain Jana will be pleased, too. I just know it."

As she rocked her child in her arms, she considered the change in Tovi's demeanor since they'd installed—and removed—the implant. She was so focused and determined now and rarely played like she once had. It was as if she were an entirely different child.

In some ways, I suppose she truly is. Once freed from Nyona's severe restrictions on her use of Ability, Tovi's development in that area had been exponential. And it was all thanks to the book Nyona had found, the pursuit of which had led the rebels to believe that she—of all people!—was working on behalf of the Conclave.

A History of Corinas…though it was only half that. Within the pages describing the country's history in dry language had indeed been paragraphs detailing the use and control of Ability. Piecing together those random passages revealed not only a training manual for Adepts—including techniques and skills Nyona had never heard of before—but also a description of how an Adept could hide her use of Ability from the Conclave's watchful eyes.

The discovery of that passage had led to Captain Jana's agreement to remove Tovi's implant—at least temporarily—to test the described methodology. The rebellion coveted Tovi's Ability, but they were understandably skittish about the risk of her using her talents for their benefit.

In the rebellion's early years, back before Nyona was born, the rebels had managed to turn a disaffected Adept to their side, but their success had been short-lived. The Conclave had some idea of where the Adept had gone, and her Ability acted as a beacon to the other Adepts searching for her. As a result, the Conclave's Guard found her within days, executed her on the spot, and destroyed the rebellion's entire base of operations. Captain Jana didn't want a repeat of that episode—and neither did Nyona, for that matter.

So, a small group had taken Nyona and Tovi to Zanita, a remote town with a three-Master tribunal who was friendly to the rebellion. Zanita was a weeklong journey to the northeast of Morell, yet still far from Corval, so Adepts only serviced the city once a month on a rotating assignment. The tribunal agreed to have its current visiting Adept look for unauthorized use of Ability as a "training exercise," and if the book's methodology had failed, the tribunal would claim any detected Ability was from a training decoy. The precaution hadn't been needed, for Tovi had completed numerous exercises with the Adept being none the wiser.

She looked down to where Tovi had fallen asleep in her lap.

Nyona stood awkwardly, cradling the child in her arms. She carried Tovi across the room, laid her on the chaise, and drew a crocheted blanket over Tovi's slumbering form.

The door opened and Mathis entered the room unannounced, as usual. His cheeks were rosy from being outside in the cold. "She's done? What happened? Why didn't you call for me? Is she all right?" He hardly paused between his questions.

"Shush. She's exhausted. Let her sleep, and we can talk outside," Nyona replied.

Mathis followed her into the hallway, silently closing the door to the room that served as Tovi's classroom behind him. The corner of her mouth twitched up in a half smile. For someone who claimed to hate being an Adept's bodyguard, Mathis watched over Tovi like an overprotective older brother. It was hard to believe he was in any way related to Sonya; the two could not be more different. From what Nyona could gather, he shared her opinion on this.

"So what happened? Did it work?" He stared down at her with dark, emerald-colored eyes that revealed his impatience.

"Sort of. She saw the Adept, and the Adept saw her, but Tovi couldn't speak. She could only shake her head."

"Hmph. Think the Adept understood that?"

"I hope so." She shrugged her shoulders. "I suppose we'll find out soon enough."

Mathis nodded. "I'll go inform the Captain."

Nyona grabbed his arm as he turned to leave. "No, I'd rather go. I could use the fresh air after being cooped up in here. Can you stay, in case Tovi wakes up? If she does, tell her I'll be back soon."

"All right," he said. "It's pretty cold out, though, so don't forget your gloves." He reopened the door and went back inside.

Nyona skipped down two flights of stairs to the front door. She grabbed her wool coat and knit scarf from a hook and put them on, then drew her gloves over her hands.

Outside, the hazy, blue-white sky promised more snow. Her breath puffed in the air before her as she walked briskly along the dirt road. No longer a prisoner, she could go where she pleased, so long as she remained within the boundaries of Morell.

Her freedom had not come overnight. Convinced that Brien's death and their capture were the Conclave's doing, it wasn't until well after she'd arrived in Morell that she'd begun to realize her error. Yet even then she'd wanted nothing to do with the rebellion. They wanted Tovi for themselves. How was that any different from the Conclave?

Kelda, Nyona thought with a small smile.

The former Master of the Conclave had been the one to change Nyona's mind. Nyona didn't remember her—she'd left the Conclave when Nyona was still quite young—but their shared experiences had convinced her of Kelda's sincerity. After many long conversations with the former Master—and now Morell's Director of Education—Nyona had come to recognize that the rebellion's purpose and her own were not so dissimilar. They all wanted the Conclave out of their lives, though the rebels sought that end for all citizens of Corinas. She and Tovi could help the rebellion achieve that goal, and in so doing, save themselves.

Besides, it wasn't as if they had somewhere else to go.

She passed a number of people on her way to the command post. Some wore Guard uniforms while others, like she, were dressed in civilian garb—yet all were involved in the rebellion to some degree. Not for the first time, Nyona wondered how this could be. The Conclave she knew wouldn't hesitate to take action against a town full of rebels. That they hadn't was nothing short of astonishing.

Mathis thought the Conclave didn't pay attention to Morell because it was so far from Corval. That seemed too simplistic an explanation. The Conclave never let something as simple as distance get it its way. *That's why I've been running ever since Tovi was born.*

Nyona reached the Guard's command post in the middle of town. While most buildings in Morell were narrow, plain rectangles packed next to one another, the command post had a broad first floor and a limited second story that rose up only in the middle of the structure. A slender watchtower reached above the second floor another thirty feet, permitting the Guards on duty a clear view of the town and surrounding valley.

A pair of Guards, bundled up against the cold, stood at the front entrance. They knew her by now, and they opened the heavy, reinforced door for her without bothering her with questions. Once inside, she removed her gloves and unwound the scarf from her neck. Carrying both in her hands, she turned left and walked down the broad corridor until she could go no farther, then turned right, then right again. She jogged up a narrow staircase to the second floor where the officers' quarters were located and knocked on the third door to her left.

"Come in," came a muffled voice.

Nyona entered Captain Jana's office, unsurprised to find her working at her desk. The woman seemed to never sleep. She looked up, then immediately set aside a stack of papers. "Sit," she commanded, pointing to the chair in front of the desk. "Do you have news?"

"Yes, Captain," Nyona said as she sat in the plain wooden chair. "It took much longer than we thought it would, but Tovi was able to break through to the Adept in Aldham when the woman from the village spoke of the attack. Tovi reported that the Adept saw her, but all Tovi could do was shake her head. Hopefully that will be enough to convey our message that the attackers weren't part of the rebellion."

Captain Jana frowned. "I doubt the Adept would get all of that from a mere gesture. Did Tovi try to speak to her?"

"Of course. She couldn't get through."

"I wonder why not? The book suggested this form of communication was simple."

Nyona gave a small shrug, hoping her annoyance was adequately concealed. "I don't know, Captain. Perhaps Tovi was exhausted from the effort of maintaining a channel for so long while she waited for the opportunity to communicate with the Adept." *Or perhaps it's because this is all new to her and you're expecting far too much, too fast.*

"Well, we can only hope it is enough, then. The Aldhamian tribunal believes the Adept will be receptive, but I had wanted to get a message through to her before Sonya is forced to take action. I am certain you would agree that it will be better for everyone if she comes willingly." She tapped her long, elegant fingers against the desk. "Are you sure you don't remember anyone named Alia from your time at the Conclave?"

"No, Captain. She would have been just a child when I entered Seclusion. It's been so long—I wouldn't remember any of their names."

"Apparently the girl suffers from an unusual affliction. Master Ciara reports she has no hair at all. I would think that would be memorable, even though there were far more Adepts back in your day."

A sudden memory of seeing such a girl in the lowest benches of the Ritual Hall sparked in her mind. Had that been a tiny Alia looking up at her with adoration during her Ascension? Such a minor detail to recall from that day, only a week after the Masters had implanted Renai—when Nyona's guilt had threatened to overwhelm her.

Remorse welled at the thought of her former friend. After the initial shock of seeing Renai at the rebel camp—and the woman's hysterical attack—Nyona had come to realize that Renai was far more damaged from a mere implant than Nyona could have ever imagined.

It's not my fault, she thought. *How could I have known what they would do?*

She and Renai had been late for their appointments in the Ward —appointments at which they'd expected to learn that they were ready for Seclusion. Nyona had recognized the signs in the both of them, and, giddy with excitement, she'd gone searching for her delinquent roommate. Yet when she'd finally found Renai inside a lower-level storeroom, she was not rifling through old scrolls as Nyona had expected. Instead, Renai was naked, straddling an equally unclothed young man, and moaning with pleasure as she moved back and forth against him. Nyona had stood there, mouth agape, until Renai realized she was there.

At that time, Nyona had believed she had no choice but to report the incident to the Masters, despite Renai's pleas to the contrary. It wasn't just because she was supposed to—indeed, Nyona had lost count of the times she'd pretended she didn't notice Renai's rule-breaking. Rather, she'd been convinced that a report was necessary to protect Renai herself and the future Adept she would one day bear.

Nyona hadn't been surprised at the young man's execution. Death was the Conclave's penalty for unauthorized contact with an Adept, even when that contact was far less than what she'd observed. But she'd never imagined the Masters would implant Renai. They'd claimed it was because she'd misused her Ability to enrapture him, but that made no sense. Renai had been so close to Seclusion—and the concurrent loss of her Ability—that an implant served little to no purpose.

I should have known better. The implantation had been nothing more than a reminder that Adepts were nothing but pawns subject to the will of the Masters. And in that, it had been a most impressive example. In her mind, Nyona could still hear Renai's screams, could still see her facedown on the table, restrained, as one Master sliced into her neck while a second Master positioned the metal device, its long prongs extending to either side like some alien insect—

"Nyona. Are you listening to me at all?" The Captain's query was not unkind.

Nyona blinked. "I—I'm weary, Captain. My apologies. I think I do remember this Adept."

"That's good to know," Jana said with a slight nod. "For now, get some rest. As I was saying, I will call upon you later to discuss in more detail how you and Tovi can assist us with the next stage in our plans."

Nyona nodded in return, already lost in her memories. Without another word, she left Captain Jana's office, returned downstairs, and exited the command post. The air chilled her bare hands and face as her feet slowly carried her home.

CHAPTER 6

SARABIE

THE MUSICIANS' STRINGED instruments filled the room with a tranquil nocturne. Women in red robes sat in quiet reflection upon red-and-gold cushions scattered throughout the lounge. Ornate lamps emitting a muted, warm light hung from delicate chains at the ceiling and under the arches that encircled the room. One archway led to the Hall of Learning, another to the Hall of Residence, and a third to the dining room. Along the lounge's remaining circumference hung heavy, red velvet drapes that billowed against the floor.

Sarabie closed her eyes and focused on the soothing sounds of the eunuchs' music. She breathed in and out slowly, in time with the phrasing of the melody. It was a practiced routine, one she'd been taught in her first days of Seclusion to help cope with the loss of her Ability, and one that worked to calm her even now. She'd been anxious all day—so much so that she'd barely been able to eat that morning, and she'd skipped the afternoon meal entirely.

Tonight would be her sixth monthly Review since she'd entered Seclusion. Each month, she'd hoped the Masters would tell her that her time had come, and each month her hopes had been dashed. After each of her failed Reviews, the Masters reminded her it was not uncommon for a woman to spend *years* in Seclusion before moving to Generation. Sarabie understood this; indeed, three of the women in her small group, who were from the Initiate prior to hers, had been waiting for almost two years. But understanding did not bring acceptance. She did not *want* to wait years.

Marta, the only person from her Initiate past Generation thus far, had moved to Generation just days after Sarabie had ascended to Seclusion. In the nearly six months since, Sarabie had seen Marta just once: last week, when some Masters had led a group of women who had completed Generation through the lounge. Marta's pregnancy bulged far from under her high-waisted robe. Sarabie had wished she could congratulate her, but women at different levels of Seclusion were not permitted to mingle.

What were the Masters looking for? She'd tracked her cycle and recorded her observations about her body dutifully in her journal for months. What was missing? Tonight, she could only hope, once again, that the Masters would finally see something in her journal that demonstrated she was ready.

A bell chimed three times, and the music dwindled away. Sarabie stood from the cushion on the floor, her leather journal in hand. She followed the other women exiting the lounge in silence, her long red robe brushing against her legs as she walked under the archway that led to the Hall of Learning.

At least her regular lessons had been going well. She'd learned her letters easily, and Master Elda told her she already read like someone who had been reading for years. Her lesson books contained histories she already knew, yet it fascinated her to *see* what she knew written on a page. Learning how to read had been the best thing about Seclusion so far. *Alia will love it—if she ever gets here.*

Don't be silly, she thought, but she couldn't deny the terrible worry she felt for her friend. Everyone else from their Initiate had been in Seclusion for months. She hoped there was nothing wrong.

Worry about that later. Sarabie left the stone-lined hallway and entered the small classroom where four other young women sat around an oval table. Her small group consisted of herself, Kati, and three women from the Initiate before theirs. All nodded in greeting as she pulled back the last remaining chair and sat down next to Kati.

"Are you well?" Kati asked quietly. "I didn't see you at the afternoon meal. Did your cycle come again unexpectedly?"

"No; I am quite well, thank you," Sarabie replied, squashing a surge of annoyance. Her relationship with Kati had soured in Seclusion. Kati's innate competitiveness had increased with each passing month, making her nearly impossible to be around. She constantly asked about Sarabie's cycle in a way that made it clear she only cared for purposes of comparison.

Two Masters entered the room from their adjacent office, ending the potential of further queries from Kati. Both Masters wore gray robes with numerous silver stripes along the sleeves. Whorls depicting high rank decorated the chest of Master Elda's.

"Good evening, ladies," Master Elda said. "As you know, tonight we will be conducting a Review. After we have looked over your journals, we will discuss our findings with each of you individually. Once we're done with your particular Review, you are free to leave and enjoy an early evening meal."

Master Lana walked around the table, collecting their journals. Sarabie looked down at the table, picking at the edges of her cuticles. No one in the room spoke, even as the minutes ticked on. Everyone else was nervous this time, too, Sarabie realized. They'd all been waiting a long time—some far longer than others.

After about fifteen minutes, the office door opened, and the former Adepts all looked up expectantly. Master Lana poked her head out around the edge of the door. "Sarabie," she said.

Sarabie's stomach lurched. Was that pity in the Master's tone? She hoped she'd be able to hold back her disappointed tears until after they dismissed her this time. With her expression carefully neutral, she entered the office and sat before the Masters. Her journal lay open before them.

"So, right to it," Master Elda said. "We have reviewed your records, and it is our determination that you are ready to move on to the next level."

Sarabie gasped. "Do you truly mean it?" she blurted, before slapping both hands over her mouth. She did not want to be impertinent at a time like this. *I am moving to Generation!* Tears welled in her eyes.

Master Elda gave a good-natured laugh. "We truly mean it. First thing on the morrow, you will move to your new room in the Generation level. Your lessons will continue there, but with different Masters. You have progressed nicely in the time you've been with us, and we expect you will continue to do well."

"Congratulations to you, Sarabie," said Master Lana. "Do you have any questions for us?"

"When will my ceremony take place?" It was the only thing that mattered.

"That is for the Masters in Generation to decide, after they have reviewed your records," replied Master Elda. "We will give your journal to them tonight, so you should know their decision fairly soon. Some women go through the ceremony in a matter of days, while others might need to wait a few weeks."

Sarabie nodded, hoping she would be one of those who experienced Generation right away. Bringing forth a new Adept was what she was meant to do, and she'd waited long enough.

"We wish you the best," Master Elda continued. "And if all goes well, as we expect it should, you will join us one day as a Master to help Adepts use their Ability for the good of all Corinas. Now, go and enjoy an evening meal, then return to your room to pack. Servants will arrive early in the morning to escort you to your new room."

So dismissed, Sarabie left the small office through a second door opposite the one she'd used to enter. She wanted to shout with excitement. Only minutes before, she'd been so discouraged, and now—*Generation!* No one else was in the hallway, so she allowed herself a few little skips before regaining a dignified pace.

With Reviews having only just begun, she thought she might be the first to arrive for the evening meal, but muted conversation greeted her as she pushed open the wooden door to the dining room. Still, only a few of the small, elegant tables were occupied, but the women already seated appeared despondent. Rather than intrude on them with news of her good fortune, she selected an empty table. She brushed away an errant string from the pristine, white tablecloth, and pushed the silver flatware farther apart.

A servant approached. Like all servants in the Conclave, he was a eunuch and long of limb, and the red tattoo that covered his right hand was nearly the same color as his hair. "Good evening, Sarabie. Would you like some wine?"

At her nod, he poured a white varietal from a decanter into a crystal goblet on the table. She didn't recall seeing this particular eunuch before, but they always knew her name. She rarely could say the same.

A cloth slipped from his arm, and he crouched to pick it up. As he stood, he paused to whisper in her ear. "Marta urgently requests that you meet her in the musicians' alcove after your meal."

She startled at his fleeting, nonsensical words. *Marta?* She reached for his arm, but he evaded her grasp and hurried back toward the kitchens.

Her hand fell limply to the table as confusion set in. Women at different levels of Seclusion were not permitted to speak to one another, and Marta had moved on months and months ago. Was it a test of some sort, now that she'd been approved for Generation? She glanced around the room, but no one seemed to pay her any attention. What could possibly be so important that Marta would break the rules and ask her to do the same?

Her breath caught. *Alia.* At her level, Marta would be privy to some outside information. If she'd learned of something bad concerning Alia, she would know Sarabie would want to hear of it right away. *That must be it. There's no other explanation.* Worry for her absent friend took hold anew.

A few minutes later, a different eunuch—this one with brown hair, but with the same red tattoo on his hand indicating his status —placed a simple meal of soup, bread, and fruit before her, disrupting her pessimistic thoughts. Despite her anxiety over Alia, she was famished and needed to eat something. She gently blew a breath of air over a spoonful of thick pea-and-pork soup to cool it before raising it to her lips. Garlic and pepper tingled her taste buds as she chewed on a small piece of meat.

Sarabie was scraping the bottom of her bowl with a piece of the warm, brown bread when Kati entered the dining room with a group of other women. Kati scanned the dining room and smiled broadly when she spotted Sarabie. She threaded her way through the tables, all of which were set with four place settings even though there were nowhere near enough women to fill them.

"There you are! Guess what? I'm moving to Generation!" Kati announced, her cheeks flush with excitement.

Of course she didn't bother to ask about my Review first. "Congratulations!" Sarabie said with a forced smile. "I am as well."

Kati squealed in feigned delight and threw her arms around Sarabie in a quick hug. "I'm so delighted! To move to Generation together after all this time! Well, not so long for me as it was for you, of course. But still, isn't it just so wonderful?"

Sarabie resisted the urge to roll her eyes. Kati had finally found a way to turn her belated entry to Seclusion to her advantage. "Yes. Actually, I'm just about to go pack for tomorrow. Shouldn't you start packing as well?" Maybe Kati would take the hint and be on her way. She needed to find that eunuch.

Kati plunked herself sideways into a chair and draped her arm along the seat back. "We've got plenty of time. Why the rush? And besides, this will be our last night together for a while." She accepted a glass of wine from a eunuch—not the one Sarabie sought— but waved him away when he inquired about food. "I'm far too excited to eat a full meal right now. I'll just have some of your fruit."

Sarabie quashed a surge of annoyance as Kati crunched into an apple slice. "What do you mean, our last night? We're both moving to Generation."

After she swallowed her mouthful of food, Kati leaned forward, conspiratorial. "Yes, but I heard we'll be secluded there even more so than here. Our only contact will be with the Masters." She raised her eyebrows, leaned back, and took another bite.

"Where did you hear that? The Masters have said nothing like that to us."

"Let's just say—sometimes, Secluded doesn't really mean *secluded*. I have friends in other levels, you know, and they tell me things."

"Was it Marta?" Sarabie whispered. Kati and Marta had been roommates as Adepts, after all. Perhaps Marta broke the rules more often than Sarabie realized.

Kati wrinkled her small, pert nose. "Marta? No. I've not heard a thing from her since she left. I don't know what's gotten into her— well, other than a future Adept." She giggled at her own joke. "No. I won't reveal my sources. It's better that way." She downed the rest of her wine in one gulp, stood up, and grabbed another apple slice. "You've just reminded me that I should go talk to the others before I'm not supposed to talk to them anymore. Enjoy your packing."

Kati trotted off to another table, leaving Sarabie alone to consider her options. Might that be all Marta wished to say? Yet it seemed foolhardy to risk the kind of trouble they'd incur if they were caught speaking to one another, just to tell her something she'd find out for herself the very next day. *It must be about Alia.*

Leaving her meal unfinished, she folded her napkin and placed it next to her plate as she stood from the table. The dining room was fuller now, and she exchanged pleasantries with some of the women she knew as she walked by, trying to keep the appearance of normality.

A melodic nocturne greeted her as she exited the dining room, and she let out a small sigh of gratitude. With the musicians having resumed play, they wouldn't notice her rummaging about the storage alcove where she was to meet Marta. She paused under an archway at the edge of the central lounge. Few women, and no Masters, were present. That, too, was a relief.

Sarabie strolled along the edge of the lounge, her hand trailing lightly against the velvet drapes that hung from the archways that encircled the room. She passed behind a small cluster of women conversing over their journals, but they paid her no mind. Her fingers caught an open seam in the drapery, and after a quick glance around the room to confirm no one was watching her, she darted behind the curtains into the small space that separated them from the wall.

She pressed her back against the stone wall and pivoted her feet so her toes pointed in opposite directions, trying to minimize the chance that her body would be visible behind the drapes. Her heart pounded as she considered excuses she might use if she were caught. Sliding one foot to the left, she inched her body to follow. She repeated the process as she slowly progressed to the musicians' alcove. Soon enough, her foot encountered open air, unrestricted by the wall behind her.

Open instrument cases and storage trunks crowded in the darkness of the alcove. Sarabie nearly yelped when someone stood up in the corner. *Marta.*

Marta hurried over to Sarabie. "I'm so glad you came," she whispered. The swell of her pregnancy pressed into Sarabie as they hugged. "I wasn't sure you would."

"Neither did I," Sarabie admitted. "But I knew you wouldn't do this if it weren't important. Tell me: Is it Alia? Did something happen to her?" Even as she asked, she dreaded the answer.

Marta shook her head. "No. Well, I heard that the Masters sent her out on a long assignment for some reason, but I don't know anything more."

Sarabie frowned. "Then why would you put us both at risk by asking to speak with me? If they catch us, we could be put out of the Conclave."

"*Shh.* Keep your voice down. Don't worry; they won't put you out. They need you. And they won't put me out, either, for I'm not to have just one Adept, but two!" Marta smiled as she placed a hand on her abdomen.

Sarabie's breath caught in wonderment. "You are honored. I am so happy for you."

"Thank you; it is a true gift, indeed. But still, I have no doubt they'd punish us somehow if we are caught, so let me get to it. I heard you are moving to Generation, and I wanted to talk to you before you did. It's impossible to get messages to the women there; they only leave their rooms when it is time for the actual ceremony."

I guess Kati was right, Sarabie thought. "How did you find out, and so quickly? I only just learned of it myself. And who is that eunuch who delivered your message? He ran off before I could ask him any questions."

"I apologize for the drama, but I'm sure you agree secrecy is necessary. Stefan serves me, and me alone, and he risked much to bring you the message. He couldn't linger long without someone noticing he wasn't where he was supposed to be. The Masters would not hesitate to dismiss him if he were caught—or worse, I suppose."

Sarabie nodded, grimacing. "That is true."

"As for knowing about your promotion, at my level, the Masters announce who is moving to Generation. I think we may know before you do. Once I heard your name, I instructed Stefan to find you immediately. After he did, he showed me a separate passage to this alcove."

"That's all well and good, but if you aren't here to tell me news about Alia, I don't understand why you're here. What could possibly be so important that you couldn't wait until the proper time to speak to me?"

The lines between Marta's brows deepened. "I came to warn you about what is to come."

The tone of her voice, even whispered, sent a chill through Sarabie. "What do you mean?"

"I believe the Masters keep the levels of Seclusion separate so those further along cannot tell the truth to those who follow. And you *need* to know the truth—the whole truth—about Generation."

"What haven't the Masters told us? In the end, it's just basic mechanics—right?"

"Yes, but..." Marta breathed deeply. Her hands had balled into fists. "They give you things so you won't resist. And so you won't remember."

Sarabie felt her brows draw together. "Resist? Why would I ever?

Generation is what we're destined for. And why wouldn't they want me to remember something I've been looking forward to for my entire life?" This conversation was making Sarabie more confused by the minute. Marta's own fecundity was the product of a system she now suggested was somehow false.

"They teach us that Generation occurs with a special partner on a special night, yes?" Marta's voice was tight and unhappy. "Well, that's not true. Generation lasts for days—and you will have more than one partner."

Sarabie suddenly regretted her decision to meet her old friend. Marta's words contrasted starkly with the picture of Generation Sarabie had held in her mind since she'd first learned, as a young Adept, of her true purpose. Without the match of a specific, unique partner, the gift of Ability still within her—trapped, and now inaccessible to her—would die with her. "That's ridiculous," she scoffed under her breath.

Marta placed her hand on Sarabie's arm. "I know it's difficult to hear, but it's true. The Conclave can't afford any failed Generations, especially after the plague killed so many women in Seclusion years ago. The Adept ranks aren't what they used to be, and the Conclave can't rule Corinas without us—erm, without them. So, the Masters are doing everything they can to make sure each Generation is successful; they can't risk losing what little Ability is left."

"Which is exactly why the ceremony is tranquil and why my partner is selected just for me! Otherwise, a new life might not even be capable of accepting the gift of Ability, let alone desire to."

Marta shook Sarabie's arm slightly, her grip tightening. "No. That's all a farce. Multiple days of Generation with multiple partners is the only way to guarantee pregnancy."

Sarabie refused to believe what she was hearing. "Why are you telling me this? I *want* to go through Generation. I'm not Alia. And are you not pleased? You're so honored to carry *two* future Adepts!"

"I know, and I am pleased, but..." Marta bowed her head. "I don't think it has to be this way. It is a slim hope, but maybe things will change if more of us are willing to—they know you are obedient—if you try to—"

"Is someone back here?"

Sarabie squeaked in fright, and Marta stepped back with haste into the deep shadows at the back of the alcove. Sarabie turned slowly, trying to remember the excuses she'd prepared.

One of the musicians squinted at her in the dark from a break in the curtain at the opposite side of the alcove. "You shouldn't be here. If you do not leave now, I will be forced to report you to the Masters."

She gave the eunuch her most innocent smile. "I'm sorry. I had just hoped to see some instruments up close." She tapped her fingers against an empty case. "I apologize for disturbing you; I will leave you to your duties." She pulled aside the curtain and stepped into the lounge, blinking at the light. The eunuch did not follow.

With her adrenaline running high, she returned to her quarters without further incident. She couldn't believe she'd risked speaking to Marta for *that*. Determined to forget she'd made such a mistake, she began to pack for her move.

CHAPTER 7

ALIA

ALIA WOKE WITH an incredible headache. She blinked her gummy eyelids, trying to ease the dryness of her eyes. Pillows propped her up on the bed upon which she lay, and a heavy, gray blanket covered her body.

"Shall I give her another dose?"

Alia turned her head toward the voice, but a sharp jolt of pain radiated from her neck, halting her movement. An old woman shuffled to the side of her bed.

"Here you are, child. Still got some pain, do you? She's sorry for that, you know." Age lined the woman's kindly face, and her white hair was gathered loosely atop her head. She slid one arm behind Alia's shoulders and eased her forward. With her other hand, the woman held a simple pottery cup to Alia's lips. An unfamiliar herb flavored the water, but she drank eagerly. Excess dripped down her chin.

"There you go. Now, sleep some more and mayhap you'll feel

better when you wake again." The woman lowered her back against the pillows and dabbed at the wetness around Alia's mouth.

"Please," Alia croaked. She hardly recognized her own voice.

"Oh, try not to talk now. Rest."

"Please," Alia tried again. "Where am I?"

"You're in a safe place, and that's all you need to know for now. Sleep." The woman's voice was firm, and she did not linger bedside to see if Alia had more questions.

Despite the confusion of her circumstances, sleep tugged at Alia's consciousness. The pain in her head lessened, and her senses dulled. Her eyes soon closed of their own accord, and she drifted back into a dreamless sleep.

Pale yellow light flickered from a lantern set on a table next to Alia's bed. The pain in her head having reduced to a dull throb, she risked turning to look around her. There wasn't much to see. The small room contained only the bed, nightstand, and a simple wooden chair. Walls of rough, unfinished stone, with no windows, surrounded her.

She raised a hand to her forehead and felt a bandage. Further prodding revealed a hard, tender lump at her temple, and the bandage thickened and continued down the length of her neck. She'd obviously been injured, yet this room looked like no ward she had ever seen. *Where am I?*

The memory of the servant's attack suddenly returned, and with it a surge of fear. Was that woman nearby? That old woman said she was safe—but perhaps she was in league with the servant. Her fingers clutched the rough blanket. A flood of questions ran through her mind, none of which she could answer.

No matter. A quick inquiry to the Conclave would tell her what she needed to know. If she *had* been abducted, the persons responsible would soon be very, very sorry. The penalty for harming an Adept was death, and she could easily identify both her assailant and the old woman. She reached for her Ability.

She failed.

Alia sat for a moment, uncomprehending. Accessing her Ability usually came as easily as breathing. Her wounds must be grievous, indeed. She tried again—and failed once more.

Her first thought was that her Ability had finally, after all this time, left her for good. Yet that didn't seem quite right. Signs of dissipation would have appeared over weeks, and she couldn't have been unconscious that long. Perhaps the medicinal herbs they'd given her interfered; that she could overcome by attaining a deeper trance to bring her closer to the source of her Ability. She closed her eyes and chased away all thoughts of the attack, her wounds, and even the room itself as she focused inward, slowing the beat of her heart and the rhythm of her breath.

This time, she felt something blocking the pathways in her mind. She pounded the mattress with her fist in frustration. Her Ability was there—she had not lost it—but it felt as if a solid wall surrounded it that her consciousness could not breach. Maybe she needed more rest. Maybe...

A sudden burst of cold panic coursed through her. *No. No.*

With shaking hands, she reached behind her head to the thick bandage at her neck. Knowing now what she sought, her fingers easily found the device's protrusions.

She collapsed back into her pillows. *Implanted!* How? Why? For all her faults, she couldn't think of anything she had done to warrant the Conclave's ultimate punishment. It had been years and years since the Masters had last implanted an Adept, yet Alia still could remember the Adept's screams.

To her horror, tears slipped from her eyes. Thrown out of the Conclave, her name would be struck from the records and all would be forbidden from speaking her name. Not even Sarabie would mourn for her.

She allowed herself a few minutes of sadness before blotting at her eyes with the sleeve of her nightshift. *That's it, then. No use wishing for things that will never be.* With stubborn resolve, she shifted her legs over the edge of the bed and stood, steadying herself with a hand against the wall.

The door opened and the old woman entered the room, carrying a tray of food. Her eyes opened wide when she saw Alia. "Child, what are you doing out of bed?" She set the tray on the chair. "You need your rest; Movani's here to take care of you," the woman continued as she gently pushed Alia down to a seated position on the bed.

"Movani, is it? There's no need to play games, good woman. I know why I'm here," Alia said. Her voice sounded calm and in control.

Movani narrowed her eyes. "You do?"

"Yes. I know the Masters have sent me away, because of..." She placed a hand behind her neck. "Because of this. I would like to petition the Conclave to learn the reason why. Can you give them that message?" She wasn't sure if this old woman would—or could—relay her request to the Masters, but it was worth a try.

Movani barked a curt laugh. "Aren't you a delight! Ha! What kind of girl are you, to decide it must be so?"

Alia frowned. "Well, I was never particularly favored, and they think something is wrong with me, anyway, so..." She closed her mouth, confused. "Are you saying I'm *not* here on orders of the Conclave?" That made no sense at all.

The woman smiled, and the creases around her eyes deepened. "I think it's time you talked to ones in the know. Movani's just an old woman caring for you. I mind my own business." She transferred the tray to the nightstand. "There's some soup and bread for you, and more of the tea for your pain if you think you need it." She snickered under her breath as she walked back out of the room. "Thinking it was her own. Ha!"

Alia's stomach growled at the smell of the soup, but she would not eat. If what the woman suggested were true, then that meant the servant who had attacked her had somehow abducted and implanted her—and if they weren't of the Conclave, Alia had no idea how they'd know what an implant was, let alone what to do with it. Fury replaced her confusion. These people must know the Conclave would come for her. They couldn't hope to keep her hidden away for long.

Her anger, quick to arrive, dissipated just as swiftly. All she needed to do was wait. Master Ciara and the other Masters in Aldham would have already reported her abduction to the Conclave, and a rescue was surely imminent. Once she got back to Corval, she was certain the Masters would know how to remove the implant. There must be *some* way.

She was musing over her plans for revenge when a man walked through the open doorway. He was slender and of average height, with long, black hair slicked into a braid that fell over his shoulder. All of his clothing was black as well, which only served to further emphasize the pallor of his narrow face. The man said nothing as he examined her with pale blue eyes. His nose was crooked, as if it had been broken long ago, and an old scar—paler even than his skin, though that seemed hardly possible—ran down the side of one cheek. Alia refused to look away from his gaze. She wanted to remember this face.

A slim, taller woman clad in tight-fitting leathers came through the door as well, crowding the small space. "You!" Alia exclaimed when she saw the woman's face.

"Ah, you remember me. Well, that will make this song and dance much simpler." The servant from Aldham pushed her shoulder-length brown hair behind one ear as she walked farther into the room. She pulled up the wooden chair and straddled it. A knife handle protruded from the top of her boot; when the woman caught Alia's eye, she pulled the knife from its hidden sheath. Light gleamed along the blade's edge. It was not a subtle warning.

Alia adopted the mask of authority she had worn her entire life. "Who are you?" she demanded.

"Oh yes, I'm terribly sorry," the woman replied in a mocking tone. "The pleasantries. Of course. My name is Sonya, your most Honored One, and this here is Hasso. We are here to make sure that you don't take any unexpected…liberties…while we wait for your new handlers to arrive and take you to your new home."

Alia looked at Hasso briefly, but he made no response to his introduction. "The Conclave is my home. And you must know there's no possibility whatsoever you will succeed in whatever it is you have planned," she announced in a voice that betrayed none of her uncertainty. "A unit of the Guard is likely en route as we speak. You cannot hope to withstand them. No one ever does."

Sonya snorted. "Are you truly that naive? The Conclave doesn't care about you. No one from the Guard—well, no one from a unit controlled by the Conclave, anyway—is coming for you. We have all the time in the world, and we *will* succeed. The sooner you accept that, the better. We're the best friends you could have now in this big, wide world." The woman grinned as she unfolded her arms from the top of the chair. "You should eat something," she said, pointing to the tray by the bed. "It seems that I hit you a little too hard, and you need to get your strength back before your journey."

Alia glared, irritated by the woman's ignorance. "You are sorely mistaken if you believe the Masters do not care about my abduction. I am an *Adept* of the *Conclave*. The tribunal will have sent a message to Corval by now, and the Conclave is already doing whatever is necessary to find me." She tried to sound powerful—or at least as powerful as she could be with no access to her Ability.

Sonya shook her head. "Hasso, she doesn't get it, does she." The man shook his head. Sonya leaned forward. "The Aldhamian tribunal sure did message the Conclave. They reported that you hid from them that your Ability was leaving you, and that when it finally left you for good, you announced that you refused to enter Seclusion and ran off with a foreign merchant before anyone could stop you. We didn't think the Conclave would believe such a farcical story, but it turns out they did. Sounds like you've been quite the handful for them all along, and they were just waiting for a reason to get rid of you." She stared expectantly at Alia, as if gauging her response.

Alia looked down at her hands, despairing yet not wanting it to show. If what Sonya said was true—and without her Ability, she had no way of knowing, one way or the other—then she truly was on her own, just as if the Conclave had implanted her itself. And if the tribunal in Aldham was involved in all this, then that meant they—

"I'm sorry, did I hurt your feelings? I certainly didn't intend to," Sonya said with thick sarcasm. "It's no matter, though, as you'll be leaving my hospitality soon. Please, eat. We have big plans for you, and we don't want anything to happen to you." She stood from the chair and whirled it back into place in the corner. "Hasso, check her implant, would you please? We don't want any infections."

Defeated for the moment, Alia did not resist as the man came to the side of the bed and fiddled with the bandage at her neck. "Who *are* you?" Alia repeated at Sonya's retreating frame. "And why did you—are you—doing this to me?"

Sonya paused at the door. "We are the ones trying to save Corinas from the Conclave's corruption," she pronounced, with no hint of mockery. "And you are going to help us."

⚜

Chapter 8

Mathis

THE FIRE IN the hearth crackled, its flames coalescing and parting in an ever-changing dance. That and the ticking of the clock on the wall were the only sounds in the sitting room where Mathis, Nyona, and Tovi waited. They had arrived at the Guard's command post nearly an hour ago, and he and Nyona had long since run out of idle topics for conversation.

At least the child kept herself entertained. Tovi sat cross-legged on the rug, reading a thin, leather-bound book. Nyona lounged in a chair behind her. She'd insisted on bringing her daughter with them, and Mathis had learned over the last six months that it was easier to accommodate her requests than to argue. That usually was the way with women.

He wondered if the Captain would have new orders for him. He'd long since finished his last mission—ensuring Tovi made it to Morell in one piece—and he itched for something new. Yet at the same time, he hoped whatever it was wouldn't keep him away from

Morell too long. Both Tovi and Nyona had grown on him, much to his surprise, and his thoughts on leaving them to someone else's care were...complicated. Sometimes, Nyona would say or do things that reminded him she came from the Conclave, but most of the time, he forgot they had once been on opposite sides. And the child behaved nothing like a real Adept.

"What is taking so long?" Nyona asked, breaking the silence. "We've been waiting forever."

Mathis shrugged. "Captain does what she does, when she does it."

Nyona rolled her eyes. "That's helpful, thanks." She brushed a lock of curly hair away from her face. Her hair had grown, and she wore the front portions pinned at the sides of her temples, with the rest flowing loose to her shoulders. "Do you think she wants Tovi to contact the Masters in Aldham again? There is no reason to come here for that—Tovi knows what to do."

"Maybe she wants Tovi to talk to Sonya."

"No, that can't be it. She knows Tovi can only reach Adepts or formers, and Sonya's neither."

"We'll find out soon enough," he said. "I bet we go up any minute now."

Nyona grumbled at his false patience, but his prediction was correct. A few minutes later, footsteps approached the sitting room from the hallway. Nyona looked toward the open door expectantly, and her expression soured.

Kelda, Morell's Director of Education and Mathis's former teacher, entered the room with Renai in tow. Kelda steered Renai to an empty chair and she sat without protest. Mathis raised his eyebrows. It had been a while since he'd seen Renai, but she was usually not so—compliant.

Kelda answered his question before he could ask it. "Hasso gave me some potions before he left, and they have proven to be most effective in keeping Renai more...docile, shall we say. I've been testing different doses, and this morning I gave her a quite high one. I didn't want to leave her behind while we go speak to the Captain in case something goes awry. She shouldn't bother Tovi."

"Wait, what?" Nyona asked, her eyes wide. "She's staying alone with Tovi? What might go awry?"

"Renai could fall further into a stupor and struggle to breathe," Kelda said calmly. "Which is why she must stay close by, but there's no need to bring her before the Captain. And in any case, we won't be leaving her alone with Tovi. Owen should be along shortly." She glanced at the wooden clock set against the wall and patted the bun formed from her gray hair at the nape of her neck. "In fact, he should have arrived by now."

"What if the Captain needs Tovi's Ability?" Nyona glanced at Mathis and gestured with her head, but he didn't follow her meaning.

"The Captain's summons did not include the child. She will remain here." Kelda gathered her long, brown robe and squatted next to Tovi. "Good afternoon, Tovi. What are you reading today? That doesn't look like a book from our lessons."

Tovi smiled at her tutor. "It's not. I found it on the bookshelves here. It's called *A Tailor's Tale*. It's about an orphan girl who's apprenticed to a tailor."

"Ah, yes. A classic story, that one. Are you enjoying it?"

"It's okay. The girl is rather whiny."

Kelda laughed, a merry sound that contrasted with the lecturing tone she'd used with Tovi's mother. "She *is* rather whiny. Keep reading, though. I think you'll like how it ends. If you don't finish while we're meeting with the Captain, take it home with you, and I'll collect it from you later." She laid a hand briefly on Tovi's head, then walked to the door and peered out into the hallway.

Tovi returned to her book, while behind her Nyona glared at Mathis. He didn't know what he'd failed to do this time, though he guessed it had something to do with Renai. He didn't like the idea of leaving Tovi behind with Renai, either, but Kelda knew her business. Besides, Renai seemed hardly aware of her surroundings today, let alone that others occupied the room as well.

Granted, unpredictability defined Renai's interactions with Nyona. Some days, Renai ignored her former roommate, but other days she hurled insults at Nyona that shocked even him. On those days, Nyona pretended Renai's venom didn't affect her, but he could hear her sobs through the thin walls of the house they shared. One day, he would ask Nyona what, exactly, had happened between her and Renai to result in such a guilty conscience. *I guess we all have our secrets. Maybe I'll trade mine for hers.*

Rapid footsteps echoed from the hall. "Ah, there he is," Kelda said.

Owen entered the room. "Sorry. I didn't realize how late it was," he said, rubbing his hand over his closely shorn hair—an unconscious habit he'd developed after unwelcome pests had forced him to shave his head. "Go ahead and go. I'll keep a close eye on them both."

"Please do," Nyona replied, and lifted one leg over Tovi's head to stand awkwardly from the chair. She kissed Tovi's cheek. "Mind Owen while we're gone, love. We'll be back soon." After a final, brief look in Renai's direction, she followed Kelda into the hallway.

Mathis paused at the door. "If anything comes up, send someone to find me, right?" he told Owen in a low voice. The last thing he needed was for Renai to visit some misfortune—even if unintentional—upon the child.

"Will do," said Owen. "Don't worry, Mathis. She doesn't seem capable of much today."

"So far." He patted Owen on the back, then jogged down the hall to catch up with Nyona and Kelda.

Upstairs, Kelda rapped the door to the Captain's office with her knuckles and walked in without waiting for a response. Captain Jana looked up from her desk. "Please," she said, gesturing to the two guest chairs. Kelda and Nyona sat. Mathis leaned against the wall between the desk and the chairs. He preferred to stand, anyway.

"My apologies for keeping you waiting so long. As you know, our plans escalated when we found you and Tovi, Nyona. An Adept, unaffiliated with the Conclave? Absolutely unheard of."

Nyona nodded, her expression guarded and uncertain.

"We received another stroke of luck when the Conclave sent an older Adept, Alia, to serve in Aldham," The Captain continued.

"Master Ciara and the others there have been helping us for years, and given what they told us of this Adept's disposition, we had hoped to bring her over to our side. Sonya went to Aldham to facilitate their work, and at the same time, Tovi tried to reach out to the girl."

"She did all she could," Nyona protested.

"No one is doubting that, Nyona. But we ran out of time. The Conclave's 'rebel' attacks have increased in frequency, and their 'rescue' efforts have resulted in the capture of some of our operatives. These tactics also have had the unfortunate effect of making affected citizens believe the Conclave is protecting them. So, shortly after Tovi attempted contact, Sonya captured the Adept. It may have been somewhat premature, but the end result is that Alia is now safe in our custody."

Mathis snorted. *Somewhat?* All eyes turned to him. "Sorry. Allergies," he mumbled.

The corner of the Captain's mouth twitched upward. "I am sure. In any case, I sent Hasso to meet with Sonya at the safe house in Dakeforth. He implanted Alia—yes, I know, Nyona, but it could not be helped," the Captain said when Nyona's expression darkened. "We hope it will be as temporary for her as it was for Tovi, but we simply cannot risk her contacting the Conclave. Interestingly, they have made no effort to locate her, so it appears they accepted the fiction of Alia losing her Ability and running away. But we cannot trust that our information is complete; they could be looking for her as we speak."

"Captain, if Alia's of the age where she will lose her Ability naturally, what good is she to us? And if not, what if she suffers ill effects from the implant, like Renai?" Nyona asked.

"If she loses her Ability soon, she can still give us more recent information from inside the Conclave," Kelda answered. "There shouldn't be any ill effects from the implant, either. Renai's implant severed her permanently from her Ability, unlike the blocking implants used on Tovi and Alia. And Renai's madness is the result of her removing her implant on her own rather than from the implant itself. Alia will not suffer the same fate."

"Trust we have considered these issues," Captain Jana said in a voice that brooked no debate. She sat up straighter in her chair and leaned forward. "Now, I did not summon you merely to tell a story, but to give you orders in light of these circumstances. Mathis and Nyona, you will travel to Dakeforth to bring Alia back here to Morell. Avrey will accompany you to provide support. We do not anticipate any interference, but take a route that avoids the main roads, just in case. Between that and the weather, I expect that this mission will take you about two weeks. Kelda will remain here to continue Tovi's training, and Owen will watch over Tovi in your absence."

Mathis kept his face a perfect mask to hide his surprise. Not because of the nature of the orders—apparently, he had become the rebellion's de facto guard for Adepts—but because Nyona was going, too. Despite his bewilderment, however, he knew better than to question orders. Nyona did not.

"What?" she exclaimed. "You want *me* to travel with Mathis to fetch this Adept? Leaving Tovi here alone? Absolutely not. There is no reason for me to go. Mathis is perfectly capable of getting her; I would just get in the way. And why can't Sonya and Hasso bring her back? They're with her already."

Mathis raised his eyebrows at her outburst. Maybe the Captain would let it slide, given that Nyona was a woman and the mother of the rebellion's most important asset. *Or not*, he thought, as the Captain's eyes narrowed.

"I will excuse your insubordination as you are critical to our success, but you *will* go on this mission, Nyona. You may not be a Guard, but you are part of the rebellion, and that means you obey orders."

"But—" Nyona tried again.

"I have made my decision." The Captain squared her shoulders and folded her hands together on top of the desk; subtle gestures, but ones that emphasized the finality of her words nevertheless. "Not that I have to explain myself, but Sonya and Hasso have other orders," she continued. "And I am sending you, Nyona, for two reasons: first, to receive messages from Tovi, and second, to earn

Alia's trust. We must win her to our side as quickly as possible. You are the perfect choice to help us achieve this, given that you have the most in common with her."

Nyona caught her lower lip with her teeth, and her eyes crinkled with distress. "Couldn't Kelda do the same?"

"Kelda has been out of the Conclave too long. It has been—what, twenty years?"

"Twenty-two," Kelda said.

"Twenty-two years. You've been out seven, and did you not tell me you remembered Alia? She might remember you, too, and that may help build trust. Now, back to your orders. Avrey has spent the morning preparing your supplies and arranging your mounts. Gather what you need from home and meet him back here within the hour. I expect you to begin your journey—"

She broke off at a pounding on the door. "Captain! Captain!"

Mathis rushed to the door and yanked it open. Owen stumbled in, carrying Tovi, her arms clutched around his neck. A few steps behind came Renai, breathless.

"What happened?" the Captain demanded.

"She overheard a conversation that might have come from the Conclave. Tell her what you told me, Tovi," Owen said as he delivered her into Nyona's waiting arms.

"I didn't mean to," Tovi apologized, her youthful features contorted with worry. "I know I'm not supposed to do anything without you, mama, or Kelda, but I wanted to play a game with Renai and I guess I just—"

"Don't worry about that now, Tovi," Nyona said, clearly struggling to keep her voice calm. "What did you hear?"

Tovi's eyes darted between Owen, Renai, and the Captain. "I heard two women speaking. One seemed mad. The other one called her something like 'Gersemi.'"

All three women started. "*Master* Gersemi?" Nyona asked, incredulous.

"The head of the entire Conclave?" followed the Captain, looking to Kelda.

"It must be; they wouldn't give a new Adept her name unless

she'd passed, and we've had no word of that," Kelda said. "Continue, child."

"They were talking about Aldham and an Adept, and it was hard to understand until I *really* focused, but when I did, I heard one say…" Tovi scrunched up her face in concentration.

A woman's deep voice resonated in Mathis's mind, drowning out the child's nervous recitation of the same words. "I'm no fool," said the voice. "Of course they're all liars in Aldham. We've known that for years. What matters now is that they fell for it, and we don't want to discourage them from their plans. Adepts are sweeping the area as we speak. We *will* find Alia, and when we do, we'll destroy them all."

Chapter 9

Nyona

STEAM PUFFED FROM her horse's nostrils, dissipating quickly in the frigid air. His hooves tossed clumps of fresh snow toward Nyona's saddle with each step despite her attempt to follow the path Mathis had already forged through the forest. She pulled her borrowed black-and-silver cloak tighter around her body to ward against the chill. *What am I doing?* she thought. *I should be with Tovi, not traversing the countryside to fetch an Adept who probably won't even remember me.*

Not that she had much choice in the matter. After Tovi had intercepted Master Gersemi's ominous conversation, Captain Jana ordered Nyona, Mathis, and Avrey to leave Morell at once. A prudent person would have abandoned the mission upon learning the Conclave knew of their plans. But Nyona's decision to join the rebellion meant that her choices were no longer entirely her own. Thus, she found herself out in the wintry wilderness, suffering from sleep deprivation on top of the pervasive cold.

Master Gersemi's words echoed in her mind with each fall of the horse's hooves. *What matters now is that they fell for it*, the Headmaster of the Conclave had said. The rebellion had been operating in Morell for years without the Conclave's notice—at least, that's what Mathis told her they'd thought.

Her horse snorted, bringing her back to the present. She clucked her tongue to urge him forward over a thick, snow-covered tree trunk that had fallen across their path. It didn't help to worry about the Conclave now; she needed to focus on completing this mission so she could get back to Tovi. Their last communication had been three days ago, and she fretted something was amiss. Mathis's reasonable suggestion that Kelda and the others were probably limiting Tovi's messages out of an abundance of caution hadn't lessened her fears.

Ahead, Mathis waited astride his horse under a thick canopy of boughs. He pulled his scarf down below his chin as she approached, exposing several days' worth of stubble. "This forest isn't far from Dakeforth," Mathis declared. "I'd guess we're about a day from the safe house."

"Good," Nyona replied, chafing her hands together. "I still don't understand why we're risking all this to get our hands on another Adept, given that Tovi is just as capable. We should have stayed in Morell with her."

"Captain's orders, that's why," Mathis said with a shrug, as if this both explained and excused everything.

Nyona rolled her eyes. "Should we stop here to eat?" Less snow covered the ground here, and it would be good to get out of the saddle. Her toes were beyond numb.

"Avrey, what say you? Is it time for lunch?" Mathis asked the boy, who had lumbered up behind Nyona. He and his mount carried most of their party's supplies, which slowed his pace considerably.

"Nope," Avrey replied. "We've got another hour before the sun's straight up. And if we need to, we can eat ahorse."

"How in the world do you even know where the sun *is*?" Nyona could hardly see any of the cloudy, gray sky through the obstructing trees.

"A trick, I guess. Never fails!" He grinned.

"Well, if we aren't stopping, then let's get going. I want to try to shave down that day estimate of yours." She briefly squeezed her lower legs into her horse and shifted her hips forward to continue past Mathis, but he caught up to her swiftly.

"You want to lead, now?"

"If I were leading, we'd be headed back to Morell."

He sighed. "We have our mission."

"I don't understand what value this Adept could possibly bring to the rebellion. She has got to be on the verge of losing her Ability, if she hasn't already. And what if she's gone mad from being implanted?"

"Kelda said that wouldn't happen, and there's no reason not to believe her. Besides, they say Renai went mad because she ripped the implant out of her neck like a damned fool, not because of the implant itself. Tovi's fine, isn't she?"

"But—" she started.

"Just stop," Mathis said, impatience clear in his tone. "I'm not thrilled about having to go after this Adept, either, but you've got to trust the bigger plan. I'm certain the Captain and the others have thought through all the possibilities. They wouldn't risk all this if they thought the Adept would be no good to us at all. So shut up about it already."

A flare of indignation burned through her. No man but Mathis *ever* talked to her like that. "That's easy for you to say," Nyona snapped. "You've lived with these people half your life. I've been with you all of, what, six months? And not, if I might add, under the best of circumstances. Remember Brien? That was a lot for me to overcome."

Mathis cast his eyes down to the snow. "I remember."

His simple words merely fueled her temper. "Besides, the last time I agreed to do as I was told, no questions asked, I was kicked out of the Conclave, the only home I'd ever known, and left to fend for myself. So I'm not going to put blind faith in your Captain, or in the rebellion, or in *anyone*, no matter what you say."

"*Shh*, calm down. I'm not asking you to put blind faith in the rebellion. I certainly don't—you should know that by now. I'm just saying that in this situation, trust that they think this Adept's worth the risk."

"You don't get it," Nyona said, feeling the anger still simmering in her blood.

"Explain it to me, then. Why'd you get kicked out of the Conclave, anyway?"

Nyona immediately regretted losing her temper. What he asked wasn't a secret—she had explained her circumstances to the leaders of the rebellion long ago—but it felt awkward telling her story to a man, even one who normally was not unpleasant to be around. "There's nothing much to explain. I couldn't produce an Adept, so they sent me on my way," she said, hoping it would suffice.

Mathis cocked his head toward her. "This sounds like a good story. Start from the beginning."

Of course he wouldn't let it go, now that she'd raised the subject like a fool. *He might as well know.* At least Avrey was out of earshot. "When I lost my Ability, I moved to Seclusion, expecting to spend only a few months there before moving on."

"Seclusion? Never heard of it. Where is it?"

"It's not a town. It's in the Conclave itself—a kind of preparation area where Adepts go right after losing their Ability. There, you begin lessons meant to prepare you for becoming a Master, such as learning how to read—"

"Wait—learning how to *read?*" Mathis said, his brow scrunching up in disbelief. "Weren't you something like twenty years old then?"

"No Adept knows how to read before Seclusion. The Masters claim the knowledge interferes with one's Ability."

"That can't be true. Tovi knows how to read, and her Ability seems just fine."

"I didn't say it was *true*. It's just what they *claim*. Anyway, after a few months in Seclusion, I got sick with the plague along with quite a few other women."

"Fires! Truly? I had no idea. You show no signs of it."

"I was lucky. Many others died. Obviously, I survived, but it took another year before they deemed me ready for Generation."

"Is that another place in the Conclave?"

"Kind of... Generation is the ceremony where you create a new Adept, and women going through the ceremony stay in a specific area."

"What, um, does 'create' mean, exactly?" Mathis asked, eyebrows waggling.

Nyona shot him a withering look. "You know exactly what it means, you disgusting pig. They pair you up with a man, and you—well, *you know*—and you end up pregnant with a new Adept."

"Where do they get the men?"

"I don't know. The Masters selected one for each of us, claiming that the only way we could create a new Adept was with that man, and only during Generation." She snorted. "Of course, that ended up being a lie, too. So for all I know, they pulled men up from off the street."

"Hmm. So. You're in Generation. What happened? Feel free to include details."

Nyona smirked. *Men.* "Sorry. I don't remember anything about it."

"Your partner must not have been that talented. *I've* never had that complaint."

She punched him on his arm. "Stop it. No Adept remembers. They give you some kind of drug to enhance your fertility, but a side effect is memory loss. Not that the drug helped me any. My first attempt at Generation failed, and my second, too. That almost never happens, and the Masters weren't sure what to do with me."

"How so?"

"Well, you can't be a Master if you don't produce an Adept."

"That's the stupidest thing I've ever heard. What does it matter if you bear a child? You'd been an Adept, you knew how things worked—right?" Mathis asked, shaking his head.

"It's just the way it is; the rules require expulsion after two failures. Yet before me, a double failure apparently hadn't happened for years and years. Given the situation with the plague, though, some of the Masters fought to give me another chance."

"I take it that didn't pan out, either."

"Right. After my third failure, no one stood up for me. I argued that I still could help Adepts harness their Ability, and at one point, it seemed the higher-ups had heard me and would change their minds, but in the end, they didn't really care. They tossed me out like trash." Their betrayal would never leave her memory. Never.

"Wow," Mathis said. "That was stupid, given that you ended up pregnant with an Adept later on. They must have picked the wrong man for you."

"Maybe." Nyona paused, thoughtful. "You know, I still don't understand it. Setting aside the Conclave's losses due to the plague, it's reckless to kick out women who can't bear children. The Masters all help raise one another's children, and there's no reason I couldn't have done that as well. No Adept at the Conclave knows who her mother is, anyway."

"Truly? So your mother could still be there?"

"She could be. She could also be dead. Many Masters got the plague, too."

A tree branch laden with snow cracked and fell to the ground a few feet from Nyona. Her horse whinnied and shied to the left, bumping into Mathis's horse, who snapped back. "Settle, settle," Mathis murmured, patting his mount's neck.

"Everything okay?" Avrey called.

Mathis twisted in his saddle to look back at the boy. "All good," he replied. "Best to keep back as you've been doing, though, in case something else falls."

"Will do."

They rode for a few minutes in companionable silence before Mathis returned to their conversation. "So what happened after you left?" he asked.

Nyona wiped away some snot from her nose with the back of her gloved hand. "I was supposed to report to someone in Corval about getting set up with a new life, but I wanted nothing to do with the Conclave's offerings. I fell in with a troupe of actors, instead, and I traveled with them for some time. That's how I met Tovi's father."

"Brien?"

"No. I met Brien later on, after Tovi and I had left the troupe.

She'd started showing signs of having Ability, so it was too danger-ous to stay with them. Brien offered to...to help keep us safe." She felt her voice crack slightly as she finished the sentence. *I'm sorry, Brien,* she thought for what felt like the thousandth time.

"That wasn't supposed to happen," Mathis said with a sidelong glance. "It was Sonya's fault, for barreling in there without a plan."

"I know, I know," Nyona said, ignoring the sting in her eyes. "I don't blame you all anymore for what she did on her own. It's just that—what was that?"

Mathis held up his left hand in a fist, signaling a halt. Nyona's horse whuffed at the sudden stop. Fear washed over her as the sound of riders grew louder. *Maybe they're just traders,* she thought, but knew that no legitimate trader would choose the forest over the roads. *Robbers,* she hoped instead. They could handle robbers.

In the distance, a dozen riders emerged from a thick copse of trees. They all wore black-and-silver uniforms, crisp and clean, the same colors carrying through the leather of their horses' bridles and reins. The group paused for a moment, and then rode closer with obvious purpose. Nyona's stomach flipped.

"Mathis, it's a Guard unit," Avrey said from right behind them, his voice low and urgent. "A *real* one."

"It was bound to happen at some point," Mathis murmured. "Keep calm. Nyona, no talking. No matter what."

Nyona nodded, remembering their plan. As the only woman in their little group, others would expect her to be in charge. Had it been traders they faced—or even robbers—it would be easy to project such authority. But Guards were different. They had their own code, their own references, and their own expectations of command that she could never hope to replicate. She took slow, long breaths to steady her nerves.

"Greetings, strangers," hailed a female rider at the front of the group. She pressed the edge of her left fist against her forehead in a brief salute, below the hat that covered her head and ears. Mathis and Nyona repeated the gesture. "I am Lieutenant Olinda, from the Napimir Unit. Where are you based?" she asked, peering at the insignia stitched on Nyona's borrowed uniform.

"Um, sorry there, Lieutenant, but Sergeant Alma here's got a bad case of laryngitis and can't speak for shit. We're from the Morell Unit," Mathis replied.

"Ah, Morell. Well, that explains the unfortunate condition of your uniforms and gear. How you can stand working out of that backwater outpost is beyond me." The woman sniffed. "Well, Sergeant Alma, if you can't talk, then your man can answer for you. I assume you have the same orders as we do; all the other Guards we've passed have. Any sign of the runaway Adept?"

"No, ma'am. We passed some other folks a while back, though, who claimed they'd heard rumors of her being in Brome."

"Brome? Ha! Wouldn't it be fantastic if we found her in the same place where we routed the rebels before? Something symbolic about that, for certain. Hmm. Maybe the rebels think we wouldn't bother to look there twice?"

Nyona feigned boredom at the prospect. Everyone knew about Brome; it served as a stark reminder of the Conclave's absolute power over Corinas. Once a popular mountain retreat, the Conclave's Guard had destroyed the burgeoning rebellion there many years ago, killing most of the rebels, many of the citizens who'd harbored them, and an Adept who had switched sides. From what she'd heard, Brome today was nothing more than heaps of collapsed walls and burned-out stores. An enterprising Lieutenant seeking to make Captain one day might be enticed to follow Mathis's false thread—which conveniently led far away from the safe house—in hopes that a bit of the Conclave's "glory" in Brome might repeat itself through her.

"That's so, ma'am. The Sergeant here, she didn't believe it none, because it sounded a little *too* convenient, if you know what I mean. So we kept going this way, to see what we see."

The Lieutenant seemed to accept Mathis's story. "That may be wise of you, Sergeant Alma, though we haven't seen anything back that way. I'm not one to hold up another's mission, though, especially someone from Morell. You really should put in for a transfer, you know, if you ever want to get ahead."

Nyona nodded and shrugged as if to say, *What can I do?* She nudged Mathis's leg with her foot and gave him what she hoped was a particularly commanding glare. She wasn't sure how much longer she could maintain her act; she could feel nervous perspiration collecting at her temples.

"Yes, ma'am. Well, Sergeant here wants to get going, so we'll be on our way. For the good of the Conclave," Mathis said, saluting with his fist.

"For the good of the Conclave," Lieutenant Olinda repeated, offering her own brief salute.

The two groups parted, each continuing on in opposite directions. Nyona wanted nothing more than to urge her horse into a trot, but she instead followed Mathis at an excruciatingly slow pace past the remaining Guard members. It wasn't until they had passed through the thick copse of trees, many minutes later, that Mathis finally gave the command.

"Ride!"

❧

Chapter 10

Mathis

In the middle of a shabby clearing of frozen mud, a squat building made of uneven timber planks leaned dangerously to one side. Cracked, opaque glass filled tiny windows on either side of the door, and a patchy thatch roof completed the ramshackle structure. Two horses, dirty and absent of any tack, occupied a lopsided lean-to that rested against the building. It didn't look like a place one would want to spend any amount of time, and Mathis could not have been happier to see it.

Sixteen hours had passed since their chance encounter with the Napimir Guard unit. They'd ridden hard and fast through the night, pausing only to eat a few bites and water and rest the horses. Despite the confidence he'd expressed to Nyona, Mathis hadn't been so certain they'd get away unscathed. He didn't tell her that, though. She was still looking over her shoulder every two minutes, and he didn't want to encourage her paranoia.

Though I suppose it's not paranoia when they really are *after you.*

"This is it?" Nyona said, sounding dismayed. "It doesn't look particularly safe."

"Don't worry. This is all for show; most is underground." Mathis swung his right leg behind the saddle and hopped off, dropping the reins. His horse wouldn't wander; the Guard trained them up to ground tie.

The plank-wood door opened. An old woman wearing a brown belted dress smiled with delight. "Mathis, my boy! I didn't know they'd be sending you!" She held out her arms toward him.

Mathis grinned and gathered his old nursemaid in a gentle hug. "It's good to see you. Are you well?" She had more wrinkles and brown spots on her face and hands than he remembered from the last time he'd seen her.

"Oh, I'm fine," she said, patting him on his back. "I live in Dakeforth proper now, all fancy like. Didn't you know? I only come out to check here every now and then, though I've been here a bit now to help care for the girl." She pushed against his arms and peered around him. "But who's this with you?"

"This is Nyona, and this here is Avrey. Nyona, Avrey, meet Movani. She helped care for me when I was young." Nyona and Avrey murmured greetings in response.

Movani tugged at his hand. "Enough of the pleasantries, then. Let's go in before someone wanders by and wonders why an old woman like me is having so many visitors. Let the boy handle the horses; be sure to hide away all the Guard trappings."

"Avrey? You got that?"

"Sure, no problem," Avrey said, scooping up Mathis's reins from the ground.

Movani led Mathis into the house, and Nyona followed. Inside, Sonya sat in one of the four chairs surrounding a rough-hewn table, her brown hair hiding part of her face as she leaned over a book. Her crisp and clean uniform contrasted sharply with his and Nyona's dirty clothes and unwashed hair. He was suddenly quite aware of how he must smell.

Sonya looked up and sighed. "Of course it would be you. No wonder it's taken so long for someone to come. And I see you've brought our new friend as well. How...interesting. Hello, Nyona."

"Hello," Nyona said in a flat voice. She'd promised to play nice for the mission's sake, but apparently she didn't consider idle pleasantries to be part of that promise. Her dirty travel uniform and disheveled hair contrasted starkly with Sonya's neat appearance.

This should be fun, Mathis thought darkly. Not that he wanted much to do with his sister, either. The less time spent around her, the better for him and Nyona both. "You know we're here earlier than you expected someone to arrive," he said. "And if the Adept's ready to go, we'll leave first thing tomorrow."

"Why the rush? Are you that anxious to worm your way into the good graces of yet another Adept?" Sonya snarked. "Besides, it's been quite some time since we last saw each other. Shouldn't we spend some time together, as brother and sister, to reconnect?" She clasped her hands together in front of her chest and flashed a most insincere smile. "I'm just dying to know why you brought *her* along."

Ignoring her first taunt, he responded to her second. "Captain Jana ordered her to come. She can get messages through Tovi, and she's also supposed to try to win over the Adept. I can't imagine you've even tried."

"I've tried. She doesn't talk much." Sonya said. She picked up her book and idly flipped through the pages. "Fires. No wonder Jana turned you into a nursemaid for Adepts. You clearly have no aptitude for anything meaningful."

"At least I follow orders," Mathis retorted with some heat. "Everything you do leads to more problems, including grabbing this Adept before we were ready. Your stupidity is probably what tipped off the Conclave."

"Don't be ridiculous," Sonya scoffed. "The Conclave is blissfully unaware of us, just as they've been for years. Blaming me for your delusions will get you nowhere. If you had any brains at all—"

"Am I in the presence of a grown man and woman, or do I see a pair of young children once again?" Movani interrupted. "Have you forgotten you are both on the same side? It'd be best to remember that when you're in front of the girl."

Mathis dropped his gaze to the floor; an old habit from childhood. "Sorry, Movani," he apologized.

"Yes. Our apologies," Sonya said begrudgingly. At least she managed to show some decency for the old woman's sake.

Mathis cleared his throat. "But back to what I said—it's true. The Conclave knows we have the Adept, and there are Guards out there right now looking for her."

Sonya sat up straight. "Impossible. Master Ciara assured us the Conclave had accepted the tribunal's report of the Adept running off with a merchant. Why would she lie to us?"

"She didn't," Nyona responded. "The Conclave told her what they wanted us to hear."

"What do you mean, 'what they wanted us to hear?'"

"Tovi overheard a conversation involving the Headmaster of the Conclave when she was using her Ability. She learned that the Conclave sent the Adept to Aldham as bait for the rebellion."

Sonya leaned back in her chair and gave an exasperated snort. "Hysteria over the words of a child? For a moment, I thought you might be serious." She picked up her book again, as if the conversation were now over.

Her quick dismissal of Tovi's trustworthiness annoyed Mathis. "She told it true. We ran into a Guard unit from Napimir on the way here. Their Lieutenant talked about how everyone had received orders to look for the Adept and the rebels who had her."

Sonya looked up from her book with narrowed eyes. "When?"

"Yesterday. They said they'd come from this general direction. I take it you didn't see anything?"

"No one's been near the cabin since we've been here. Movani? Could you please ask Hasso to come up?" Movani nodded and shuffled through a second door at the back of the room. "He's down with the Adept," Sonya explained.

This day just gets better and better. He'd hoped that Hasso's initial absence meant the medic had already gone off on some other mission. At least Mathis would be free of both his sister and Hasso on the morrow. He had no intention of remaining at the safe house any longer than necessary.

"Is he treating her? Has she shown any ill effects from the implant?" Nyona asked.

"No—well, at least, no *unintentional* ill effects," Sonya said wryly. "The implant works as it should, and there's been no infection. She sleeps a lot."

"Her behavior is unchanged?"

"How would I know? She still acts like an entitled little bitch when she's awake, so I suppose so."

Nyona glared at Mathis, as if his sister's slurs were his own. Though Sonya had a point; Adepts were an entitled bunch. Nyona still had a streak of that in her, though he'd never say so to her face. Tovi was the exception; she was good-natured and hardworking. It embarrassed him now to think of how bitter he'd been when the Captain first assigned him the task of guarding the child.

Sonya tapped her fingers against the table. "I hope you understand, of course, that the Adept cannot know her people are looking for her. Not even a hint of it," she said. "She thinks the Conclave has willingly abandoned her, and we'll never get her to cooperate with us if she finds out that's not true."

"I'm surprised she believed you in the first place," said Mathis.

"I'm not," muttered Nyona.

Sonya grinned. "I found it extraordinary. Apparently this Adept already believed the Conclave wanted to be rid of her, and that's why they sent her all the way to Aldham. Why, I have no idea. Obviously, they aren't shy about removing Adepts through other means."

Floorboards creaked as footsteps approached, and the back door opened. "Here he is," Movani said, ushering Hasso into the room. "The girl's fast asleep."

"Hello Mathis, Nyona," the medic said in a soft, whispery voice. *I'm sorry*, he'd once claimed in that same, detached tone. *I didn't know.* Mathis shook his head, discarding the memory.

"Hasso." Sonya gestured toward Mathis and Nyona with one hand. "They claim Tovi overheard someone in the Conclave talking about how they set us up to take the Adept. Then, they apparently ran into a Guard unit yesterday who was asking about her, and supposedly, there are more units doing the same. Have you seen or heard anything when you've been in town?"

"I would have told you, if so." His rebuke was gentle. "Dakeforth has been quiet."

Sonya curled her fingers and held them to her chin for a moment, thoughtful. "Well, if it *is* true, then we need to get her, and us, out of here right away." She laid her hands flat against the table. "We'll all leave for Morell tomorrow."

Fires. Mathis needed to stop this idea before it gained traction. "Captain made no mention of you two returning. If she'd wanted you to, she would've asked you to bring the Adept back yourselves. You should continue with your original orders."

"Clearly, given what you've reported, *our* orders are outdated. Unless you'd like to recant this tale of yours?"

Mathis scowled and shook his head once.

"That's what I thought." Sonya smirked before turning back to Hasso. "We need to go with them and find out what Jana wants us to do now. The plans must have changed, and maybe the reason we haven't had any messages since we left is because none could get through."

"More of us would mean a better chance—better protection, right?" Nyona asked. Mathis shot her an annoyed look, but she didn't notice. Why would she want to spend any more time with his sister than she had to? She hated Sonya, and with good reason. *The encounter with the Guard unit must have rattled her even more than I thought.*

"Under these circumstances, I agree," replied Hasso. "If we want to get the Adept back to Morell without incident, it's best to present ourselves as a more fulsome Guard unit in the event we run across others."

"It's decided, then," said Sonya, smacking the palms of her hands against the table. "We'll leave for Morell in the morning. But first things first: it's time for you to meet Alia."

CHAPTER 11

SARABIE

SNOWFLAKES CLUNG TO Sarabie's window, fresh ones replacing the old as they warmed and slid down the surface of the glass. She idly traced a line of liquid with her finger. The snow had been falling since last night, transforming the garden in the midst of the Generation wing into a beautiful, silent haven.

Sarabie let the heavy curtain fall back into place and considered the meal of bread, soft cheese, and smoked bacon waiting for her at the table. Why they thought she could eat anything this morning was beyond her. Perhaps she would drink some of the tea they'd given her to ease the nervous anticipation that had taken root in her stomach. She poured the hot liquid from the covered teapot into a white porcelain cup rimmed in gold. A sip revealed mint, chamomile, and a few notes she couldn't identify by taste alone. It was delicious.

I wonder how it will begin today.

After a little more than a week here, the Masters had declared her ready for Generation. Sarabie was more than ready to move on. While she marveled at the elegance and luxury that surrounded her —a far cry from her previous quarters—she had not left her room since her arrival to this wing of Seclusion, and she'd seen no one but Master Nivi and a few eunuchs.

Marta had been right about all that. The thought caused a spike of anxiety to shoot through her, and not for the first time. *What if she's right about the rest?* She had thought often of Marta's claim that Generation was not as the Masters taught them it would be. She'd concluded Marta must have been confused, but that didn't eliminate her periodic doubt.

Sarabie drank the rest of her tea before it cooled, then poured some more. Today was her special day, and she would *not* let Marta's unfounded accusations spoil it for her. Generation *was* special, and right now, there was a man—*one* man—waiting to help her create a new Adept. She'd looked forward to Generation ever since she had learned as a child that one day, her Ability would fade. Generation gave her life purpose now that she had no Ability to call her own.

Sarabie was finishing her third cup of tea when the outer bolt to her door slid open. Master Nivi walked into her chambers, unannounced as usual. Her sponsor smiled as she approached. "Good morning, Sarabie. Are you feeling well? You've not eaten your breakfast!"

Sarabie smiled back. "I couldn't possibly, Master Nivi. It's okay, though. I'm fine."

"You should eat something. Today is a very special day, and you don't want it to be spoiled by hunger pains. Did you enjoy the tea?"

"Yes, Master Nivi. It's quite good." Sarabie tipped the teapot to pour herself some more. A drip fell into the cup.

"Ah, you're out. I'll have more brought right away."

"Oh, please don't trouble anyone; I've probably had enough tea for one morning."

"Nonsense. We will waste no effort to make sure you have everything you need today, including more tea to chase away the chill of the morning. I'll be right back." Master Nivi retreated from the room, closing the door behind her, and the bolt slid back into place.

Sarabie surveyed the food before her once more. She supposed Master Nivi was right; she didn't know what the rest of the day would bring as far as meals went, and the tea had settled her stomach somewhat. As she nibbled on the edge of a piece of bread, she decided she was glad Master Nivi had ignored her. More tea would be most welcome.

She reached for another chunk of bread, and was surprised to find none left. No cheese or bacon remained, either. She must have been daydreaming as she ate; she did not remember eating all that food. The inside of her mouth felt dry; where was Master Nivi with her tea?

As if her thought acted as a summons, Master Nivi appeared, carrying a new teapot. "Oh! You ate. Wonderful. You're probably thirsty now, yes? Here you go."

Master Nivi poured fresh tea into Sarabie's cup. The hot liquid burned Sarabie's tongue, but she drank it all without pause. She held up her empty cup, and Master Nivi refilled it for her. Her face felt flush. Maybe she should have waited for the tea to cool.

"It's quite an honor, Sarabie. She only visits a few people before their ceremony. I expect she'll be here any minute."

"Who?" Sarabie asked.

"Master Gersemi, of course. Whom did you think I was speaking of?" Master Nivi smiled. "Your cup is empty. Would you like some more? Of course."

Sarabie was halfway through another cup when Master Gersemi strode into the room, light reflecting from the silver designs embossed over the entire surface of her gray robe. Master Nivi stood and bowed her head; Sarabie thought she should stand, too, but it would be such an effort. Master Gersemi would understand.

"Good morning, Sarabie," Master Gersemi said in a deep voice. "I came to wish you a successful Generation."

Master Gersemi continued, talking of destiny and duty. Sarabie tried to focus on her words; she did not want the Headmaster to think she didn't appreciate the visit. The last time Sarabie had seen her was during Marta's Ascension ceremony, months and months and months ago, and Sarabie had never been this close to her. Alia had because she so often found herself in trouble. *Not me. I'm good.*

"I think you've had enough tea, my dear," said Master Gersemi. She pried the empty cup from Sarabie's clutching fingers and set it aside. "How do you feel?" she asked.

Sarabie pondered the question for a moment. Feelings were so subjective. What she felt right now might not be what she felt a few moments from now. She curled her toes in the thick pile of the rug beneath her chair. So many threads. Where had her slippers gone? They must be somewhere...

"Master Nivi, I believe it's time." Master Gersemi leaned down and kissed Sarabie on both cheeks. "May today bring the Conclave great fortune through you," she said. She turned and walked from the room.

Master Nivi squatted to place slippers on Sarabie's feet. "Do you need to use the lavatory before we leave?"

Excitement coursed through her. *I'm leaving!* She stood, grinning, then clutched the Master's arm for support as a wave of dizziness passed through her.

"Sarabie. I asked if you needed to use the lavatory."

"Oh. Yes. Yes." She had drunk quite a bit of tea. Better to take care of things now. Master Nivi led her to the lavatory and helped her use the chamber pot. She wondered where the Master would take her next. Maybe she'd visit the lovely, lovely garden, the one with all the snow.

"No, we're not going to the garden," said Master Nivi, as she steered Sarabie toward the door.

Sarabie clamped her lips together to keep them from betraying her again. Outside in the hallway, a tall eunuch wrapped his arm around her shoulder. As he guided her down the hall, she twisted to look behind her. Master Gersemi was speaking to a Master Sarabie didn't know, gesturing to punctuate her words.

"...and when we do, we'll destroy them all," Master Gersemi snapped. She noticed Sarabie then, and frowned before turning and walking away swiftly. The second Master glanced toward Sarabie as well before scurrying after Master Gersemi. Light scattered from the lamps positioned on either side of the corridor as they passed.

Why would Master Gersemi want to destroy anything on this lovely day? Sarabie turned to ask the Masters, but her legs tangled in the attempt. Only the strong grip of her supporter kept her from falling to the ground. All other thoughts fled as she concentrated on putting one foot before another as they followed Master Nivi.

They turned down a dimly lit corridor. The stone walls were much rougher here, with lamps ancient and few. At the end of the hall, the eunuch helped her navigate down a spiral staircase. The steps went on forever. Sarabie tried to count them, but gave up after forgetting the number three times. Did she hear water? That made no sense; they were inside, after all. She had to be imagining things.

At the bottom of the staircase, their path took a confusing set of turns until they reached a short footbridge suspended by metal chains. A black door set in an arch stood at the opposite end. Sarabie's first step on the bridge's wooden planks caused it to sway, and she grasped the ropes on either side, certain she would pitch headfirst into the stream below. The attendant murmured some-thing reassuring, and somehow, somehow, she made it across.

She poked at the crisscross pattern carved several inches into the door's dark wood. Master Nivi batted Sarabie's hand away, then knocked on the door three times—or perhaps five. It opened, revealing a few more steps. Sarabie wearied of steps.

A narrow pool of light illuminated a small, round table and a woman wearing the gray-and-silver robes of a Master. Master Nivi paused before the second Master, and Sarabie drooped her body toward the ground, hoping to rest. To her annoyance, the eunuch pulled her upright. They had been walking for such a long time.

"Whom do you bring before us?" intoned the unknown Master.

"This is Sarabie, who was once an Adept," Master Nivi replied.

"Has she passed the necessary tests?"

"Yes, she has met all requirements for entry."

Tests? Sarabie didn't remember taking any tests. Well, whatever it was, Master Nivi covered for her. Perhaps she had misjudged her sponsor.

"Is she prepared?" the woman at the table asked.

"No, she is not."

Confusion drifted into Sarabie's consciousness. She tried again to sit, but the eunuch's arms thwarted her once more.

The strange Master raised a small, dark square from a tray on the table. She passed it to Master Nivi, who then held it to Sarabie's lips. It smelled of cloves and anise, and it stuck to the roof of her mouth before dissolving. Flavors of chocolate and spice exploded over her tongue, and even some kind of spirit. Delicious.

No one said anything for many long minutes. Sarabie stood motionless, uncertain if they expected her to do something. The eunuch still wouldn't let her rest. Maybe they'd give her more of that chocolate.

Master Nivi pushed up the left sleeve of Sarabie's robe with one hand. The Master held a small knife in her other hand, its hilt decorated in gold and silver. Sarabie watched, fascinated, as the Master drew the blade slowly across Sarabie's forearm, parting her pale skin. Blood flowed from the wound and dripped to the stone floor. A giggle escaped from Sarabie's lips. Shouldn't it hurt when you bleed?

"Is she prepared?" the other Master repeated.

"She is prepared," pronounced Master Nivi. She set the knife on the tray.

"Proceed."

The door behind Sarabie boomed shut. Master Nivi supported her as the other woman spread a salve on the cut and wrapped a strange, shiny bandage around her arm. The two Masters escorted her out of the beam of light into another dark corridor. They weren't nearly as strong as the servant had been. She hoped he didn't think her rude for failing to wish him farewell.

Another door opened, and they stepped into a hot, humid room full of light. Sarabie squinted and blinked. Her eyes adjusted, and she marveled as she took in her surroundings. White marble walls, veined with silver, continued up and up to an impossibly high ceiling made of frosted glass. Vines dotted with fragrant yellow flowers crawled up narrow columns that formed a circle inside the room. Globes of light floated in the middle of the columns, and below them—below them was a bath like she had never seen. It was fitted into the ground itself, and steam rose from its surface. She wanted nothing more than to immerse herself in that water, and to her delight, she found herself already naked.

The Masters helped Sarabie to the edge of the bath, where two eunuchs appeared to take her hands. She put one foot in the hot water, then eased the rest of her body into the bath. One eunuch cradled her head against his chest, and she let her feet drift up toward the surface of the water. Finally left in peace, she fell asleep.

Sarabie woke, disoriented. She lay on top of a bed piled with pillows and blankets, her bare skin glistening with aromatic oil. Red velvet covered the walls, or perhaps it was purple; in the dim lighting, she couldn't tell which. A sweet-smelling incense filled the room. She tried to sit up, but the room spun and she gave up the attempt. The bed was quite comfortable, after all. She closed her eyes.

The door opened. A handsome eunuch with long, reddish-brown hair entered the room. She waved him away; she needed nothing at this time but rest. If he didn't leave, she'd report him for bothering her. He wasn't even wearing a proper uniform, and he'd somehow hidden the tattoo on his hand. If the Masters saw him dressed in that short, black robe edged in silver, they'd punish him for certain. She opened her mouth to issue a command, but her lips and tongue would not form the words.

She then noticed the strawberries he carried in a silver bowl. *My favorite!* He offered one to her, and she took a bite without raising her head from the pillow. It was a bit overripe, but she didn't care. She hadn't eaten strawberries in *ages*.

Sarabie sighed in satisfaction as the eunuch placed the empty bowl on the side table. He walked to the foot of the bed and unfastened the clasp at the side of his robe. It fell to the floor. *A man!* He was in even more trouble than she first thought. Everyone knew that a man found inside the Conclave's walls faced immediate execution. Yet she hoped that wouldn't happen to him; his presence strangely pleased her. There was something—*something*—she should remember, but she couldn't grab hold of the thought.

The man climbed onto the bed and crept closer to her. *What is he doing? He'll get me in trouble, too.* His hands slid up her legs, and she tried to kick him away, but her muscles refused to act. The man's hands traveled even higher, exploring, and she felt her body responding to his touch. *The Masters will know, they will come.*

He shifted his body and pushed her legs farther apart. His hair fell against her chest, and she heard nothing but his panting as he moved his body back and forth against hers. *The Masters will know, they will come, they will throw me out.* Wait—no they won't. There was a reason for that, if she could only remember what it was. The man grasped her hips close to him, holding her for what seemed an eternity.

She blinked, and found herself alone again. Incense grew thick in the air. Everything was as it should be. Maybe she would remember why after a little more sleep.

Sarabie woke underneath blankets. Her head pounded, and her mouth was parched. Steam rose from a teacup on the side table next to the bed. She reached for it and drank without waiting for the liquid to cool. The tea was sweeter than she liked, but tasted of mint, chamomile, and something else she could not name. Or was it familiar? *I'm so tired.* She put a hand to her head and lay back against the pillows.

The door opened. A eunuch entered the room, clad in a black-and-silver robe, just like the other one. Or had that been a dream? It was so hard to remember. The eunuch brushed a lock of blond hair from his eyes and presented her with a small bowl of strawberries. *My favorite!* He fed the berries to her one by one with plain, unadorned hands. How had he managed to hide his tattoo?

The eunuch set the bowl to the side and removed his robe. *A man*, Sarabie thought, unsurprised. He stood at the foot of the bed and shoved the blankets aside. Goosebumps appeared on her bare skin, yet her limbs felt dull and heavy. He pulled her toward him by her ankles and spread her legs apart. She thought she might be dreaming; she did have such vivid dreams sometimes. *The Masters will come…they will know…*

Sarabie woke when the door opened. A eunuch, garbed in a black robe edged in silver, stood beside her bed. His dark hair was nearly the same color as his robe, and he held a small bowl of strawberries in one hand. *My favorite!* As he placed a berry in her mouth, she wondered why he wore a robe instead of his uniform. She could not think of a reason, though it seemed like she should...

CHAPTER 12

MATHIS

NERVOUSNESS SURGED THROUGH Mathis, as if he were headed into a fight. This fight wouldn't be physical—at least, he didn't expect it to be—but his body didn't know the difference. The Adept he was about to meet, born and raised within the halls of the Conclave, would be nothing like Tovi, and anxiousness kept his adrenaline running high.

Despite what he'd told Nyona the other day, he doubted the wisdom of Captain Jana's orders. How in the world was he supposed to earn this Adept's trust for the rebellion when he could never have any trust for her?

Mathis joined Sonya in the small sleeping chamber located just off the safe house's front room. A bed with flat pillows and threadbare quilts took up most of the space in front of the door, leaving little room for Hasso and Nyona to join them. At the foot of the bed, a small wardrobe was jammed against the wall, its door askew from the top hinge. The cabin's patchwork floorboards masked the seams of the panel that granted access to the tunnels hiding beneath the aboveground facade.

Hasso crossed over to the wardrobe and contorted his arm to reach a spot inside of it. A latch below the floor made a loud click, and Nyona jumped back as a panel slid open near her feet.

"Hurry now; it will close soon, whether you're all the way through or not," instructed Sonya before she disappeared down the ladder.

"Go ahead," Mathis told Nyona, and she rushed into the opening as if she feared the panel would decapitate her at any moment. He moved to follow her, not wanting to leave the two women alone for very long lest they remember how much they dislike each other. "You coming?" he asked Hasso from the top of the ladder.

"No," Hasso answered in his peculiar, soft voice. "I'll remain with Movani and the boy, in case there's trouble. Go, and good luck." The panel clicked again and closed.

Mathis hurried the rest of the way down to where Nyona and his sister waited, nearly missing the last rung in his haste. A lamp cast long shadows against rough, pitted stone walls. "Hasso's staying upstairs," he reported.

"Of course he is," Sonya said, as she led them down the tunnel at a rapid pace. "Someone with appropriate experience should always be above ground, if possible. Movani and the boy aren't going to be of much help if someone unexpected shows up. I swear, Mathis. It's like we weren't trained by the same people."

We weren't. His training came from regular Guards, not from people like Hasso. He opened his mouth to tell her exactly what he thought about her particular brand of training, but Nyona tugged on his sleeve and shook her head. Why did she care what he said to Sonya? Nonetheless, he held his tongue.

Lamps set at regular intervals along the right side of the tunnel lit up as they approached and flickered out once they passed. They soon reached a larger, open space carved from the stone. Three passages branched out from the space in different directions, two of which were dark. Sonya turned down the illuminated one on the left, which eventually brought them to an iron-banded door.

"Before we go in, remember: talk to her, be friendly, but reveal very little. If something happens on the way to Morell, she can't tell them what she doesn't know." Sonya lifted the bolt and pulled open the door.

Mathis eased around his sister into the tiny room. Muted light emanated from a small lantern set on the nightstand. The Adept slept in the bed, covered by a gray blanket. She lay on her side, facing them, her hands tucked under the pillow that cradled her head. A white bandage peeked out from above her nightshift, and above that...

"What's wrong with her?" he whispered, shocked.

"I told you, she sleeps a lot. You really need to listen," Sonya chided.

"No, not that. What's wrong with—" he gestured around his head. "She's got no hair. She's got no *eyebrows*, even."

"Oh. That. I have no idea. Do you?" Sonya asked Nyona.

"No. She was like that as a child, too."

Fires. The Adept's pale skin and lack of hair seemed to make her features float on her face. She looked half a child, though she was supposed to be around twenty years old. He stared, fixated, and nearly jumped when the Adept opened her eyes.

"Oh good; she's awake!" Sonya waved her arm in a grandiose fashion toward the girl, who blinked in confusion. "May I present to you her most Honored One, or shall I say, *former* Honored One, Alia." The Adept winced as she pushed herself upright, though it could have been from the bandage on her neck rather than from Sonya's barb. "Alia, this is Mathis, and this is Nyona. They're here to take you to your new home."

Alia glanced at Mathis, then with a slight frown, considered Nyona as she sat in the room's only chair. Mathis hoped the Adept recognized her, given that Nyona's main purpose on this mission rested on their shared background.

"Well then," Sonya said, patting Mathis familiarly on his back. "Why don't the three of you get to know one another better, hmm? I'll be back in a bit."

Alia leaned against the headboard as Sonya left the room, then wrapped her arms around her knees and pulled them close to her chest. She darted her eyes back and forth between Nyona and Mathis, waiting. As the silence grew longer, the urge to speak intensified. How did one go about winning someone's trust after abducting her? With Nyona and Tovi, it had just *happened*, though he suspected it had more to do with Kelda's help on that front than anything he'd done.

"So," he said, before clearing his throat. "Um. You've probably figured out we're not exactly, aligned, so-to-speak, with the Conclave. We hear you might not be, either—aligned, that is—and that's why we brought you here. To see if you might want to join our cause." He immediately realized how ridiculous his words sounded. *As if it were as simple as that.*

The Adept looked at him with distain. "I don't know what those traitors in Aldham told you, but you are fools if you think I will join you," she said. Her voice was low yet strong, and her pale green eyes bore into his own. "My loyalty is to the Conclave."

"Even though they don't care about you?" The Conclave might be looking for her now, but she didn't know that, and besides, the Masters *had* used her as bait to attract the rebellion. They must have considered her expendable. "Listen, all we learned from the tribunal was you weren't always on board with the Conclave's orders and you tended not to follow the rules. So we figured you'd eventually come to us if properly introduced. But plans changed, and, well, now you're here. I apologize for how it came about, though."

"Apologies are mere words when they come from someone with no honor," Alia said with contempt.

Indignation warmed his cheeks, and he responded without pause. "No honor? It's not us who lack honor, girl. It's your precious Conclave who kills innocents and sends its lackeys to murder people for daring to disagree!"

The Adept blinked at his onslaught. "The Conclave ensures the good of Corinas," she said, a hint of hesitation creeping into her voice.

"Alia," Nyona interjected softly. "Those are just words repeated out of habit. I know. You might not remember me, but I remember you. You were still a young child when I entered Seclusion many years ago."

Alia's eyes narrowed as she released her knees from her grasp. "So this is the game. I'd wondered when I heard your name. But you cannot be Nyona of the Conclave. She died during the plague; it's recorded in the histories. Try again."

"Is that what the Masters told you all? I suppose it was easier than the truth." Nyona gave the girl a small, sad smile. "I did get sick while in Seclusion, but I survived. Obviously."

The Adept shook her head. "No. You are one of them. A rebel. I know you're lying."

"No—you don't. It's incredibly difficult to learn how to assess someone's honesty without Ability. I've been there, and it takes a lot longer than the time you've had. And even with practice, you can never be sure. Besides, you *do* know the Masters don't always tell you the truth of things—don't you?"

Alia said nothing, but it was clear Nyona had hit a mark. Mathis nodded his head for her to continue. She was much better at this than he.

"So consider this." Nyona leaned forward in the chair. "Do you remember, back before the plague, when the Masters implanted an Adept named Renai in the Ritual Hall?"

Alia's jaw dropped slightly before she closed her mouth again.

"Do you remember?" Nyona pressed.

"Yes," Alia said, reluctant.

"Then you might remember the Masters forcing a young woman —Renai's roommate—to stand beside her on the platform, next to the table they laid her on. You might remember how the Masters forced the roommate—me—to hold the knife as they cut into her neck. You might even remember how Renai screamed. Do you?" Nyona asked, her voice breaking at the end.

Fires. Nyona had never spoken of this before. He knew she'd been Renai's roommate, but he didn't know she'd been made to help implant Renai. If the Conclave was willing to torture its own, no wonder it cared little to none about what it did to the citizens of Corinas.

"I remember," Alia whispered, her eyes wide. "It was the last time they did it in front of us." She stared at Nyona for several long moments. "You *are* Nyona. I see it now. But—how—why did they say you were dead? And why are you here?"

"As for the former, I can't say. They expelled me for failing Generation. As for the latter—well, it's a long story, and one I won't get into now. But suffice it to say, I believe these people have the right of it, and helping them helps us all."

"I don't understand," Alia said, looking briefly at Mathis. "The rebels have been attacking villages. And that woman you were with abducted and *implanted* me." The volume of her voice increased as she spoke. "How can any of that be right?"

"It's not us attacking those villages," Mathis said, annoyed. How could anyone accept such nonsense? The rebellion would never attack the people it sought to save.

"I saw them! A petitioner came to us in Aldham, seeking aid for her village. She said it was the rebellion, and she spoke true!"

"The petitioner spoke the truth as she believed it to be," said Nyona. "Just as you—only a few minutes ago—believed that I was dead. I have no doubt there was an attack on the village. But it wasn't the rebellion."

Alia scratched at her bare scalp above her furrowed brow. "I-I don't know. This doesn't make any sense. Who else could it be?"

"Are you truly that naive?" Mathis asked, exasperated at the Adept's stupidity. "It's the Conclave, trying to discredit us. *Think*, girl. Doesn't that sound like the sort of thing they'd do, if they thought it would end the challenge to their rule?"

"Mathis," Nyona rebuked. "Please."

Mathis pressed his lips together and folded his arms across his chest. Insulting Alia was not the way to win her over, but he couldn't stop himself from speaking up. How could someone be so blind to reality?

"Assuming what you say is true—and I'm not saying it is," Alia said, "it still wouldn't forgive the fact that someone working for you attacked me and did—this to me." She pointed to the back of her neck. "After that, why in the world would I agree to help you?"

"Trust me, she's not working for me and Mathis. If it helps, we don't like her much, either," Nyona said with a wry smile. "As far as the implant goes, I'm not happy with that decision, but it wasn't mine to make. I can assure you, though, that others in similar circumstances have made the choice we're now asking of you."

Alia scrunched up her mouth into a pout of disbelief. "I highly doubt that. In any case, even if I wanted to help you, I couldn't. I don't know anything about anything, and I'm no good for anyone now that I'm implanted. Thanks to you." She leaned back against the headboard again.

"We can remove it," Mathis said.

The skin above her eyes where eyebrows should have been leaped up. "What are you talking about? Implants are permanent."

"Not yours. When—if—we can trust you, we'll remove it. Otherwise, you can spend the rest of your days with a piece of metal stuck in your neck." *Assuming she doesn't follow in Renai's footsteps, anyway.* To be sure, the implant would be the least of her problems if she chose not to join them. He couldn't imagine the Captain would allow her to live.

Alia scrutinized him. "If you can remove it, someone else can, too. Someone who won't force me to betray everything I know in exchange."

"An Adept's duty is to Corinas, not the Conclave," urged Nyona. "You won't be betraying Corinas by helping us. You'll be *saving* Corinas."

Alia rolled her eyes and made an exasperated sound. "That's easy for you to say. You've clearly made your choice." She shook her head. "Look, it's true I don't agree with everything the Masters say and do. And I know I have few options now that they've expelled me from the Conclave on account of that fiction of me running away. But I also know what happened to the last Adept who joined the rebellion. Give me one good reason why I should risk death for you and yours."

Nothing came to Mathis's mind. The Conclave undoubtedly would execute her if they caught her helping the rebellion. Of course, the same was true for them all. He supposed he was used to the constant threat, but the same couldn't be said for her. He hoped Nyona would know what to say.

Yet Nyona said nothing as she sat there rigidly, her eyes staring at nothing. *Fires. Not now.* How was he going to explain this without revealing the child? "Nyona," he said, shaking her shoulder, hoping to break her from Tovi's communication.

Alia peered at Nyona, then gasped. "She's receiving a message from an Adept!" she accused. "What is the meaning of this? Is this a test? I said I was loyal!" She kicked the blankets away from her legs.

"Don't you dare leave that bed," Mathis bellowed, holding a hand out at Alia. *Hurry, Tovi. I need your mother back.* As if the child had heard his plea, Nyona suddenly slumped in her chair. He caught her arm before she fell. "Nyona," he said urgently. "Don't say anything. Let's go upstairs, first."

"No. No. It doesn't matter if she knows," Nyona said in a shaking voice as she lifted her head. "Alia, make your choice. Come with us or stay, it makes no difference, but you must decide *now.*"

What is she doing? He tried to forestall whatever it was. "I think it's best if we—"

"I said, it doesn't matter if she knows," Nyona yelled, shaking off his grip. "Master Ciara has fled Aldham. The other two Masters in the tribunal are dead at the Conclave's command, but not until after they were tortured—and they talked. The Conclave knows we are here with Alia." Nyona's face contorted. "And they know about Tovi. We must flee, *now!*"

CHAPTER 13

ALIA

CONFUSION SWIRLED IN Alia's mind as her captors argued with each other. In a matter of minutes, she had gone from being certain Nyona was a horrendous liar to realizing the Masters were the ones who had lied—about Nyona's death, anyway. And if they'd lied about that, what else might they have said to avoid certain unpleasant truths?

Old fears and suspicions bubbled to the surface. *Why* did *the Masters send me so far away?* With the rest of her Initiate in Seclusion, it was only a matter of time before it became her turn. They could have assigned anyone to confirm the suspected rebel activity in Aldham. Why send her? Perhaps the Masters never intended for her to return home to Corval.

Yet it was plain the rebels also left much unsaid, such as the fact that they'd already turned one Adept, who'd just communicated with Nyona. Their reaction clarified they weren't working for the Conclave, despite their Guard uniforms. Alia scanned her memory for Adepts who might have been susceptible—and available—to the rebellion, but none came to mind. In fact, she was the only Adept she could think of who had ever voiced any disagreement with the Masters at all. Most were mere sheep.

And yet—the rebels claimed the implant they'd given her wasn't permanent. If that were true—and she *needed* for it to be true— then the Masters might remove it despite having already expelled her from the Conclave. The implant would be a sure sign of the rebellion's lies about her, and the Conclave would welcome her back...

Would they? her doubting inner self asked. *They wanted you gone, however it happened. These people may be your only chance to gain back your Ability before it's gone for good.*

Was she willing to take that chance?

"You must decide now, Alia," Nyona repeated. "Will you come with us?" Footsteps pounded outside.

The man with Nyona ducked his head under the doorframe. "Trouble?" he called.

"We thought *you* were in trouble," a woman yelled. A few moments later, Sonya and Hasso reached the door. "What in fires is going on?" Sonya demanded of the man, shoving him back inside the room. "We heard you yelling all the way upstairs through the air vents. You'd better hope no one is skulking about outside." Bright spots of color flushed her cheeks.

"Nyona received a message from Tovi, and—oof," he grunted as Sonya whacked his arm.

"You're speaking gibberish, Mathis. Have you eaten enough today?" She dug her fingernails into him.

Mathis winced. "Ow, dammit, let go," he said. "She already knows. Shut up for once and listen."

"If you think I'm going to stand here and let you order me to—"

"Let him speak." Hasso's unassuming voice did not sound as a command, but his words served to end Sonya's rant nonetheless. "I trust he would not bring this up in the girl's presence if it were not important."

Mathis stepped away from Sonya and her scowl, placing himself near the foot of the bed in one of the few remaining spaces in the crowded room. "Let Nyona tell you. She's the one who talked to Tovi."

Confusion returned. Alia knew of no Adept named Tovi who was old enough to communicate.

Nyona's face had taken on a sickly pallor. "They know where we are," she said, without preamble. "Our orders have changed. We're to leave immediately—with or without Alia."

"What? How? If that Guard unit you ran into has something to do with this..." Sonya's threat remained unvoiced.

"It wasn't us," said Nyona. "The Conclave acted against the tribunal in Aldham. They were tortured and gave us up before they were killed."

"Ciara is dead?" Hasso asked, louder than Alia had ever heard him speak. Sonya and Mathis looked at him askance.

"No," Nyona replied. "Masters Kyra and Ardell are dead. Master Ciara escaped. We will meet her...later," she said, glancing in Alia's direction.

"I'll bet Ardell talked," Sonya said under her breath. "I never trusted that one."

"Show some respect, Sonya," Mathis snapped. "They died for the cause. Not everyone can withstand what the Conclave dishes out, no matter how hard they try, as you and Hasso well know."

An uncomfortable silence filled the room. Alia felt as if she'd stepped into a long-running dispute for which she had no frame of reference. It astonished her to see Sonya, whom she'd assumed was the leader of this ragtag band, cowed for the second time in a matter of minutes—and by two men, no less! While something about Hasso demanded respect, Mathis seemed to be someone whose only competence involved physical matters.

Sonya cleared her throat. "What are the new orders?"

"We need to leave right away," Nyona said. "We're not to bring Alia against her will, but either way, we're to...activate the access catch?"

"Are you certain that's the order?" Mathis said, surprise in his tone.

"Yes, I'm certain. What does it do?"

"It cuts off access to the tunnels," Sonya replied. "Activating it ensures no one can get underground—or out—until it is deactivated. And deactivating it is a lengthy and complicated process. I hardly know how to do it myself." Her lips curled up in a self-satisfied smirk.

"Oh," Nyona said, frowning.

Alia suppressed a shudder. She hadn't realized she was underground. While Nyona had made it sound like she had a true choice, it appeared now her choices were to go with the rebels now or be locked away down here for who knew how long. Maybe she'd be trapped underground, alone, for weeks, months—or even the rest of her life. She breathed deeply to calm herself.

"Enough chatter, then. Let's get going," Sonya said. "It won't take me long to activate the switch after we leave, and then we'll be on our way home."

"Our orders changed about that, too. We're not going home."

"What?" Sonya and Mathis said in unison.

"Where are we going, then?" Mathis asked.

"Why don't we discuss this upstairs?" Hasso suggested, his voice quiet once again. "Alia has not yet made her choice, after all."

"True." Nyona turned back to Alia in a rush. "We must have your answer now—*right* now. Will you join us?" Her hazel eyes pleaded with Alia to say yes.

Alia didn't have time to agonize over a decision. She believed Sonya's threat that the room would become inaccessible once the rebels left. Even if the Conclave knew she was here, the Guard might not find her before she starved to death.

Only one choice remained.

She wouldn't *truly* join the rebels, of course. She just needed to get out of here, away from these walls. If the Guard found them en route to wherever it was they were taking her, she'd explain her captivity. If they weren't caught and she remained with them—well, she'd do or say whatever they asked of her if it meant they'd remove her implant like they promised. And once they did, she'd contact the Masters and tell them what she'd learned. *They'd take me back for certain, then, no matter what lies have been spread about me.* They'd want her for Generation, if for nothing else.

"I will go with you," she announced in a high-pitched, thin voice, yet no one else seemed to notice how unusual it sounded.

Nyona sighed in relief while Mathis nodded his head once, folding his arms across his chest. Sonya merely rolled her eyes. "Well, goody for us, then. We'll leave as soon as possible. Hasso, remain here and watch her. Nyona, Mathis, come with me." She turned on her heel and stalked out of the room.

Nyona stood, normal color returning to her face. "You've made the right choice, Alia. Your assistance to the cause will be invaluable —for us and for you." She patted Alia's leg through the blanket, then left the room with Mathis.

Hasso pulled the now-empty chair closer to the bed and sat down. Alia plucked at the blanket covering her, avoiding his eyes. She hated being alone with him, and not just because he'd given her the implant. He reminded her of something she hadn't yet been able to place, and those misplaced memories cast an aura of disquiet over him.

"I know what you're up to, child."

She glanced at him, only to find him staring at her with his strange, ice-blue eyes. "Whatever do you mean?" she asked, trying to seem nonchalant.

He chuckled, an eerie sound coming from a man who didn't smile. "I thought I'd warn you before you decided to do something stupid. You might be able to fool some of the others, but your implant will remain in place until *I'm* certain you can be trusted."

"I'm not trying to fool anyone," she protested. "I said I'd go with you."

"Yes, you did, though under obvious duress. Yet even had it not been so, your agreement does not equal trust. The Conclave's web is strong, and its fangs bite deep. You'll have to demonstrate you've escaped that web, and that you no longer fear the repercussions for doing so, before I'll even consider restoring your Ability...or recommending that you remain alive at all."

A cold feeling of dread crept over her at his words. He requested the impossible. Even if she were to join the rebellion in truth, she would live the rest of her days in fear of retribution. People didn't defy the Conclave without consequences. Look at what had just happened to the Masters in Aldham. And years before that, to the entire city of Brome.

"Heya, Hasso," a red-haired youth called from the threshold, disrupting her morbid thoughts. "I've got travel clothes for the Adept." He entered at Hasso's nod and stared, eyes wide, as he approached Alia's bed carrying a bulky canvas sack. She frowned in annoyance. Plenty of men had no hair, but no one looked twice at them. The boy dropped the sack on the bed and stepped back in some haste.

"If I'm to change, may I have some privacy?" she asked coolly.

"Certainly. Come, Avrey. We should change as well." Hasso guided the boy out into the hall and pulled the door shut behind them.

Alia opened the sack. Inside was a set of clean undergarments, some thick stockings, an undershirt, a long-sleeved tunic, trousers, a leather jerkin, and at the very bottom, a pair of winter boots. Other than the undergarments, the clothing was all in shades of brown and green. She never wore anything but white as an Adept, and it had been years since she'd worn trousers. It had been on a lark, she recalled, and the Masters hadn't been particularly happy about it.

She grasped the bottom of her nightshift and lifted it over her head. As she pulled the garment away from her body, it caught the bandage at her neck and tore it away from her skin. Wincing, she tentatively raised her hand. As her fingers explored the raised edges of an inch-long incision pulled together with stitches, her arms dotted with gooseflesh. A sudden urge to dig inside the wound and yank away the device possessed her.

Alia exhaled and dropped her hand to her side. If it were that easy, all those who had ever been implanted would not have remained so for long. She must wait—and hope she was not waiting on a lie.

The bandage trapped in the neckline of her nightshift held no trace of blood or other fluid. She crumpled the fabric into a wad and threw it across the room. Worried that someone would walk in at any moment, she dressed quickly, surprised to find that everything fit. She fumbled with the lacings on the jerkin, but figured her efforts were sufficient so long as it remained closed.

Alia had just pulled on her boots when someone knocked at the door. "Are you decent?" a man asked in a deep voice.

"Yes," she replied, smoothing the front of her trousers. "You may —"

The door opened before she'd finished granting permission. Mathis stood in the threshold. He'd changed from his black uniform into clothing similar to hers, though he also wore a brown cloak.

"Time to go," he said, gesturing toward her.

She needed no further encouragement to leave her prison. Mathis placed his hand on her back as she walked by, and she struck his hand aside on instinct. "How dare you touch me," she snapped.

He raised an eyebrow. "We're not big on following the Conclave's social norms. So you'd better get used to it. I'm your designated escort, after all." With that, he seized her arm and led her from the room. Every inch of her being protested at his blasphemy, but she did not resist. He was right; if she was ever going to get these people to trust her, she needed to let go of some things. Her boots clunked awkwardly against the ground as they walked through a dimly lit stone tunnel.

They reached an open space where Nyona, Sonya, Hasso, and the redheaded boy waited, also garbed in brown-and-green clothes. The boy handed Mathis a thick wool cloak, and he started to wrap it around Alia's shoulders.

"Wait," Hasso said. "What happened to your bandage, child?"

"It came off when I changed."

He walked over and pressed cool fingers against the flesh around her wound. "It's not yet ready to be exposed." He reached into a pack at his waist and pulled out a fresh strip of cloth and a bottle of adhesive. Within moments he'd deftly re-bandaged her neck, and Mathis then clasped the cloak around her.

"Are we ready now?" Sonya asked, impatience clear in her voice.

"Seems so," Mathis said. "Avrey, you sure we have enough sup-plies?"

"Yeah, we should be okay. We've got what we came with, and Movani's leading the horses out now. That plus the field packs from here should keep us until we get to vo—"

Sonya smacked Avrey on the back of his head. "Fires, we *just* talked about this. Clearly you've been spending too much time with my idiot brother. Come on. Cover her, and let's go."

Brother? There was no resemblance between the two as far as Alia could see, but that perhaps explained why Sonya had been willing to accept Mathis's earlier command.

Mathis unfolded a black piece of fabric. "Sorry," he said gruffly. "Can't let you see the path we take to get out. I'll uncover you once we're aboveground."

She recoiled and held back a shriek as he pulled a hood over her head. The closeness of the rough fabric was far worse than the walls of her underground prison cell. What she assumed was Mathis's hand guided her forward, yet she stumbled as she walked, disorient-ed. Her breathing quickened as they continued for what seemed an eternity. The light penetrating the cloth of the hood diminished, and a musty scent filled her nose. Someone grunted, and the squeak of unused gears assaulted her ears. A chain rattled.

"You've got about twenty steps to go up now," Mathis said. "Use the railing. There you go. I'll be right behind you."

Alia grasped the railing as if her life depended on it. The steps were steep, and each one required her to pull herself up with the assistance of the railing. By the time her foot came down into empty air, her heart threatened to burst from her chest. No one offered her any respite, however, and she was led farther uphill. Sounds of her own ragged breathing filled her ears.

Mathis finally stopped her forward momentum. More chains rattled, followed by a dull whirring noise. Light flooded in from above and shadows moved around her. Mathis placed her hands on two vertical wooden bars spaced shoulder-width apart.

"This ladder will get you aboveground. Use your feet to find each rung; there's only about ten of them. I'll wait below in case you fall."

Freedom beckoned with light and the sound of wind rustling through trees. Using a last reserve of energy she didn't know she possessed, she flew up the ladder, desperate to breathe fresh air. Someone helped her off the last rungs, and she collapsed onto the ground. She tore at the bottom of the hood with her fingers.

"Wait, wait. Let me help." The hood lifted, and Alia sucked in haggard breaths of cold, clear air. Nyona crouched next to her with a look of concern. "Are you okay? Here, get out of that patch of snow before your clothes soak through." Alia accepted Nyona's assistance to stand while she focused on regaining control.

Mathis pulled himself out of the hole in the ground and joined them. To one side, the old woman who'd cared for her held the reins of two horses, while the boy managed three others. Dark evergreen trees surrounded them, and far beyond the hill where they stood was a small house and ramshackle stable nestled in a low clearing devoid of trees.

"Is that where we came from?" Alia asked.

"Yes. It's quite some distance, isn't it?" Nyona replied. "Though I think we walked about twice that, didn't we, Mathis?"

"Probably so. It's not a direct route, and uphill, besides."

Hasso climbed out of the ground, followed by Sonya. She didn't stand, however; instead, she pivoted to lie on her stomach next to the opening. Her shoulders twisted as she manipulated something below ground.

"I'll be on my way, then," the old woman said, handing the reins she held to the boy. She reached up to Mathis and gave him a hug. "You take care of yourself, now, my boy. I'm sure to see you again soon." The woman embraced Sonya, too, then nodded in farewell to the rest of them. She wrapped her cloak around her and was soon lost from view amongst the trees.

Sonya jumped up from the ground as a panel spotted with dirt and patchy vegetation slid to cover their egress. She brushed her hands clean against the side of her trousers and kicked more dirt and snow over the covering. "It's done."

At first, Alia thought the distant rumble was a figment of her imagination, brought on by the stress of their escape. But the sound grew louder and louder, until it seemed the very ground beneath her feet began to shake. All at once, the house and the grounds surrounding it collapsed into the earth with an enormous *boom*. A plume of dust and debris rose high into the air and a flock of startled birds took flight from the trees around them.

Alia gaped at the destruction. If she had chosen to remain be-hind...

"*Fires*, Sonya," Hasso cursed.

"Erm." Sonya's cheeked were flushed, and she looked sheepish under Hasso's withering glare. "That was—not supposed to happen."

"No kidding." Mathis turned to Alia with a sardonic grin. "Aren't you glad you threw in your lot with us?"

Chapter 14

Sarabie

THE DOOR BOLT grated against wood as it slid open. As she did every day, Sarabie rolled over in her bed and pretended to still be asleep.

Dishes rattled as the door creaked open. Someone crossed the room with muffled steps and set a tray on her table with a clink of metal against wood. Fabric swished, and bright light suddenly penetrated through her eyelids from an uncovered window. With a grunt of irritation, she pulled the blankets up around her face.

"Sarabie, you must get up today," the servant announced from beside her bed. Sarabie glared with one partially open eye. A eunuch with white-blond hair and eyebrows stood holding her slippers and a bed robe. The red tattoo on his right hand stood out garishly against his pale skin, as did the black fabric of his servant's uniform.

She closed her eye. "Go away. I wish to remain abed." He should know that by now.

"I'm sorry, Sarabie, but you must get up," he repeated. "The Masters have scheduled you for an appointment in less than half an hour."

At his words, a twinge of excitement filtered through her despondency. *An appointment?* After so many weeks, an appointment now could only mean one thing. Today, they'd finally tell her that everything she'd gone through had been worth it. Her lips twitched upward briefly.

"Please, Sarabie," the servant pleaded. "I'm to escort you, but we must first do something about your hair. And you should eat something as well."

"All right," she said, then propped herself up on one elbow, causing her dark, tangled hair to cascade along her arm. She wrinkled her nose. It had been days since she'd changed out of this nightshift.

The eunuch placed slippers on her feet and helped her to stand, then eased the bed robe around her shoulders. "Very good, Sarabie. It's a lovely day outside. Why don't you come sit near the window to eat while I do your hair?" He pulled one of the padded chairs away from the table.

Sarabie sat in the chair and considered the tray of biscuits, fruit, and tea before her. As usual, he'd brought far more food than she would ever want, though her stomach rumbled in disagreement. She selected a small biscuit and nibbled at its edge as the eunuch began working at the knots in her hair with a comb.

Outside, the sun stood high above the stone walls surrounding the small interior garden. Bright green and deep purple leaves filled the branches of two trees, shading the rosebushes that still had not yet responded to the arrival of spring. Two brown birds dove past the window to land at the edge of a bobbing branch, turning their heads this way and that in quick motions before flying off again. Sarabie hoped her new quarters would include access to a garden for walks—she was moving up, after all, and once the Masters confirmed her status, there'd be no reason to keep her so shut away.

She reached for another biscuit and winced when the servant's hands failed to follow her motion. "Ow!"

"My apologies, Sarabie."

"No, it's okay. It's not your fault." She was mildly embarrassed at how messy she'd let her hair become. Perhaps she'd ask the servants in her new quarters to wash it after she moved. She smiled to herself. Today would be the first good day she'd had in a *very* long time.

After the eunuch finished with her hair, including several generous spritzes of lavender-scented water, he helped her remove her sweaty nightshift and dress in fresh undergarments and a red robe. The face staring back at her from the long mirror was thinner than she recalled, and shadows lingered under her eyes. To her satisfaction, however, no trace of bruising remained around her neck, even with her hair pulled back into a low tail. She turned to the side and drew her hands lightly over her still-flat stomach. Soon she'd need a whole new wardrobe; robes that fastened tight across the waist would not do when her belly began to swell.

"Are you ready?" the eunuch asked.

"Yes, please. I don't want to be late."

He opened the door and allowed her to exit the room first. The corridor extended to her left and right a short distance before curving out of view. She didn't know which way to go; she'd only been outside her room twice since her arrival. The last time, she hadn't paid any attention, and the first time—well, the first time, she didn't recall leaving. *I wish I didn't remember the rest, either.*

The eunuch gestured to the right. As he escorted her down the hall, she wondered if anyone she knew might be behind the doors they passed. She missed seeing her friends and the others from her Initiate—even Kati, who on her best days was merely tolerable.

And Alia…Alia, she missed most of all. She still couldn't believe her friend was never coming home. The announcement of Alia's dismissal from the Conclave, not long after Sarabie's disastrous Generation, had only driven her further into her depression.

She blinked away the moisture that threatened at her eyes. Now was not the time to think of such things. Today she could finally expel some of her sadness, and she desperately yearned for that release.

They turned into a short corridor that ended in a floor-to-ceiling window of opaque glass blocks that allowed in filtered sunlight. Four red doors alternated along both sides of the hall. The eunuch opened the first one to the left. "Good luck," he whispered as she passed by him to enter the examination room. She felt a little bad that she'd never learned his name, though it didn't matter at this point, as she'd never see him again.

Inside the room were three upholstered chairs and a padded table. A narrow counter with drawers below it butted against one of the walls. The room had no windows, but none were necessary given the bright balls of light suspended from the ceiling. Sarabie sat in the chair nearest the door and began tapping her fingers in sequence against the armrest.

Her wait soon ended. Master Nivi entered the room, accompanied by a young Adept. The child's bright white robe made the Master's gray robe, with only three silver stripes on one sleeve, seem dingy in comparison. As with her last appointment, Sarabie didn't recognize this Adept, who looked to be about five years old. That was no surprise, of course—Generation Adepts lived apart from the rest. It must be a lonely experience.

"Good morning, Sarabie," said Master Nivi. "This is Adept Kenna." Sarabie nodded her head toward the girl, who smiled shyly in return as she sat in one of the two remaining chairs.

Master Nivi took the last chair and opened a notebook bound in dark green leather. She flipped through to the middle and then ran her finger down the page. "I see here that it's been nearly six weeks since your Generation. Your first appointment, right after your ceremony, suggested it had been successful. Adept Kenna will perform the assessment today to confirm those results. It won't take long, and then we can discuss moving you to your new rooms." Master Nivi flashed Sarabie a bright smile. "I'm sure you're looking forward to seeing your friends again!"

"I look forward to learning the results, Master Nivi." Sarabie responded. Once they told her she carried a future Adept, she could be happy again. She could forgive everything that had happened to her and everything she wished to forget.

"Go ahead, my dear," Master Nivi instructed the Adept.

The girl hopped down from her chair and stood before Sarabie. She placed her hands on Sarabie's abdomen, her fingers spread wide, and closed her eyes. For the first time in a long while, Sarabie missed being able to access her Ability. Yet no one remained an Adept forever—and in any case, what remained of her Ability would soon transfer to her child, if it hadn't already.

Hardly any time had passed before Adept Kenna removed her hands. Sarabie tried to make eye contact with the child, but the girl turned to whisper in Master Nivi's ear. A moment of doubt crossed Sarabie's mind; she'd assumed the Adept would simply announce the good news.

"Thank you for your service, Adept Kenna," Master Nivi said stiffly. "You may leave us now." The child bobbed her head and left the room without once looking Sarabie's way.

After the door closed, Master Nivi ignored Sarabie and flipped back through her notebook. An uncomfortable silence developed. As the minutes ticked by, Sarabie fought to keep her tears at bay. She felt as though she might be sick.

Master Nivi finally looked up from her book and sighed. "I'm afraid I don't have good news."

Sarabie burst into tears. She covered her face with her hands, embarrassed to make such a display in front of the Master. *I cannot go through it again. I just can't.* "How...can it be...it didn't...work?" she asked between sobs.

Master Nivi rummaged inside one of the drawers under the counter and handed Sarabie a handkerchief. "I'm terribly sorry that I'm not better prepared. This happens so rarely. It's been many years, in fact, according to my records."

"What...do you mean?" Sarabie wiped away tear after tear as she tried to regain control. "Everyone knows Generation can...fail." Her ragged voice sounded strange to her ears.

"Yes, but that's not the problem. Your Generation didn't fail. You *are* pregnant—just not with a future Adept."

The handkerchief dropped from Sarabie's limp fingers. "What? But...what?" Her mind could not form a coherent question.

Master Nivi paced back and forth, the room's short confines limiting her to only a few steps in either direction. "This was not supposed to happen for anyone in your Initiate. We ran all the tests!" She slapped her notebook on top of the counter. "I must consult with Master Leyta. Wait here."

Sarabie grabbed the edge of her sponsor's robe as she strode toward the door. "Please," Sarabie blurted. "I don't understand. How can I be pregnant, if not with an Adept?"

"You're carrying a male child." She pulled her robe away from Sarabie's clutching fingers.

Sarabie's jaw dropped. "That's impossible!"

"It's not impossible, but it's very, very rare. And it never occurs without careful planning. Though I suppose that's not quite true, now, hmm?" Master Nivi patted Sarabie's shoulder. "Don't worry. We'll take care of everything. I'll be right back." Without another word, Master Nivi swept from the room.

Sarabie sat in stunned silence. *How can this be?* Adepts beget Adepts; that's how it worked. How else would Ability pass from generation to generation? What did it mean to carry a boy? She'd never seen a male child anywhere in the Conclave. More and more questions, most seemingly absurd, filled her mind as she waited for Master Nivi to return.

At least she *was* pregnant. Despite her unsettled situation, there was some solace in knowing she wouldn't have to go through Generation again.

The door opened, and Master Nivi returned with a second young Adept and a senior Master whom Sarabie didn't know. Silver stripes encircled the new Master's sleeves from shoulders to wrists, and patterns of silver dotted the body of her gray robe as well. It wasn't quite as intricate as the pattern of rank on Master Gersemi's robe, but a casual observer would be hard pressed to notice the difference.

"I am Master Leyta," said the older Master. "I understand we may have an unexpected situation. Adept Tara, please perform an assessment. We must be certain."

"Yes, Master Leyta." The Adept, a few years older than the last, placed her hands on Sarabie's abdomen. Her brow furrowed in concentration. This assessment took longer, but the results were the same. "It is confirmed," she said. "Sarabie carries a male child."

"You're certain?"

"Yes, Master Leyta. It's quite clear."

"Ah well, then. Thank you for your service, Adept Tara; you are dismissed. You too, Master Nivi. We shall speak later about where things went wrong."

Master Nivi bowed her head. "Yes, Master Leyta." Keeping her eyes toward the ground, she handed her notebook to her superior and hurried out of the room once more.

Once they were alone, Master Leyta sat in the chair opposite Sarabie and took Sarabie's shaking hands in her own. "I realize this must come as somewhat of a shock for you, my dear. But don't worry. This wasn't your fault, and given that you've proven yourself to be fertile, we won't count this against you as a failed Generation. Be assured that this problem is easily remedied if we act quickly." She sat back in the chair, opened the notebook, and perused several pages.

"Remedied? What do you mean?" Sarabie hoped she didn't sound as hysterical as she felt.

"It's quite simple, really. All we have to do is terminate this pregnancy and prepare you for another ceremony. If we do it soon, you'll still be able to pass your Ability to a future Adept the next time." She pulled a pencil from behind her ear and scribbled something in the notebook. "The medics can take care of the former this afternoon, and I'll begin the preparations for your second Generation. I suspect we'll then meet again in about a month's time under better circumstances."

Sarabie's throat constricted. "I can't."

Master Leyta looked up with a befuddled expression. "Why ever not?"

"I just—can't." Explaining required the exploration of memories she'd spent the last six weeks trying to forget.

"You are not making any sense, Sarabie. You *must* do this if you want to fulfill your duty to the Conclave."

"I will not."

Master Leyta pressed her lips together. "I don't think you quite understand what you are saying. If you do not do what is necessary, you will remain isolated until this boy child is born, forgoing the chance to reunite with others in your Initiate. And after, we will take the child as we do all others, but you will not become a Master. Instead, you'll be expelled from the Conclave with your name stricken from the rolls."

Sarabie gasped. "Only people who fail Generation twice are dismissed. You said this wouldn't be counted against me!"

"Refusing to participate in a second Generation is grounds for dismissal, no matter the cause." Her expression softened slightly, and she reached for Sarabie's hand and squeezed it. "Please understand, we do not wish for you to leave. You are precious to us. We want nothing more than for you to stay, to give us the gift of an Adept, and to take up your duties as a Master. But none of that can happen if you don't start anew."

Sarabie's emotions swirled in confusion. If she refused to do what Master Leyta requested, she'd lose her home and everything she knew. But if she agreed...she squeezed her eyes shut against the memories. "I can't," she whispered.

"But you *can*. I promise, the medics know what to do. It will be quick and you won't feel a thing."

"No—that's not it. I don't care about that."

"Then tell me why you are refusing to do what you must!" the Master said, exasperated.

Might this woman understand if she knew? No matter how badly she wished not to speak of it, she had to try if she was to have any hope of remaining in her home. "I can't go through Generation again," she said in a small voice. "I...remember what happened the first time. Not all of it, but I remember the men...not man, *men*, plural, and one of them—he—he—*hit* me, and he—"

"That's enough." The Master held up her hand. "My dear, you are mistaken. What you *think* you remember are merely delusions brought on by the fertility medication we gave you before the ceremony. Usually, this medication only causes memory loss—it's unavoidable, unfortunately—but on rare occasions, it causes delusions. Whatever you think you saw or experienced, let me assure you, it did not happen." She shook her head and clucked her tongue. "I wish you had spoken of this sooner; the Adepts here in Generation are trained to deal with this, but it's too late now to do anything about it. Yet if this truly is the basis for your refusal, know there simply is no reason for it."

Sarabie hesitated, considering. It *had* been very difficult to stay awake during the ceremony. Could her memories truly be nothing more than a dream?

Yet the purple-and-yellow bruises around her neck, which had taken weeks to fade, certainly had been real. And those bruises matched her memory of the man's sadistic laughter as he choked her when she was helpless to fight back. She shook her head, denying the Master's claim.

Master Leyta sighed. "I'm sorely disappointed, Sarabie. From everything I've heard about you, I never expected you would fail us so utterly."

Silent tears slipped down Sarabie's cheeks. It was true she'd always done whatever the Masters had asked of her—but she couldn't do this. Even if it meant she'd be cast out and that her Ability, dormant and waiting, would be lost forever.

"Well then." The Master snapped her notebook closed with the pencil trapped inside. "Your servant will escort you back to your chambers, where you'll have one week to reconsider. After that, it will be too late."

— ❧ —

CHAPTER 15

NYONA

TOVI SAT ON a large, lichen-covered rock with her arms wrapped around her legs, which were bent at the knee. Steady wind pulled strands of hair free from the ribbon that gathered it behind her head, yet her black-and-silver jacket protected her from the chill. She pulled her black leather boots up closer to her as small waves splashed up against the rock. She seemed at peace this cloudy day— a marvel, considering everything she had endured in the last few months. Her daughter's strength filled Nyona with pride.

"What are you thinking about, love?" Nyona asked, tucking the escaped tendrils of hair back in place under the ribbon. It was likely a futile gesture.

"How pretty the ocean is. I'll be sad to leave."

"We can come back down here tomorrow, if the weather holds."

"No, I mean—leave the island."

"Why are you worried about leaving already? We only arrived a few weeks ago."

"Because we always do."

Nyona's throat tightened. She hugged her daughter's shoulders, but could provide no words of comfort in response. If she tried, Tovi would know them to be false, even without using her Ability. They'd run before, and this time, Tovi understood why.

How could one comfort a child who was well aware that capture meant the certain death of everyone she knew and loved?

"Nyona!"

Mother and daughter both turned their heads at the shout. Mathis strode down the slope of the ridge above the beach, striking in his new Guard uniform. He seemed to stand taller wearing it, and its unusual silver emblems drew attention. "The Captains want you two back," he said as he approached. "One of the scouts on the eastern shore spotted a ship."

"Ours?" Nyona asked with alarm. *Please, let it be ours. Don't let Tovi's premonition come true so soon.*

"They think so, but just in case, they want Tovi to confirm Master Ciara is on it before it gets too much closer. Captain Levina's already on her way to meet the scout, but Captain Jana's waiting for you at the outpost to show Tovi where to look."

"I can try looking from here," Tovi offered. "I bet I can find her on my own."

"No, love." Nyona ran her hand along the crown of Tovi's head. "The tide is coming in, so it's time to head back, anyway. Let's wait to see what Captain Jana wants to show you." An unguided search would not only drain Tovi's energy, but also put her—and all the rest of them—at much greater risk of detection.

The Tovi of old would have pouted at being denied, but this child accepted Nyona's response without complaint. *Six years old.* Nyona hardly believed it; so much had changed in that time. She'd considered mentioning Tovi's recent birthday to Mathis, but making it a reason for celebration still felt foreign to her. The Conclave didn't recognize birthdays—no Adept knew the precise day she'd been born, after all.

It hadn't helped that they'd also been running for their lives at the time. *Next year,* she promised herself.

Nyona helped Tovi hop down from the rock. They walked hand in hand, their boots crunching against tiny gray, white, and amber pebbles as they made their way toward the forested ridge. The curious pine trees on this island were unlike any she'd seen before. Their trunks grew straight from the ground to a point about twice Nyona's height, then they gently curved, along with their branches, toward the center of the island in the direction of the prevailing wind.

"How much time do we have?" Nyona asked Mathis as they followed him at a quick pace along a narrow path between the trees. She eyed the ground as she walked to avoid turning an ankle on the uneven, rocky terrain.

"The wind's against them on that side of the island, so I'm guessing about an hour. I'm sure it's them, though, and the Captains must think so, too, else we'd be headed underground already. They're just being overly cautious."

"As they should! If the last few months have taught us anything, it's that being overly cautious might be a good idea."

"Not disagreeing with you. But Sonya and Master Ciara were supposed to arrive any day now, so it's most likely them. No one comes to Vose on a lark."

"But what if the other Masters told the Conclave about it before —?" She hesitated, aware of Tovi's presence. Her daughter knew how the Masters had died, but Nyona preferred not to mention it around her. She didn't even like to think of it herself.

"They didn't know, and apparently Master Ciara didn't, either. Fires, even I didn't know about this place until we got the order to come here. Vose's connection to the rebellion is on a need-to-know basis, and the Masters in Aldham didn't need to know." His face soured. "Apparently, Sonya did."

"I hope you're right," she said, wishing she shared his confidence. Remote and obscure, Nyona hadn't even heard of Vose until Mathis showed it to her on a map. The Conclave had established the island outpost long ago, when its power was new and it was worried about foreign threats. None had ever presented itself in the many generations since, yet Vose continued its isolated watch.

But Morell had been remote, too, and its location had provided no security in the end. Now that the Conclave knew not all its Guards were loyal, why wouldn't they send Adepts to every outpost to find out if the taint of rebellion had spread? What if there was an Adept on that ship right now?

Don't be stupid, she thought as the outpost's stone wall came into view. From what Alia had told them, the Conclave didn't have enough Adepts to complete such a task all at once. And even if they sent Adepts in waves, Vose was as far from Corval as one could get while still being considered part of Corinas. Without more information, this small Guard outpost would not be high on the Conclave's list of places to look.

"I hope Master Ciara is well, at least," Nyona said, dismissing her negative thoughts. "She's been through a lot."

"She knows it could have been much worse," Mathis muttered. "Though maybe she feels differently after having had Sonya as a traveling partner for the past month."

Nyona smirked. "True. Do you think Sonya managed to avoid doing something stupid this time?" She doubted it; Sonya's volatile behavior was sadly predictable. The woman did nothing to further the rebellion's goals as far as Nyona was concerned.

"She never does. Why would this time be any different? I'll never understand why Captain Jana keeps giving her these critical missions. I thought for sure that would change after she bungled the mission with you so badly."

Guilt flared at the reminder of Brien's death. Between their frenetic flight from the safe house and the constant worry that the Conclave would come upon them at any moment, Nyona had not thought of him in weeks. Had he already become that easy for her to forget? She had loved him, in her own way, but she suspected now that her feelings toward him had been due to his unquestioning dedication to Tovi more than anything else.

If Sonya had not made such a terrible mistake, he would still be alive. *If I hadn't allowed him into my life, he would still be alive.*

Nyona sighed at the return of such despondent thoughts. What was done was done. She needed to focus on the present.

Two Guards standing on either side of an open space in the outpost's wall nodded at their approach. Remnants of wood and metal clung to the edges of the stone behind them—the last hints of a gate that once filled that space.

The un-gated wall surrounded a collection of buildings made of gray, weathered wood. Small houses provided living quarters, and the kitchen and mess hall were in a long building nearby. On the other side of the outpost stood the storage facility, a flat-roofed building that held the armory and workshop as well as a large barn. Four horses were tied to a rail next to the barn: one gray, two a speckled white-and-tan, and the last, much smaller than the others, a black so dark it almost looked blue.

"Why is Midnight saddled?" Tovi asked. "We *are* leaving the island, then?" Her voice wavered.

"No, no, love. We're not leaving." Nyona shot Mathis a look, hoping that what she'd just told her daughter was true.

He squinted his eyes and nodded slightly, indicating he under-stood her concern. "That's right. The horses are just to make things faster today. Once you confirm Master Ciara's on the ship, Captain Jana wants the three of us to go with her to greet them when they land. We'd never get there in time if we walked."

"Alia's not coming?" Nyona asked, itching the side of her nose.

"Hasso said it wasn't necessary. We'll be coming right back."

"Hmm," she grunted. Hasso continued to distrust Alia, despite her model behavior. She'd been quiet and cooperative during their escape from the safe house, and she'd become even more so since their arrival on the island. The young woman had paled upon meeting Tovi, and her reaction to Renai—well. While Alia had been only a child when the Conclave implanted Renai, Nyona had no doubt it had created an indelible memory.

Of course, Tovi could determine where Alia's true loyalty lay, but it wasn't worth the risk now that the Conclave knew of Tovi's existence. Nothing suggested the techniques they'd learned from the banned book, *A History of Corinas*, failed to mask Tovi's use of Ability, but truth assessment required more than the ordinary use.

The door to the officer's quarters banged open and Owen

skipped down the steps. He stopped short when he spotted them. "There you are! Captain Jana sent me to find out what was taking you so long." He gestured toward the house. "Come on!"

They rushed to cover the final distance. Owen held the door open and they entered a spacious sitting room. Captain Jana bent over a wooden table, her arms straight and her hands flat against the table's surface, studying a large map spread before her. She looked up. Puckered skin ran from her jawline up the side of her left cheek, stopping just below her eye. The wound she'd taken during a fight with the Conclave's Guards after leaving Morell must have been hideous. Nyona owed a debt of gratitude to her and to the other rebels who had been injured—or had died—during that fight; without their sacrifices, Tovi would not have made it to Vose alive.

"I trust Mathis has brought you up to speed," Captain Jana said as she straightened. Without waiting for a response, she continued. "Tovi, let me show you where you should focus your efforts." Tovi joined her at the table and stood on her toes. Captain Jana pointed to a spot on the map. "Here is our little island. You spent the morning on the western beach, over here, but the ship is approaching from the southeast, between these other islands, here…and here." She jabbed the map twice with her thumb. "Make it a very narrow, focused inquiry, okay?"

Tovi nodded and closed her eyes.

Nyona's heart fluttered, though she was confident Tovi would mask her efforts from the Conclave. In truth, her anxiety stemmed from what they'd do if the ship did *not* carry Master Ciara. She didn't think there'd be enough time to get off the island, and the maze of tunnels hiding beneath the outpost—assuming the Conclave didn't know about them, which she doubted—would only sustain them so long before they ran out of supplies. *Please let it be her. Please.*

They waited, silent, as time seemed to stretch. She smiled at Mathis when he looked her way, trying to appear calm. He moved next to her and reached for her hand. His calloused palm squeezed hers briefly before letting go.

Right as Nyona was beginning to wonder if it was time to panic, Tovi gasped and opened her eyes.

❧

CHAPTER 16

MATHIS

THE SOUND TOVI made when she came out of a trance always startled Mathis, though he liked to believe he hid it well. She couldn't help it; her intense efforts to mask her use of Ability left her breathless. Knowing that didn't help his nerves, though.

Nyona rushed to her daughter's side and helped her into a chair. "There, there, love," she said, as Tovi gulped in air.

It didn't take long for her to recover. "It's them," Tovi told the room. "They're close—the ship anchored and they're about ready to get in a rowboat."

Mathis exhaled slowly. He hadn't *really* been worried that the ship carried someone unexpected, but he welcomed the confirmation all the same. Nyona's wide grin made obvious her own relief.

"The winds must have shifted in their favor," Captain Jana said. "I want to be there when they land. Tovi, can you ride?"

"Yes."

"Then let us be off. Owen, stand post outside the women's

houses in case you are needed. Kelda and Ysitra are with Alia and Renai, so there should not be any trouble, but I would rather take the extra precaution. We will be back shortly."

"Yes, Captain," Owen replied before he headed out the door.

Captain Jana ushered the rest of them outside, and they followed her to the horses waiting near the barn. Mathis lifted Tovi onto the saddle of the small, black mare the child had named Midnight. Alia preferred that docile animal as well, though no amount of practice would ever make her a competent rider. He still couldn't believe the Conclave didn't teach Adepts to ride. It was almost as stupid as not teaching them how to read. *How have we allowed these idiots to rule us for so long?*

"Everyone ready?" Captain Jana called. She squeezed her legs against the sides of her horse, a white-and-tan gelding the twin of Mathis's own. They crossed through the gaping hole that had once been the eastern gate, a reminder of how decrepit the outpost had become. If they remained at Vose for much longer, they really should fix the gates. The wall was pointless without them.

Mathis took the rear position to keep an eye on Nyona and Tovi. The child didn't need guarding at the moment, but she was still his charge. Besides, he *wanted* to keep her safe. Especially after he'd almost gotten her killed by thinking he was so damned clever.

His attempt to misdirect the Guard unit they'd run into on the way to the safe house had worked, but not in the way he'd hoped. Instead of turning north toward the ruins of Brome, the unit had turned west—right into a group of rebels fleeing the Conclave's surprise attack on Morell. From what he'd heard, the fight on the road had been fierce. Despite being undermanned and exhausted, the rebels had emerged victorious, leaving no Guard alive to report their escape. Captain Jana wore the most visible scar from the confrontation, yet at least she had her life. His friend Jekros and many others had not been as fortunate.

As he thought about those who had died in the fight, anger displaced his guilt. He should have *been* there instead of ferrying a recalcitrant Adept across the countryside. It was obvious she didn't want to be with them, and he'd noticed how carefully she watched and listened to everything around her. Nyona and Kelda seemed to think she'd come around, but for once, he agreed with Hasso. None of them should trust Alia.

Small puffs of dust rose from the horses' hooves as they made their way to the coastline at a brisk trot. Ships bearing supplies for the island always came from the east, and the dirt road, with none of the rocky obstacles marring the path to the west, facilitated transport between the shore and the outpost.

At the edge of the forest near the beach, two horses with tack matching their own stood near a tree. While all Guard emblems were unique to a specific unit, the ones marking the Vose Guard were distinct, embellished with an old-fashioned style he'd not seen anywhere else. The emblem repeated on their uniforms—even those of support staff like stable hands. That was the role Tovi played in this charade, being too young to pass as a proper recruit.

Captain Jana dismounted and dropped the reins of her horse on the ground near the two others. Mathis hopped off his mount, ready to help Tovi, but she'd already slid off her saddle on her own. They spaced out their horses then mimicked the Captain's action; trained to ground tie, the horses wouldn't wander with their reins touching the ground.

They hurried down the gentle slope on foot. A wooden board-walk connected the end of the dirt road with a dock extending into the ocean. Captain Levina and Hasso waited on the beach itself, close to the water.

Captain Levina shaded her eyes from the bit of sun peeking through the clouds with one hand while she waved furiously toward a rowboat with the other. She turned as their boots crunched against the rocky beach, squinting. "Finally!" she called. "Took you long enough; they're just about here."

"Sorry for the delay," responded Captain Jana. "We had to fetch Tovi from the other side of the island."

"I didn't mean to keep you all waiting," Tovi said softly, despite the fact that she couldn't have known the Captains would need her that morning. Nyona frowned and drew a protective arm around Tovi's shoulders.

Captain Levina waved her hand with an easy grin, dismissing any perceived slight. "Don't worry, child. We hung back until we could see for ourselves, but I didn't really doubt our scout in any case. See there, Jana? She looks well, poor thing." Captain Levina put her hand to her brow again, just below her gray-and-blonde hair, and continued to peer out toward the water.

The rowboat had already moved a good distance away from the larger boat anchored well out in the ocean. Mathis assumed the blonde woman in brown travel clothes was this Master Ciara they all kept talking about. She wouldn't be one of the two rowers, and she certainly wasn't the woman with shoulder-length brown hair, dressed in black, with her back toward the shore. Somehow, even across the waves, his sister's posture communicated her arrogance. Successfully rescuing Master Ciara had likely inflated Sonya's already immense ego.

The rowboat came ever closer to shore. Behind it, a line of brown pelicans flew low above the waves. One by one, the birds dove into the water before rising again, most gulping down fish from a successful catch.

Small waves carried the boat over the final distance to the shore, and its bottom ground against pebbles when it finally reached land. The two rowers let from the boat, and with Hasso's assistance, dragged it farther onto the beach. Once set, Hasso offered his hand to Master Ciara. She accepted it with a warm smile, and Mathis was shocked to see the medic briefly reciprocate as he assisted her from the boat.

Sonya needed no such help. While Ciara made her way toward the Captains, Sonya moved in the opposite direction, far from the boat. Hasso joined her, and the two spoke quietly. Mathis couldn't hear their words, but he was certain nothing good would come from their conversation. Nyona had been trying to convince him that Hasso truly regretted all the things he'd once done in the name of the Conclave, but seeing the medic interact with Sonya only reminded Mathis of why he'd hated the man for so long.

Master Ciara embraced each of the two Captains in turn. "Jana. I'm so relieved you have recovered," she said, smiling broadly. "And

Levina, my old friend. It is so good to see you. It has been too long. Far too long."

"Is that a crack about how I have more gray hair now than I did five years ago?" Captain Levina laughed. "I hate that it's true. Joking aside, though, you're well? No incidents since you left the mainland?"

"Just a small internal matter we can discuss later."

"I can't imagine what that might concern," Captain Levina remarked with a raised eyebrow, tilting her head to look past Ciara.

Mathis suppressed a snort. Engrossed in her conversation with Hasso, Sonya didn't even notice Captain Levina's attention. *Captain Jana could learn from this one.*

"Truly, it can wait," Master Ciara said, sweeping her long, blonde hair over one shoulder to cascade down her chest.

"Fine," Captain Levina agreed amicably. "No reason to stand out here in the sun, then. Sonya!"

"Yes, Captain Levina?" called Sonya. Mathis could have sworn he heard a smidge of deference in her tone. He had to have been mistaken.

"Pay the men and help them shove out." The Captain tossed a jingling sack purse to Sonya, who scrambled to the side to catch it. It took every fiber of Mathis's being not to laugh out loud.

"Can I introduce myself to your companions before we go?" asked Master Ciara. She smiled as she squatted before Tovi. "Tovi. I am so pleased to meet you in person. Thank you for helping us make our way here." She embraced Tovi briefly before holding her out at arm's length. "Such a lovely child you are. And those curls!"

Tovi blushed under the attention. "You're welcome. I'm sure others would have helped if they could; I was just the only one who could talk to you."

"And modest, as well." Master Ciara stood and cast her smile toward Nyona. "You must be Nyona. Tovi favors you."

"Thank you, Master Ciara. I don't believe we've had the chance to meet before."

"Oh, we probably have met, but it would have been when you were quite young. I was not often in Corval. And please, just call me Ciara. My time as a Master is over." She turned her gaze to Mathis. "I'm afraid I don't know your name, though you do look somewhat familiar. Have we met?"

Mathis shrugged under her scrutiny. "Can't imagine why we would have."

"Ciara, this is *Mathis*," Captain Jana interjected, placing an unusual emphasis on his name.

"Mathis?" Ciara whispered, her eyes darting past him and back. "I didn't realize you would be here. My goodness."

"What?" he said, confused. Had Sonya told her something bad about him? He wouldn't have put it past her to do that.

"It's nothing," Ciara said in her normal voice, recovering quickly from whatever shock his name had given her. "I remember now that we did meet once, when you were just a boy. You've certainly grown since then! And didn't you used to wear your hair in a tail?"

He nodded, surprised that someone he didn't remember at all would recall such a minor detail.

"Yes, yes, I remember you now. It's been a long time!" She looked at him for a moment longer, then turned back to the Captains. "May we speak for a moment before we go?"

"Surely," Captain Levina said, and the three of them moved away to huddle in conversation.

"What in the world was that all about?" Nyona whispered.

"I have no idea," Mathis said, keeping his voice down as well. The strange interaction with Ciara had left him feeling vaguely concerned for no apparent reason. "I don't remember ever meeting her."

"Well, it was apparently memorable for her. When do you think your paths crossed?"

"I joined the rebellion when I was thirteen, and gained most of my height by fifteen. I started to wear my hair short sometime around then, too." He'd been rather preoccupied those first few years with adjusting to his new life, and given his parents' execution, he would have gone out of his way to ignore Ciara, anyway. Back then, a Master was a Master in his eyes, no matter their affiliation.

"Hmm. Well, I'm sure you'll figure it out eventually. Or you could just ask her."

"That's true," he replied, distracted by movement to the side. As Sonya chatted with the rowers, Hasso sat on a driftwood log, watching Ciara and the Captains. Mathis suddenly remembered the medic's reaction when they'd learned the Conclave had attacked the tribunal in Aldham. The man had turned white—a feat, given his already pale complexion—and his first question had been to inquire about Ciara's fate. *Curious.*

"Mathis?" Captain Jana called, jolting his attention away from Hasso. "Are you listening?"

"Come again?"

Captain Levina grinned as she walked by him, but Captain Jana regarded him in a way that suggested he'd hear about his inattention later. "I said, ride double with Ciara back to the outpost, then bring her straight away to speak with Alia."

Taking Ciara to see Alia was about the last thing he wanted to do, but he nodded once at the order, not wishing to push his luck with the Captain. He'd hoped that with all the excitement of a new arrival, he'd get a break from pretending he wanted the Adept to trust him.

Ciara mistook the reason for his apparently obvious displeasure. "I realize it will be awkward," she said. "Yet it's something I must do right away. I need to apologize to her for—well, everything. I should have known they'd sent her to Aldham as bait."

"I don't think she's looking for an apology from you," Mathis said, eyeing his sister as she returned to the group with Captain Levina.

"If you're talking about Sonya—and given how you've ignored each other so far, I'm betting you are—I wouldn't worry," Captain Levina said with another grin. "Sonya knows she's made mistakes, and she knows what she has to do to make up for them. Isn't that right, Sonya?"

"Yes, Captain," Sonya replied, strangely subdued.

What's this now? Had Captain Levina actually held Sonya accountable for one of her many misdeeds? The notion filled him with an absurd glee. He gestured toward Ciara, wanting to demonstrate to the Captains that *some* people could follow orders. "All right, then. Let's go."

The former Master followed him back up to where the horses waited at the edge of the forest. He hoisted himself into his saddle and then pulled her up behind him. She rested her hands lightly at his waist for support, and he urged the horse forward.

As they rode along the dirt road back to the outpost, he wondered what it was Sonya had done to get herself in hot water this time. It must have been something particularly noxious, though maybe Captain Levina simply was far less tolerant than Captain Jana. His companion knew, of course, but he doubted she'd answer a question from someone like him. It was worth a shot, though.

"So what did Sonya do to get herself in trouble?"

"I'm sorry, but I can't really comment."

Ah, well. It was as he expected. While she wouldn't answer that inquiry, perhaps she'd answer the other question nagging at him. "How do you know Hasso?"

"Pardon?"

"Back on the beach, you didn't ask to be introduced to him like you did with the rest of us. So how do you know him?"

"Oh. I've known him for a long time."

"Really?" He'd never seen Ciara in Morell, but maybe Hasso had visited Aldham. Mathis wondered if she knew of Hasso's past. "How long?"

"Goodness—years and years. We joined the rebellion at the same time."

His breath caught. *If that's true, then...*he took a deep breath and let it out slowly to steady his nerves. "You and I must have met around that same time, then, if I was still a boy with long hair?"

"Oh—yes, yes. It must have been then," she said, her falsely cheerful tone failing to cover up her lie.

His heartbeat thudded in his ears. "Funny. Hasso didn't join the rebellion until I was nineteen. Hardly a boy at all."

The fingers around his waist loosened before tightening once again. "I—I must have been confused then, I only meant—"

"That you'd met me as a boy because I *was* still a boy the day the Conclave executed my parents? So tell me this: Did they die on your orders, or were you only there to see the show?"

The horse took several steps before Ciara responded in a quiet voice that barely rose above the sound of the horse's hooves. "I did not give the order. But I did see it carried out. There was nothing I could've done to prevent their deaths."

He'd expected the answer. Still, it took every bit of self-control he possessed to continue riding toward the outpost instead of turning around and killing his parents' murderer with his bare hands.

CHAPTER 17

ALIA

ALIA STRUGGLED TO tamp down her annoyance. Everyone stared at her, waiting for her response. Mathis stood at the door, sullen as usual, while Kelda and Tovi nodded their heads encouragingly. Renai squatted on the floor and plucked at loose threads in the rug only she could see.

"Now is not a good time," Alia finally said.

Mathis crossed his arms at his chest. "Why? You're not doing anything but sitting here with Tovi. I don't see why you can't spend a few minutes talking to the woman."

Anger flared anew at his continued insolence. She owed him no explanation, but the truth was that she wanted nothing to do with Master Ciara—not now, and not ever. The Master hadn't been friendly in Aldham, so Alia couldn't imagine why she'd be friendly now, after so much had happened. Besides, the woman had repeatedly lied to her face. Why should she trust anything Master Ciara said now?

"I don't want to see her," she said with finality.

Tovi scooted closer to Alia on the sofa and took her hand as if she were the child. "It's okay. Ciara's nice, I promise. Isn't she, Mathis?"

Mathis grunted.

Alia returned Tovi's smile with some effort. "I'm sure she's nice to you. What's not to like?" She turned her attention back to Mathis. "Nonetheless, I don't want to talk to her right now. Sorry." Why was Master Ciara in such a hurry to speak to her, anyway? The woman had just arrived. Didn't she have more important things to do, like scheme with the Captains?

Mathis ran both hands through his short, brown hair, leaving bits of it stuck up along the crown of his head. "Look. I'm just the messenger here, so I'm not going to argue with you. That said, this outpost is small, so you'll end up seeing her eventually. Might as well do it now when she's in the mood to apologize."

Alia narrowed her eyes. "Apologize. Now there's a word you don't hear around here often."

"Alia," Kelda rebuked from her chair. "We have apologized—many times—for the circumstances that brought you to us."

"Hmm, she's not talking about that. Are you, friend?" Renai's singsong voice put Alia on edge. "She's talking about—*you know.*" The woman pointed to the long scar at the back of her neck. She smirked from where she sat on the floor, a thin shirt providing her with the bare minimum of decency. Her feet were filthy.

Alia pressed her lips together. Renai was uncannily perceptive at times, despite her madness. Alia wasn't talking about her abduction; she believed the rebels when they said Sonya had acted on her own. But no one other than Nyona had ever expressed any regret about her implant or the fact that she still had it, after all this time.

If it were up to Nyona, or even Kelda, Alia would likely already be free of her implant, she knew. The former residents of the Conclave understood her torment, and neither believed she would betray the rebellion to the Conclave.

Alia realized everyone was staring at her. "Never mind all that, Renai. I simply do not wish to see her."

Mathis threw his hands up into the air. "Fine. I have more important things to worry about right now," he said, clipping the ends of his words in annoyance. "A piece of advice, though. Being unfriendly to Ciara won't help you get that implant removed any sooner. She's got more influence around here than you know." He ran the fingers of one hand through his hair again, creating an even wilder look. "Fires," he muttered, before stalking out of the room. The front door slammed shut.

Kelda regarded the space Mathis had just occupied with a slight frown, then shook her head. "I know Mathis can be irksome—particularly so at the moment—but he speaks the truth. Ciara and Hasso have a—history, shall we say, and Hasso will listen to her opinion when it comes to you. Much more so than he'll listen to me, or Nyona, or even the Captains."

"Or me!" piped Tovi.

"Yes, or even you, Tovi," Kelda said with a small smile toward the child before turning her attention back to Alia. "Truly, Alia: Is it too much to ask that you give Ciara a few moments of your time? You have nothing to lose, and everything to gain, if she is willing to bend Hasso's ear."

Alia sighed in exasperation. She hated that a man controlled her fate. Why did the rebels allow him such power? It defied reason. It didn't help matters that Hasso distrusted her just as much now as the day they'd met, if not more. Indeed, his pale eyes seemed to constantly suggest that there was nothing she could say or do to alter his opinion of her. It infuriated her.

Yet none of that mattered if there was any possibility that Master Ciara might convince Hasso to remove Alia's implant. She dug her fingertips into her palms. "Fine," she said with false calm, as if the decision had been no trouble at all. "I'll talk to her. Perhaps she'll surprise me."

Kelda grinned. "She might. She's not like the other Masters you've known—first off, she's been in Aldham, not Corval, for over twenty years. Her willingness to take such a remote post showed she wasn't power-hungry like most Masters. If she believes you are truly with us now, like we do, then I'm sure she'll be able to convince Hasso of it as well. I'll go fetch her." The older woman pushed herself out of the padded armchair and stepped around Renai. Her black skirt swished around her ankles as she left the room.

Alia quashed the guilt that had emerged at Kelda's words. Nyona had believed almost immediately that Alia was done with the Conclave, and it hadn't taken much effort to convince Kelda of it as well. Tovi, of course, had merely followed the lead of her elders. It was a good thing no one had apparently considered having Tovi perform a truth assessment upon her.

Granted, Alia *had* abandoned her initial plans to escape as soon as she could and report the rebels to the Conclave. And after spending many weeks with them, she now understood why they believed what they did—and even agreed with many of their views, especially as they concerned the Masters. But that didn't mean she'd decided to actually *join* their cause and abandon the Conclave altogether.

No one had ever explained to her how eliminating the Conclave would solve the rebels' perceived problems. The Conclave had always been there, and she couldn't imagine a Corinas without it. The Conclave *was* Corinas. While she could do without the Masters, did the rebels really think they could hold the country together without *Adepts*?

The rebel's own young Adept sat on the opposite end of Alia's sofa, close to where Renai sprawled on the floor at the foot of the padded chair. Tovi's dark curls partially obscured the wrinkling of her nose as she watched Renai pick at her filthy toes. The child's hair had been a trigger for Alia's memory of the time in Aldham, right before the rebels took her, when she'd read a petitioner concerning a purported rebel attack. That it had been Tovi who'd inserted herself into the reading, and not an Adept of the Conclave, had shocked Alia to her core. According to what the Masters had taught her, this child should not exist.

Tovi caught her watching and smiled. "Hello?"

"I'm sorry. I didn't mean to stare."

The child crisscrossed her legs on the cushion and leaned forward. "What are you thinking about?" she asked. "Are you worried about meeting Ciara? You shouldn't be; she's very nice. I like her."

"I'm not worried about meeting her; I just don't really *want* to. But that's not what I was thinking about."

"Then what?" Tovi placed her hands on her knees and rocked side to side.

Alia heaved a sigh. "I was thinking about you, silly child."

"Really? What about me?"

"Aren't you full of questions today? Fine. If you must know, I was thinking about how amazing it is that your mother had you outside of Generation." With sudden embarrassment, Alia realized Tovi might not be aware of her origins. "Your mother *has* talked to you about that...right?"

"Yes. Adepts are born inside the Conclave, and Mama got kicked out because she never got pregnant during the ceremony. But she did later, with me!" The child grinned as she rocked.

"Indeed, she did. And that's never happened before, as far as I'm aware. You're quite special."

Tovi's smile turned shy at the compliment. "Mama says it just shows Generation isn't necessary."

"Hmm. Well, all I know is that if I were still at the Conclave, I might be getting ready to go through Generation myself right now."

"Why?" Tovi's brow scrunched in confusion. "You haven't lost your Ability yet."

"True, but I expect to lose it soon." Alia swallowed against a momentary surge of frustration. The implant blocked her from using her Ability, but it didn't block her knowledge of its presence. Every day, she tormented herself with that reality.

"Why?"

"Everyone else from my Initiate has been in Seclusion—the place you go when you lose your Ability—for a long time now, including my best friend. For all I know, she's already given birth to a new Adept." Engrossed in her new life as a Master, Sarabie probably had no idea of Alia's circumstances. If the Conclave had truly sent Alia to Aldham as a trap for the rebellion, she wouldn't have advertised it to a novice Master.

Tovi scooted closer to Alia. "You have a best friend? What's her name? I've never had one, other than Mama."

"Her name is Sarabie," Alia said, sympathy welling up for the child. Unlike Tovi's isolated existence, Alia's own childhood had at least included the companionship of other children her age. And it was her lifelong friendship with Sarabie more than anything else that kept her from truly considering the rebels' offer to join them. A decision to turn against the Conclave meant turning against her only true friend.

"She must be nice. Do you miss her?" Tovi got on her knees and cupped her hand around Alia's ear. "If you want, I can see how she is," Tovi whispered.

"What?" Alia said, jerking her head away in surprise. "Oh, no, no. Your mother and the Captains would be furious." Alia looked askance at Renai, but the woman's focus remained on her feet as she hummed an incoherent tune.

"We don't have to tell anyone," Tovi said, her voice quiet. "I know how to—"

The front door opened and multiple sets of footsteps echoed in the hall. Tovi darted back to her end of the sofa right before Kelda entered the room.

"Here we are!" Kelda announced. Master Ciara followed Kelda into the room in an almost timid fashion. She no longer wore her blonde hair gathered on top of her head as she had in Aldham. With her hair flowing freely in curls over the shoulders of her plain, black uniform, she reminded Alia of Marta, dressed all in black, during her Ascension ceremony. They shared the same blonde hair and pale skin.

"Good morning, Alia. Thank you for agreeing to speak with me," Master Ciara said. Her voice contained none of the authority she had wielded as the head of the Aldhamian tribunal.

Alia shrugged. "Kelda wanted me to."

"I'm glad she was able to persuade you." Master Ciara's smile dimmed when she noticed Renai on the floor. "Is that...?"

Kelda nodded. "Yes. Renai, this is Ciara. Oh, stop glaring so. She had nothing to do with what the Conclave did to you."

Master Ciara's eyes welled with tears. "They have so much to account for. So very much," she whispered. The woman wiped at her eyes as Kelda wrapped one arm around her shoulders.

"Indeed, they do, and they will one day—hopefully sooner than later," Kelda said.

Alia suddenly wondered if the story Nyona and Mathis had told her was, in fact, true. She'd assumed the rebels had exaggerated the circumstances surrounding the two Aldhamian Masters' deaths. The sentence for treason against the Conclave was always death, but not in the manner the rebels had described. Alia grimaced at the thought of what those women might have actually experienced.

"Better now?" Kelda asked. Master Ciara nodded. "All right, then. We'll leave you and Alia alone to talk. Renai, Tovi, let's see if we can find something to eat."

Renai scrambled up from the floor. "Did the cook make cake today?"

"No. There is no cake, just like every other day." Kelda sighed, then shook her head as she led Renai and Tovi from the room. Renai's chatter about potential desserts continued until the front door blocked out the sound.

Master Ciara sat down in the padded chair. Alia remained where she was, refusing to be the one to speak first. An awkward silence filled the room.

"I suppose I should start," the Master said at last.

"You *did* ask to speak to me." Alia failed to hide the bitterness in her voice.

Master Ciara winced. "That is true. I wanted to tell you why— no. The reasons are unimportant. I am here simply to apologize. I should have known Sonya would act prematurely. She almost always does. I also should have recognized that the Masters had sent you to us as a trap. It was far too convenient for us to receive an older Adept known to be rebellious herself, and even more, ru- mored to be Sempiternal. How could we resist? But I should have seen through all that, and my willful blindness placed you in greater danger. For that I truly am sorry."

The way the Master had emphasized that unusual word—*Sem-*

piternal—provoked Alia's attention. "I don't understand what you mean."

"Well, if you had come to us willingly, as we'd intended, then you would still have access to your Ability. You'd then be able to use it now to help protect yourself from the Conclave."

"No, not that. What did you mean when you said I showed signs of being 'Sempiternal'? I've never heard of—whatever that is."

Master Ciara furrowed her brow for a moment, then waved her hand in dismissal. "My apologies. It's not something they mention during the history lessons an Adept hears during Ritual. It's not part of the Seclusion curriculum, either, as a matter of fact—it's only once one has completed Generation, and is in the final preparations for becoming a Master, that one learns of Sempiternals."

"But what is it? And why do they think I have it? Is it because I have no hair?"

"No, I don't think it has anything to do with your lack of hair. Being Sempiternal is not a disease, though the Conclave might disagree on that point."

Alia raised her eyebrows. "What's that supposed to mean?"

"Just that it's not something you would have welcomed, had you remained in the Conclave. You see…if you are Sempiternal, then you'll never lose your Ability."

Alia snorted at Ciara's absurd statement. "That's impossible. All Adepts lose their Ability around the age of nineteen. Everyone knows that. Otherwise, the founders of Corinas would have never consented to the Conclave's rule."

"It's not impossible, but it's not common, either" the Master continued. "The Conclave does what it can to make sure few are born. You see, three hundred years ago, a group of Sempiternals tried to seize control of the Conclave at a time known in the histories as the Great Uprising. Truth be told, it really was more a case of the Conclave rising against Sempiternals."

The Master's words were absurd. *But it might explain much.* Most obviously, it would account for why she, of all her Initiate, had not shown any signs of losing her Ability. It also might explain the hostility she had felt coming from many of the Masters her entire life. But something still didn't make sense. "If even a few Sempiternals have been born since then, why haven't I heard of any?"

"Because the Conclave usually implants an Adept suspected of being Sempiternal not long after she turns twenty. The implant was actually created after the Great Uprising as a way to deal with any future Sempiternals."

"That's not how the Masters use it now."

"So they say, but the Conclave would *never* implant someone they might later use for Generation, no matter how badly the Adept behaved. An implant blocks the transfer of latent Ability to a new Adept. So, what you saw as a punishment was, in reality, a way to eliminate a suspected Sempiternal—after she'd provided the usual time of service as an Adept, of course."

"Wait a minute. The Conclave implanted Renai. Does that mean *she* is Sempiternal?"

"I don't think so; she shows no sign of having Ability now, though her madness may be hiding what's buried in her mind. When she was still an Adept, though, Master Gersemi and a few others suspected she was. So, when Renai was caught having sex with a boy outside of Generation, and not for the first time—well. It provided the excuse to get rid of her. I suppose they thought it gentler than killing her outright."

"*Killing* her? You must be joking. They would never kill an Adept!"

Master Ciara's expression turned stony. "I'm afraid I am not. I said the Conclave *usually* implants a suspected Sempiternal, but the other option is death. And if they know for certain an Adept is Sempiternal, then an implant is not an option at all."

A feeling of dread flooded through Alia's insides. "Are you saying that if the Masters believe I'm Sempiternal, they might...they would...?" She couldn't finish the thought out loud.

Master Ciara smiled sadly. "Yes. My dear, had you remained at the Conclave, you most certainly would be dead by now."

<hr>

CHAPTER 18

SARABIE

A STREAK OF red passing by the window caught Sarabie's attention as she waited for the Masters to arrive. She glanced outside. A small, red bird hopped along the ground, pecking at the dirt. After a few moments, it launched back into the air and escaped over the wall surrounding the garden. If only she could escape her fate so easily.

The Masters had given Sarabie one week to reconsider her decision to not go through Generation again. Served infrequently by a different eunuch each day, she'd spent the week in quiet reflection, considering her two equally awful choices for a decision she'd never thought she'd have to make. Yet in the end, the prospect of enduring a second Generation filled her with such intense terror that merely imagining it left her fighting hysteria.

Without warning, the bolt of the door to her quarters slid open. She stepped away from the window, nervously clasping her hands behind her, then in front, then back again. The door opened, and

Master Leyta and Master Nivi marched into the room. The former seemed impatient, while the latter appeared hopeful. Sarabie almost felt guilty, knowing that her answer would disappoint them both. *Almost.*

Master Leyta stopped her forward rush a few feet from the window. "Good morning, Sarabie. I trust you have used the past week wisely?"

"I believe I have, Master."

The Masters exchanged an indecipherable look. "Then you've changed your mind?" Master Leyta asked. "You will do what is necessary to fulfill your duty to the Conclave?"

A growing tightness in her throat threatened to curb her words. "I will not."

Master Leyta frowned. "Well. It is as I feared it would be, then."

"Sarabie, are you certain of this?" Master Nivi asked, her eyes pleading.

"I am." Sarabie said. *As certain as I can be, when my options are bad or worse.*

Master Leyta wrote something in the notebook she carried. "All right, then. You'll move today to new rooms until your pregnancy comes to term. I will make the arrangements now. In the interim, we will provide you with the training you will need in your new life. Rest assured we will not leave you without usable skills." She closed her notebook, and without another word, turned and walked toward the door.

The Master's matter-of-fact recitation irked Sarabie. She'd expected more of an effort to change her mind, even though such an attempt would have been futile. Instead, they seemed content to let her go, as if she had not spent all of her life in service to the Conclave. Was she so worthless to them? Anger burst past her numbness.

"How can you throw me away so easily?" she asked, her voice shaking. "Do you not care about me at all?" A thought struck her, rebellious and spiteful. "I'll tell everyone outside about what really goes on here. I'll reveal all your secrets!" She knew she was lashing out, but she felt unafraid of the consequences for the first time in her life. What could be worse than what they already intended to do?

Master Leyta paused with her hand on the door latch and half-turned, her mouth curled up on one side. "My dear, you are a foolish child indeed if you think you know even a small *fraction* of our secrets. In any case, we take precautions to ensure someone in your—situation—cannot reveal what she should not. You'll not recollect your time here at all."

Sarabie gasped. For a moment, no words would come. "Eliminating any memory is a high crime. No Adept would ever do as you say, even if she knew how," she said when she found her voice again.

Master Leyta chuckled. "There are some things most Adepts are never taught—things reserved for those few Adepts who live their lives in the Generation wing. They have the power to do such as this."

I am a stranger in my own home, Sarabie suddenly realized. The last few months had brought to light so many things she'd never even suspected. What other secrets slept within the walls of the Conclave? Now, she'd never know. A tear slipped down her cheek, exposing her defiance for what it was: short-lived.

Master Nivi, who had remained silent throughout this exchange, reached out and touched her arm. "Sarabie, you can still change your mind. She's not given the orders yet. Tell us now that you'll stay, and all will be forgiven and forgotten."

I could never forget. "I'm sorry," Sarabie said, determined to keep her voice respectful after her outburst. "I accept I will remain isolated until the child is born, and after that I will live my life outside the Conclave, with no memory of my time as an Adept. I will obey the Masters in this." She bowed her head. Defiance had gotten her nowhere; perhaps cooperation would.

When she looked up, Master Leyta squinted at her, as if she were questioning Sarabie's veracity. "I'm sorry you've refused your duty, child. Yet you should know that your acceptance of what's to come doesn't mean we won't be keeping a close eye on you." The Master opened the door and stuck her head out into the hall. Her words were inaudible, but Sarabie didn't have to wait long to learn what they were.

"I've requested the preparation of your new rooms," Master Leyta declared. "I've also sent the notice of dismissal. Once your name is stricken from the rolls, an announcement will be made that you have been dismissed for refusing to repeat Generation."

Sarabie clenched her jaw. As if her exclusion were as simple as that! Hearing their version of it made her wonder whether Alia really had chosen to leave the Conclave of her own accord. Alia was willful, but even so, it was entirely out of character for her to run off with some foreign merchant.

Master Leyta continued as if they were discussing the weather. "Tomorrow morning, your new lessons will begin. There is no time to waste, as you have much to learn before you leave us." Master Leyta's expression softened. "Sarabie, despite what you might think at this moment, we do not wish for you to have a difficult life. It simply is that we must be firm with our rules for the greater good of the Conclave."

"I understand, Master Leyta." With great effort, Sarabie managed to keep her tone humble.

The older woman seemed to accept her response. "This will be the last time we meet. I wish you luck in your future. Master Nivi, please escort Sarabie to her new chambers. The servant is expecting your arrival." With that, she left the room as if she'd already dismissed Sarabie from her consciousness.

Master Nivi turned to her, her eyes full of pity. "I suppose we should go."

"I'll gather my belongings," Sarabie said woodenly.

"No—I'm sorry, but you can't. You're not allowed to bring with you any reminders of your past life. We'll provide you with new things—everything you'll need going forward."

The Master's attempt to put a positive spin on what was yet another disappointment fell flat. Sarabie had few possessions, but they were *hers*, and she hadn't realized she'd have to leave them all behind. There was the tiny clock Alia had found buried in the sand on the coast of Corval during one of their first adventures together as children. A beaded hair comb she'd received as a gift from a grateful tribunal while on a long-term assignment. And her Crown of Ascension, with its garnets decorating the silver band.

Outside in the hallway, Sarabie turned toward the right, but Master Nivi pulled at her sleeve to draw her to the left. Panic surged within her; the path she'd taken to Generation was to the left. *It's not a trick. Even they wouldn't do that.* Or would they? She was, after all, denying them the continuation of her Ability. Why wouldn't they force her to do what they wanted? Her heart pounded as Master Nivi led her down the hall.

They turned down a narrow offshoot from the main corridor. It curved back toward the direction from which they'd come, as if they walked along the perimeter of the Generation wing, then turned and jogged randomly. She searched her memory of her Generation ceremony—which admittedly was fuzzy—and found nothing whatsoever of this corridor. Her breathing eased.

After several minutes of walking in disorienting silence, they passed under a simple arch and entered a small, round room. An iron-and-glass lamp hung from the center of the high ceiling. Three plain, identical wooden doors were spaced along the curved wall before them. Master Nivi passed through the center door, and twenty more steps brought them to a second round room. Its appearance was similar to the first, except it contained four identical doors instead of three. The Master opened the second door from the left.

Thirty-five more steps, and they passed under an arch into a third round room. It was not much larger than the first two, but unlike those barren chambers, tapestries lined the walls and an upholstered chair rested against the wall. Vertical bars blocked access to the room's only door.

"We will wait here," said Master Nivi.

Sarabie stood awkwardly behind her. The smooth metal bars made her nervous. She hadn't envisioned she'd be treated like a prisoner. She dreaded to see the conditions behind the door.

She jumped when a tapestry to her left moved. The pale-haired eunuch who appeared from behind the tapestry bowed deeply to

Master Nivi, and when he stood upright, Sarabie recognized him as the one who'd served her after Generation and who'd escorted her to her fateful appointment with the Masters. *Was that only last week? It seems a lifetime ago.* Did he know why she was there?

"Master. Due to the sudden nature of the summons, I've not been able to complete all of the necessary preparations, but I've done enough to begin residence."

"Then let us proceed," said Master Nivi.

The eunuch removed a key from the chest pocket of his black jacket and fitted it into a tiny hole to the right of the door. As the lock clicked, the bars over the door slid down into hidden recesses in the floor with a slight sound of metal scraping against stone. He opened the door and stepped back into the round room with another bow.

Sarabie stepped over the threshold slowly, nervous to discover the state of her prison cell. To her surprise, while the room contained none of the opulence she'd experienced in the Generation wing, it appeared comfortable. A quiet sigh of relief escaped from her lips.

Master Nivi joined her and nodded as she looked around the room. "This will serve you well as you wait for the child to be born. You'll take your lessons and meals in here, and then there is a separate bedroom and bath through that door over there." She pointed to the back corner of the room. "When the time comes, that's where you'll give birth."

"The windows are in the bedroom, then?" Sarabie asked. None were in the main room.

"No. There are no windows here."

"Surely I'll be able to go outside, then?" They couldn't lock her away from the sun...could they?

"Again, no. I'm sorry. You won't leave this suite until the time comes for you to leave us for good. You won't be alone, though; in addition to the instructors and medics who will visit regularly, Calio here will act as your companion. If there is anything you need that is within his power to obtain, ask."

Calio smiled at Sarabie, but she couldn't muster the effort to respond. Besides, she understood "companion" was merely the

Master's euphemism for "guard." The reality of her decision started to sink in, threatening to overwhelm her.

"All right, then." Master Nivi turned to face Sarabie. "I'm truly sorry about all this. I wish I could change the way things are; we had such hopes for you." She sighed deeply. "Well, we must do as we must. I will not see you again. I do hope you find a way to live a full and happy life."

After the Master left the room, the door closed, and the bars rattled and thunked into position. Several minutes passed as Sarabie stood in the same spot, staring at the door. *Trapped.*

"Are you hungry, Sarabie? It is nearly time for the midday meal. I can request it, if you like."

"I'm not hungry." She turned her head toward the bedroom door. "I would like to rest. Is the bed prepared?"

"Yes, of course. I will show you."

The bedroom was nothing like the one she'd had in Generation, or even as an Adept. A single pillow rested at the head of the small bed, though the blankets covering the mattress looked cozy and warm. True to Master Nivi's word, there were no windows in the wooden panels covering the walls. In addition to the bed, the room held a nightstand, a wardrobe against the far wall, and a dressing bench at the foot of the bed.

Calio opened the wardrobe to reveal several brown robes and other clothing folded neatly on its shelves. He removed a robe and held it out to her. Sarabie stared at it, confused. "I'm just taking a nap. I don't need to change." Even if she were sleeping longer, she'd change into a nightshift, not...whatever that was.

"My apologies, but you must first change into a new robe before you rest. I've been instructed to return your current robe to the Masters right away."

She eyed the dingy fabric he held with distaste. A coarse weave the color of mud, it contrasted starkly with the soft brilliant crimson fabric she now wore. It made her long for the robe she'd worn during her Ascension ceremony, made of the finest silk, which she'd never worn a second time. The Masters had probably thrown it away already, along with everything else that might suggest there had once been an Adept named Sarabie. Her fingers clutched at the fabric at her sides.

"Please. They are waiting."

"Fine," she said. Any defiance on her part would make no difference in her own situation, and would only threaten to get him in trouble as well. She unfastened the crimson robe from her waist with trembling fingers, then untangled her arms from the sleeves and threw the robe to the floor. The room's cool air chilled her bare skin. Not wanting Calio's assistance, she snatched the murky-colored robe from his hands. Tears of frustration and loss coursed down her cheeks as she dressed in her new attire.

Calio bent to retrieve her discarded robe. "Thank you," he murmured, backing out of the room and shutting the door behind him.

She slipped under the blankets on the bed, then touched the glow lantern on the nightstand to deactivate it. Only a thin line of light from under the door penetrated the inky darkness of the windowless bedroom. Her quick breaths sounded absurdly noisy in the quiet.

As she lay in the dark, she held one hand to her abdomen. It still seemed impossible that she carried a boy. So much had happened, she had nearly forgotten the source of her current calamity. *It wasn't supposed to be like this.*

Sarabie squeezed her eyes tight against her tears. Would she ever be able to forget her Generation ceremony? The last man's laughter as he'd choked her echoed in her mind and made nightmares of her dreams every night. None of the Masters had even been willing to *consider* it might have occurred as she remembered, instead claiming it to be mere delusions. That, and her punishment now, showed they simply didn't care about her. She wondered if they ever had.

Perhaps it will be good to forget this life.

Mentally exhausted, she drifted into sleep.

Sarabie.

She rubbed at her eyes and lifted her head from the pillow. Had Calio called for her?

Sarabie. Can you hear me?

Realization set in as she came fully awake. An Adept! It had to be.

"Yes," she whispered into the dark, worried Calio might be standing right outside the bedroom door.

The eunuch cannot hear you. He is cleaning something in the other room.

"Who is this?" The only person she could think of who might risk contacting her was Marta. She was so honored now, carrying twins. Perhaps after learning of Sarabie's dismissal, her friend had enlisted the aid of a young Adept who didn't know any better.

You do not know me, but I am with someone you do know. Alia.

"Alia!" she yelped, then clapped her hands over her mouth.

She wishes to know where you are. She does not recognize my description of this place.

"Oh." Sarabie hesitated as reason caught up to her elation. If Alia was with an Adept, then she was still part of the Conclave after all. Was this some trick or test? Why would the Masters bother? She bit her lower lip, thinking. It was all terribly confusing.

It's not a trick. Alia's really here with me. Do you remember that time you covered for her when she stole fruit from the kitchen?

Sarabie grinned at the memory, feeling tears well up in her eyes. It had been the one time she'd participated in Alia's schemes, and she'd been so scared of being caught that she'd never done it again. Only she and Alia knew that story, proving the Adept's words as true. "I remember. Oh please, tell me: where is she? Is she okay?"

She's fine. She says not to believe what they have said about her.

A weight lifted from Sarabie's heart, one that had been in place ever since the Masters claimed Alia had run away after losing her Ability. "I knew it!"

She wants to know if you are still in Seclusion.

"Yes, sort of..." Sarabie couldn't find the words to explain, but she didn't need to—not while connected to an Adept. She opened up her mind to allow the mystery Adept to plumb her recent memories.

No response came after many long minutes. Perhaps the Adept

was too young and couldn't maintain the necessary connection, or perhaps she and Alia had been caught by the Masters residing wherever they were.

Sarabie. The impression of the Adept's voice was fainter than before.

"Yes?"

We will come for you.

❧

CHAPTER 19

NYONA

NYONA CROSSED THE open space separating the officers' quarters from the other residential buildings. She passed a few Guardsmen in quiet conversation, the wind obscuring their words. Periodic clanging of metal on metal came from the armory. A horse whinnied.

She'd spent the morning with Kelda and Ciara in the Captains' quarters as they examined *A History of Corinas* for information that might help them decide what to do with Alia. *Sempiternal.* A strange term, and one she'd never even heard before a few days ago. It still struck her as preposterous that some Adepts retained their Ability forever, but the book seemed to discuss it as fact. And so far, they'd found the information in the book to be entirely accurate.

Less surprising was learning how closely the Masters guarded this secret. The unwritten contract between the people of Corinas and the Conclave was premised on the idea that nature limited an Adept's power. If the citizenry had any idea that someone a Master's age, with all her experience and knowledge, could actively use Ability...well. Perhaps the rebellion wouldn't have to work so hard to find recruits.

The house she shared with Tovi, Kelda, Ciara, and Alia was small —more of a cabin, really—yet its weathered, gray timbers provided sturdy protection from the island's frequent wind and rain. None of the other houses were much larger, though they didn't need to be. Vose didn't have many regular inhabitants.

The door to her house flew open just as she reached it. She held out her hand to prevent it from smacking her in the face.

Renai jumped back from the threshold. "Oh!" she cried. "I'm terribly sorry, of course. I'd never want to do anything that might cause harm to befall *you*."

"I'm sure," Nyona muttered, hoping for a quick end to their interaction. On Renai's more lucid days, she seemed to go out of her way to make oblique references to their shared past, resurrecting the guilt Nyona held concerning Renai's implantation and dismissal from the Conclave. "Why are you here?" Renai stayed in the same house as Hasso, so he could keep an eye on her.

"I was looking for—" Renai said before becoming distracted by a Vose Guardsman who was clomping down the steps of a nearby house. She arched her back against the doorframe as he walked in front them, her breasts straining against her thin shirt. "Hi there," she cooed. The man wisely ignored her and increased his pace. The Captains had warned them about Renai's...predilections.

"What are you looking for?" Nyona asked, hoping to draw Renai's attention so she'd at least get out of the way.

"You. Do you know what your daughter's been up to?"

"What do you mean?"

Renai tilted her head. "Something. Or nothing. I don't really know. She's been spending an *awful* lot of time alone with Alia lately. Maybe you should ask her? They're together in Alia's room right now."

Nyona raised her eyebrows at Renai's tone. She seemed to suggest something was amiss with Tovi's developing friendship with the older Adept—a friendship they'd all encouraged in the hopes it would draw Alia closer the rebellion. Not that Nyona should read anything into the tone of Renai's voice; it was inherently unreliable as an indicator of what she meant. Nonetheless, it didn't hurt to check in on the girls. "I'll speak to Alia. Thank you."

Renai grinned broadly, then skipped down the steps and continued in the direction of the man who'd rebuffed her.

Nyona entered the house and walked down the short hall to Alia's room. She knocked on the door. A chair scraped against the floor, and the door opened inward a few inches. Alia peered out into the hallway with one eye, her eyebrow-less face ghostly in the dim light. "Yes?"

"Is Tovi with you?"

Alia's eye squinted. "Who told you that?"

"It's no matter. Answer me." Alia's odd behavior put more authority in Nyona's voice than she'd normally use with the Adept.

"Um, well, she was, but now—"

The hairs on Nyona's arms stood on end with sudden goosebumps. She shoved open the door, pushing Alia aside. Tovi sat on the bed, rigid, with her back to the wall. Curls clung to her forehead on beads of perspiration. Her eyes were closed.

"What's going on?" Nyona cried, rushing to the bed. "She's not supposed to use her Ability unless she absolutely must. Why didn't you stop her?" Tovi had been so well behaved lately Nyona had almost forgotten how willful she could be.

"Because she wanted to do it for me."

Nyona rounded on Alia with a ferocious anger. "You asked her to do this? You are endangering her life? *All* of our lives? What are you trying to do? Have I been wrong about you?" She could feel herself shaking. *Is she a spy, like Hasso and Mathis believe?*

"No! You don't understand. She offered to do it. I told her no, but she kept asking, saying she wanted to help, and—well, I'm sorry, but I couldn't help myself. I had to know if she was well. And she's not!"

"What are you talking about?"

"My fr—"

Tovi gasped, then gulped for air, blinking.

"Tovi! Are you alright, my love?" Nyona hugged her tightly, then loosened her grip so as not to impede Tovi's recovery. "It's okay. Just breathe."

Tovi took several deep, shuddering breaths. "I...told her," she said in a halting voice.

"Told who, what?" Nyona demanded, twisting around to glower at Alia.

The Adept's face displayed a mixture of hope and fear. "My friend, Sarabie. Tovi told her we would come for her."

What had Alia gotten her daughter into? "Start at the beginning. Now."

Alia adopted the formal posture of an Adept addressing a Master, with her hands held behind her lower back. "I had mentioned to Tovi how much I missed my best friend, Sarabie. She entered Seclusion long before the Masters sent me to Aldham, and I think of her often. Tovi offered to check in on her, and I...I just wanted to make sure she was well. It wasn't supposed to take but a few minutes."

Nyona felt the blood drain from her face, and a sour gurgle crept up from her stomach. "You asked Tovi to contact someone in the *Conclave*?" Such an effort, from so far away, would require an enormous outlay of Ability. "How could she possibly mask that kind of effort? Why would you encourage her to do such a thing?"

Alia furrowed her brow. "She seemed so confident she could keep herself hidden, and all we planned for her to do was find and observe Sarabie for a few moments to make sure she was okay. We didn't plan to contact her."

Nyona, still furious at Alia's carelessness, turned to her daughter. "Have I not told you a hundred—a thousand!—times you mustn't use your Ability without permission? Especially now, when they are looking for us. Why would you be so..." She bit back her words. Tovi was still a child; she wouldn't understand the possible ramifications of acceding to Alia's desires.

Tears welled in Tovi's eyes at her mother's harsh words. "I only wanted to help. I—I imagined what it would feel like, to have a best friend. No one noticed me, I promise. I was so, so careful."

Confronted with her daughter's heartfelt, wistful words, Nyona's anger vanished. Tovi hadn't experienced anything remotely resembling a normal childhood, and she'd never had any friends. She'd had a few playmates back when they still lived with the troupe of actors that included the man who'd given Tovi her large green eyes and full smile. But once Nyona had realized Tovi had Ability, she'd done everything she could to keep her daughter away from potentially prying eyes, no matter how young.

Nyona took a deep, shuddering breath. "I will trust you were careful," she said, reaching out to touch one of Tovi's damp curls. What else could she say? What had happened was unchangeable. At this point, all she could do was learn as much as she could, then report the transgression to the Captains. She grimaced at the thought.

She moved over to the room's empty chair and sat facing her daughter. "So, what happened? Why did you contact this girl after all?"

"I couldn't find her for a long time," Tovi said. "And when I finally did, I needed to talk to her."

"Why?" Nyona asked, renewing her resolve to remain calm as Tovi looked to Alia for guidance.

"She came out of her trance and told me that Sarabie and a man —a servant—were inside some rooms with no windows, and that there were bars on the door."

Nyona had never heard of such a place in the Conclave. "Are you sure you were looking in the Conclave?" she asked Tovi. She looked directly into her daughter's eyes, refusing to allow her to defer again to the Adept.

Tovi squirmed under her gaze. "Yes. Alia showed me where it was and what it looked like."

"*Showed?*"

"I allowed her a peek into my memories," Alia admitted, her eyes downcast.

"So in addition to using her Ability to search and speak to your friend, she also used it to read you?" Nyona asked, her voice flat. *The Captains will not be pleased about this at all.* Despite Hasso's repeated requests, they'd refused to let Tovi learn how to perform a truth-seeking upon Alia, citing the high risk of detection. Nyona couldn't fault their logic; truth-seeking required a tremendous amount of Ability, especially where the target sought to hide her true self. Yet there wasn't much difference in technique between a memory read and a truth-seeking.

"It was only a little bit, Mama. Just so I knew where to look."

"That's true," Alia offered. "It took only a few moments to show her, and then she broke contact with me." She continued the story in a rush. "But after she told me about what she saw, I said I had never heard of rooms like that in the Conclave, and that something must be wrong. The next thing I knew, Tovi was back in a trance. I didn't dare break it and send a surge of Ability who-knows-where."

Tovi's eyes displayed a stubborn resolve. "I *had* to. I had to ask her if she was okay."

"Was she?" Nyona asked, though she already knew the answer.

"No." Hurt and confusion intertwined within that single syllable, and fresh tears sprung to life in Tovi's eyes.

Nyona grasped her daughter's hands. "Tell me."

"I don't know...I tried to explain to Alia—"

"Sarabie opened her memories to Tovi in full," Alia interjected, a tear cascading down her cheek. "It was—too much to divulge to her, I think. Tovi couldn't explain everything she saw. But it seems Sarabie's Generation was—well, *violent* is the only thing I can decipher, and with multiple partners, but the Masters refused to help her. They told her she was misremembering—suffering from delusions. Then she found out she'd fallen pregnant with a *male child*. I don't understand how that's even possible, but because of it, the Masters wanted her to go through Generation again. She refused, so they locked her away in these rooms where she'll stay until the child is born. After that, they'll expel her."

Dismay surged through Nyona over the thought of Tovi being exposed to even more violence as a result of her ill-advised attempt to help Alia. An Adept trained from infancy as a tool of the Conclave might be accustomed to encountering that sort of human depravity, but not Tovi.

It was a fantastic story. Memory loss was a common side effect of the fertility drugs used during Generation. Nyona's own memories of her three ceremonies were fuzzy and vague, but even so, she was confident she'd recall multiple partners if she'd had them. And certainly she would recall if any partner had been violent.

Yet the Masters reacting badly to anyone refusing to do as they'd ordered was definitely in character. And as the mother of a child who herself was an impossibility, she was not one to judge Sarabie's claim of carrying a male child. Yet still—what Alia reported sounded...insane. The question required asking.

"How do we know your friend is right in the mind? Perhaps she's being imprisoned for her own protection." Alia scoffed while Tovi shook her head. "It's not unheard of," Nyona countered. "Consider Renai!"

Tovi continued to shake her head, denying Nyona's words. "She's not like Renai. I could tell."

Nyona doubted her daughter's ability to make such a determination, but chose to let that go for now as well. Turning back to Alia, she asked, "So then after hearing all this, you had Tovi tell her we'd come for her? Why did you even think that might be a possibility?"

"Everyone's always saying we need more people for the cause," Alia argued, dropping her formal posture. "Here's our chance to get another insider! She'll have more recent information than me. Plus, she's recently been in Seclusion *and* Generation, so she can tell us what she knows about all that. We have to rescue her now, though, before the child is born, and bring her here—or at least someplace safe, where the Conclave won't find her."

Nyona snorted, the ridiculousness of Alia's suggestion overshadowing Nyona's surprise at hearing her speak like a true member of the rebellion. "Even if the Captains were crazy enough to sign on to your plan, we're about as far from Corval as we could be. It would take months to travel there, even if we could do so openly, which we can't."

Alia stepped forward. "That's why someone should leave now! If we don't get to her before she's expelled, it will be pointless."

"Why? It's far more likely that the Captains will agree to have someone pick her up once she's out of the Conclave's control. That wouldn't involve as much risk, and we could take our time."

"But we *can't* wait. She'll be of no use to the rebellion after her child is born," Alia pleaded.

"Why ever not?"

"The Masters will erase her memory before they expel her."

Nyona sat up straight, shocked. "To tamper with an individual's memory is absolutely forbidden. You know that. When someone is expelled, the shame alone prevents people from talking about their former lives. I still remember my life in the Conclave, obviously. Even *Renai* remembers some of it."

"Maybe they didn't do it back when you all were expelled, but they're doing it now."

"I'm sure it was simply a threat to try to get your friend to acquiesce to their demands," Nyona reasoned. "Tampering with memories goes against one of an Adept's foundational precepts. No one would do it."

"Why are you, of all people, insisting that what Sarabie revealed cannot be true?" Alia said, her voice growing louder. "Just because *you've* never heard of something happening doesn't mean it's false. When you lived in the Conclave, you'd never heard of an Adept being born outside of Generation, right? Yet here sits Tovi. And what about an Adept who keeps her Ability forever? You've probably not heard of that. Would you call Ciara a liar if she told you I was one of them?" Splotches of bright-red color dotted Alia's cheeks, and she was breathing hard.

"Ciara told me a few days ago," Nyona said reluctantly, recognizing Alia's point. "So, no, I wouldn't think her a liar."

Alia pounced on her admission. "See? So please, stop trying to associate Sarabie's memories, as improbable as they may sound, to the delusions we hear from Renai on a daily basis. Renai is broken. Sarabie is not. At least, not yet."

"Please, Mama, can't we ask the Captains to help her?" Tovi asked. "She needs us."

"Help who?"

Nyona looked up to see Mathis standing in the doorway, his

head nearly brushing the top of the wooden frame. She was pleased to see him; he'd been keeping to himself of late, and she'd not had much by way of opportunity to talk to him since Ciara arrived. He'd stopped checking in on Tovi as often; Nyona didn't know if that was because he'd grown tired of his duty or simply felt it was no longer necessary. She thought he'd enjoyed spending time with them both, but perhaps he'd only done so because he'd been forced to.

She glanced back at Alia and Tovi. Two sets of eyes implored her to agree with their scheme. *I suppose I'm going to have to tell the Captains all about this, anyway.* It wouldn't be that much more to pass along Alia's request.

"I think you'd better sit down," Nyona told Mathis.

❧❦❧

CHAPTER 20

ALIA

ALIA'S VOICE SHOOK with frustration. "So that's it? You'll give it no consideration or thought whatsoever, just—no?" She twisted her wrists so her palms faced the ceiling in a gesture of exasperation. "I hear all the time how pleased you all are to have found me and Tovi. Sarabie is another, and only recently an Adept herself. But if we don't hurry, she'll be lost!"

Mathis looked down at her as if she were daft. "Look, it wouldn't matter if this friend of yours was the key to destroying the Conclave's rule for good. She's in Corval. We're on an island on the opposite side of the country. It would take months to get there, and in case you've forgotten, we're actually trying to stay *away* from the Conclave at the moment."

It was much the same as Nyona had said, yet she'd already agreed to bring Alia's request to the two rebel Captains. Given that decision, Mathis's opinion shouldn't matter at all. Yet here she was, arguing with the man because Nyona seemed to care what he thought. "A few months is acceptable, so long as we get there before her child is born. A small group travels fast; we certainly did on our way here."

"That's because we were running away from the Conclave, not toward it." Mathis muttered. He raised his eyebrows, as if he'd just thought of something. "I suppose you'd casually volunteer to be part of this rescue attempt, hmm?" Sarcasm dripped from his words. "Sounds to me like a ploy to get back home and serve up some members of the rebellion for torture and execution at the same time." He folded his arms across the front of his chest.

"Mathis," Nyona rebuked. "That's not what she's trying to do."

Alia's cheeks grew warm. It was true that she'd once planned to escape and turn the rebels in to the Conclave. But so much had changed over the last seven weeks. Besides learning about how the Masters had used her as bait without her consent and how they'd ordered attacks on innocent villages, her time with the rebels had brought knowledge of Tovi's mere existence, her own possible Sempiternal status, and now Sarabie's mistreatment. She felt utterly betrayed. The Masters hadn't lied to her once or twice—they'd lied her entire life.

They'd even lied about demonstrably false things, such as how Adepts weren't capable of learning to read while they still possessed Ability. At first, Alia thought her success at learning letters from Kelda meant she'd lost her Ability for good, but then she discovered Tovi could read, too. Why would the Masters lie about something like that? It was almost as if they wanted Adepts to remain ignorant of the world around them.

Of course they do, stupid. Masters hated to be questioned. An ignorant Adept wouldn't know she could.

Fury grew deep in Alia's chest. What else did she believe as truth that was, in fact, not? If Mathis had paid any attention at all, he'd understand why she now had no desire to return to the Conclave. Supposing the Masters let her live—which Ciara insisted would not be the case—she would question everything they said. And she would *never* acquiesce to Generation.

"Mathis, can't we please try to help Sarabie?" Tovi asked, her head resting against Nyona's shoulder as they sat on the bed. "She is so very sad."

Mathis's emerald eyes seemed to soften at the child's plea, but none of that emotion transferred to his tone when he spoke to Nyona. "If you think this is such a great idea, you present it to the Captains on your own. Somehow, I doubt they'll be willing to risk everything to rescue someone who's not even an Adept anymore."

"That's probably true, but I don't see why we can't ask." Nyona cocked her head. "For all we know, this might fit in with whatever they've been planning of late."

Mathis nodded begrudgingly. "They have been pretty tight-lipped since Ciara showed up." His upper lip curled slightly in a sneer, as it tended to do whenever he mentioned the former Master.

"So if it turns out they intend for us to head for the mainland soon," Nyona said, "maybe they'd be willing to go east. It's worth asking."

Mathis scowled, his thick, dark eyebrows diving deep toward his eyes. "Even if we all went east, a smaller group would have to split off to make it to Corval in time. Who would you be willing to send on that suicide mission? You? Me?"

Nyona returned his glare. "That's not fair. If I thought there was no chance at all for success, I wouldn't have agreed to bring Alia's request to the Captains."

"So who, then? Sonya? You know full well she likes to move fast —usually without even bothering to think."

"I'd never advocate for Sonya's involvement, and neither of us can leave Tovi. Perhaps they could send some of the Vose Guardsmen, and maybe Owen. He has a good head on his shoulders."

"I still don't like it. This idea is crazy enough to sound like it came from Renai." Mathis eyed Alia again with suspicion. "With that implant, are we sure she's *not* going crazy like Renai?"

Alia sighed in exasperation. "This didn't come from me. Tovi's the one who talked to Sarabie, and we're all certain of Tovi's sanity." She was finished arguing with this man, and turned back to Nyona. "Please ask the Captains. If they say no…" Her voice caught. "At least I did what little I could to try to help her," she finished quietly.

"We will ask, and we'll ask now. Come, Mathis. I want you with me, though I will do all of the talking. You can just stand there, glowering." Nyona brushed the hair from Tovi's face and kissed her on her forehead. "Why don't you go out into the sitting room and wait for Kelda? It's almost time for your reading lessons."

Tovi scooted off the bed and hopped to the floor. They followed her into the hallway that led to the sitting room in the front of the house, and then Mathis and Nyona continued out the front door. Alia paced back and forth, full of nervous anticipation. Would the Captains actually consider her plea? The thread of hope she held was thin, indeed.

After what seemed like many long minutes, the door opened again and Kelda walked into the sitting room. She wore the same sort of plain, black Guard uniform as everyone else, yet she opted for a long skirt instead of pants. Her gray hair rested in a familiar bun at the nape of her neck, and a brown leather knapsack hung from her shoulder.

"Good afternoon," she said. She sat in the padded chair, hiding the swirling blue and green patterns of its upholstery. "I'm afraid there's been a change of plans. I'm needed in the Captains' quarters, so we'll have to postpone our lessons until tomorrow. I wanted to drop off the material I found, though, so you can practice without me." She lifted the flap of the knapsack at her feet. "Are you ready for something new?"

"Yes!" Tovi said, oblivious to the import of Kelda's words.

Alia, on the other hand, felt a fluttering of her heart. There was only one reason for Kelda to attend to the Captains right now. The former Master had once lived in the Conclave; she would understand that what had happened to Sarabie—and what would happen to her in the future—should never occur.

Kelda reached into her knapsack and removed a book with a collage of four pictures on its cover, each brightly colored in painstaking detail. She held it toward Tovi. "This one is for you. It's a set of folk stories from the early days of Corinas. I think you'll quite enjoy them. The language is a little more advanced than what you're used to, but I'm certain you're up for the challenge."

Tovi accepted the book in her small hands and opened it reverently, revealing pages of small, clear print bordered with intricate patterns in red and gold. She took herself and the book back to the sofa, and as she began to read, her lips never moved. Alia envied her skill; when Alia tried to read unfamiliar words—which were almost all of them—she had to sound them out loud.

Kelda next removed from her bag a small, black book and presented it to Alia. It was disappointingly plain in comparison to Tovi's volume. "What is this?" Alia asked as she flipped though the pages. It didn't look like a book at all. Scrawled handwriting covered the pages, and many of the pages toward the back were blank.

"So far, you've only read from printed books. Those are easy to read—assuming you know the words, of course." Her lips twitched upward at her own joke. "I'd like you now to try reading something written by hand. That's how most of the citizenry communicates, you know. It might sound a simple thing, but because everyone's handwriting is different, it's good to practice so you learn to recognize the same letters despite variances in style. So. This is my notebook, with passages I've copied from a printed book. Try to read it."

"I will try later," Alia said. With everything else going on, she had no interest in trying to read something so foreign. At this stage, she'd only read large, perfectly printed words. Despite her successes in that, she found it difficult to let go of the conditioning she'd received since childhood that letters were impossible for Adepts to understand.

"Go ahead and try the first few words while I'm here," Kelda encouraged. "I'm certain you can do it."

The sooner she did as Kelda asked, the sooner Kelda would return to the Captains. Alia turned to the first page. "Th-The." *That wasn't so difficult.* Feeling somewhat more confident, she moved to the second word. "Co-n...d...ah...voh? Con-davoh?" That didn't sound like a word at all, but it was difficult to see the letters any other way after coming up with one version. She peered at the writing, then noticed a tiny separation between some of the letters she hadn't detected at first. "Oh!" she said, as recognition bloomed. "Conclave!"

Kelda smiled. "Yes! Excellent! See how I connect some of my letters? Some people do that even more. You corrected yourself nicely; try to read a few more."

Alia scanned the rest of the line, already finding it easier to locate familiar words than it had been only moments ago. She frowned as she read on. "Kelda, what is this book?"

"It is the true story of the Conclave."

Alia brushed her fingers down the page over the indentations of Kelda's penmanship. "Did you copy this from the book Nyona found?" She'd never seen it, but had heard plenty about it.

"Yes. It truly is a treasure. There's much and more within its pages, and we're still trying to piece it all together. I thought you might like to practice your reading on a few portions we've already gone through. Some of the sections in here discuss the Great Uprising, which I think you'll find particularly interesting. And once you've finished with that, I'll give you the notebook I'm working on now, which has sections about Ritual, Ascension, and even a bit on Generation."

It was the opening Alia was waiting for. "Kelda—you were a Master when you left the Conclave, correct?"

"That is correct. But it was a very long time ago. I can barely remember it these days," she said with a bark of laughter.

"Do you remember your Generation ceremony?"

The older woman raised her eyebrows. "You must be spending too much time around Renai if you're asking about that. Though it's no matter, as I don't remember it at all."

"Does the book about the Conclave—the full version, not this one—mention people who *do* remember?"

Kelda shook her head. "Not in the portions I've read so far." She folded her hands in her lap. "Alia. There's no need to be coy. I saw Nyona and Mathis on my way here, and she told me what you wish us to do."

Her somber expression revealed what Alia feared would be the Captains' reaction as well. "You don't agree," she said glumly.

"No. I'm sorry. I'm willing to accept that what Tovi saw was true, but I cannot find any wisdom in your plan. Not now."

Tovi looked up from her book at the mention of her name, her face scrunched up with worry. "But Kelda! I promised Sarabie we'd come for her."

"I know, child. And believe me, if we cannot, I will be very sorry. But I'm afraid that is the likely outcome. I doubt there is anything we can do for Alia's friend before it's too late." Kelda picked up her knapsack and shrugged it over her shoulder.

Alia opened her mouth to protest further, but then the door banged open. Owen strode a few paces into the room, then stopped short. "Why are you here?" he asked Kelda. "I thought you were with the Captains and the others."

"I'm leaving now," she said, standing. "Keep reading, the both of you. It will help to keep your mind off things you can't control. We'll resume our usual lessons tomorrow." Owen held the door open for her.

He shut the door firmly then rested his hand against the wall. He craned his neck to peer down the hall. "Is anyone else here?"

"No," Alia said. "Nyona and Mathis are already with the Captains, as you probably know, and I'm assuming Ciara is with them, too. Renai's out doing whatever it is that she does, and we haven't had any other visitors today besides her and Mathis. Why? Are you looking for someone in particular?"

He shook his head. "Just curious." He ran one hand through his moppish, blond hair, which did nothing to smooth its appearance. "So they'll be gone a while, you think, talking to the Captains?"

"I imagine so," she said, though she hoped it would not take them too terribly long to make their decision. Helping Sarabie was the only thing that mattered now. If the Captains agreed to save her, maybe they'd send Owen, as Nyona suggested. It would be good for Sarabie to travel with someone pleasant after everything she'd been through.

Alia went to join Tovi on the sofa. Before she sat down, she bent over to remove her shoes so she could rest her feet on the cushions without dirtying the fabric. As she stood, a sharp pain surged into her chest from the middle of her back. The shoe dropped from her hand. She reached behind her, fumbling.

Tovi screamed—a high-pitched, hysterical sound.

Alia held up her hand and found her fingers wet and red. *What?* Her senses felt numb. Owen positioned himself between her and Tovi. The same wet, red substance coated the entire length of his knife's blade. Tovi scrambled away from him as Alia fell to her knees. With Owen blocking the front door, the child pivoted and ran down the hallway with Owen in pursuit.

The door flew open. Sonya started, then bellowed, "Hasso! To me!" Sonya dashed to Alia's side, sliding along the floor in her haste. "Where's the child? Where's Tovi?"

Alia struggled to gather enough breath to speak. Her heart pounded in her ears. When she opened her mouth to answer, she coughed a red spittle that spotted her hands. An acrid, metallic taste coated her tongue. All she could do was weakly lift one hand toward the bedrooms, and Sonya sprinted away.

It's so hard to breathe. Bewilderment and pain scattered her thoughts. Her breath grew more labored still, and the pain in her back intensified. Intending to lie down, she crumpled to her side. With each thick breath, specks of red stained the light-colored pile of the wool rug.

Pale blue eyes appeared before her face. Lips moved, but she couldn't hear the words over the sound of her own heartbeat. She struggled to draw in enough air to speak, and a darkness crept in from the edges of her vision. Hands connected to a long, thin piece of metal moved closer to her chest. *What is that?* she thought, before nothingness overcame her.

Chapter 21

Mathis

THE DOOR TO the makeshift infirmary opened. A figure covered by a gray blanket lay prone in the narrow bed, and a woman in black sat next to the bed with her back to the door. Hasso entered the hallway and closed the door silently behind him. A cloth with smears of blood was draped over his shoulder, and his braided hair was looped in a black knot at his neck. He glanced at Mathis before addressing Ciara, and in that brief moment, Mathis assumed the worst.

"She's finally stable," Hasso pronounced, and Mathis let out a breath. "Ysitra will stay with her until she wakes, in case her condition deteriorates. She lost a lot of blood, but the lung collapse was due to a fractured rib rather than Owen's knife. She's lucky he didn't hit any major organs. I drained the rest of the excess air from around her lungs and cleaned and patched her wounds the best I could. She seems to be breathing comfortably now."

Ciara exhaled sharply and pressed the palm of one hand to her chest, her expression one of open relief. "Thank you, Hasso. I'll inform Levina at once." She squeezed past Mathis and Nyona. Sconces along the wall threw her shadow as she hurried toward the Captains' study.

"Can we see her?" Tovi asked, her body pressed firmly against Nyona's. She'd essentially refused to leave her mother's side since yesterday's events. If the child hadn't suctioned herself to Nyona, Mathis was certain Nyona would have done it for her. There still might be others on the island in league with Owen; Sonya and Captain Jana hadn't yet finished their questioning.

"No," Hasso responded. "She needs undisturbed rest right now. There will be time enough in the future for visits; she'll remain abed for at least the next few weeks." He pulled the soiled cloth from his shoulder and folded it into a rectangle. "I'm going to attend to Jana and Sonya. You know where to find me if I'm needed."

As Hasso walked past, Mathis noticed the weariness etched around his eyes. The intensity of his efforts to save Alia's life had given Mathis some pause. Hasso had expressed in no uncertain terms that he thought Alia was a spy for the Conclave. For him to drive himself to near exhaustion to save her made little sense—unless he had changed his mind.

Mathis still had not. *At least not yet.* He admitted to himself, however, that the events of the past twenty-four hours had revealed that he wasn't the best judge of character. How could he claim to know Alia's motivations, someone he'd known for less than two months, when he'd failed to understand the true nature of someone he'd known his entire life?

He tamped down a surge of grief. Why would Owen do such a thing? If his childhood friend had attacked only Alia, perhaps there could have been some explanation—some plausible justification for why he thought Alia needed to die. But nothing could ever justify his attempt on Tovi's life. Nothing at all.

Grief and anger were not the only emotions warring within him. Maybe if he hadn't been so focused on avoiding everyone after Ciara's admission that she had overseen his parents' execution, he would have noticed something—anything—revealing Owen's intentions. And if he'd continued his normal practice of spending large chunks of his day with Nyona and Tovi, despite the fact that they shared living quarters with Ciara, he might have been there to stop Owen from attempting to do the unthinkable.

Instead, it had been Sonya who'd heard Tovi's screams, Sonya who'd alerted Hasso to Alia's injuries, and Sonya who'd killed Owen as he tried to draw his bloody knife across Tovi's throat. He was glad she'd been there—it was far better than the alternative—but it should have been him. *He* was supposed to be Tovi's protector, not Sonya.

"Mathis? What are you thinking about so hard? I said let's go; Kelda might be back by now." Mathis looked down, shaking his head slightly. Nyona was peering up at him with an annoyed, impatient look on her face.

He cleared his throat. "Sorry." He gestured for Nyona and Tovi to proceed before him. "What is Kelda looking for, anyway?" he asked, changing the subject.

Nyona narrowed her eyes at him, but didn't press. "A bit of her research, I think. She said she'd come across something that might explain—what happened." Her arm tightened around Tovi's shoulders as they walked.

They entered the Captains' study, and Captain Levina raised her chin in greeting. Ciara and Kelda, intent on a large sack splayed open on a round table in the center of the room, didn't notice their arrival. As Nyona and Tovi sat down, Mathis remained near the door, determined to stand guard. *I will not fail them again.*

"I know it's in here somewhere," Kelda grumbled. She handed Ciara a book with one hand while rummaging through the sack with the other, never once taking her eyes from her task. Her cheeks were rosy, and hairs that had escaped from the bun at the nape of her neck drifted freely around her face.

"There must be at least thirty in here," Ciara complained as she set the tome on top of a leaning tower of discarded books piled on the table. "Can you at least remember the color?"

"Aha!" Kelda pulled a red, leather-bound book from the sack. "This is it. I'm sure of it." She opened the book, licked her thumb and forefinger, and hastily flipped through the pages. "It's somewhere in the middle...it was after I'd finished some passages on Generation, so it should be here soon... Ah! All right. Here it is." Her finger traced along the page. "This is from a section of *A History of Corinas* that I picked out from the surrounding narrative just last week. I haven't figured out where it fits in with the rest yet, so I'm not entirely certain of the context. It's quite interesting, really, because the diction is a little different from what we've seen from the other passages, suggesting it was written at an earlier time. It reminds me of a book I once read back in Corval about the First Initiate—"

"Kelda. Just tell us what it says," Captain Levina said, a bemused smile at her lips.

"Oh. Yes." Kelda squinted at the page and began to read aloud. "*Nonetheless, males retain minutia that mark them as ours. Verily, in the untutored mind, it lies fallow, and, if left dormant too long, becomes incapable of germination. Diligence is necessary if one seeks to develop the useful capacity for acquiring conveyance, and with perseverance and ascendant age, it may flourish to include transmission.*"

Kelda looked up expectantly. "Do you see?"

Mathis did not, and a look around the room revealed he wasn't the only one. The Captain's face was blank and uncomprehending, and Nyona's brow was furrowed in confusion.

But Ciara clearly saw, as her jaw had dropped slightly. She grabbed the book from Kelda's hands, rereading the passage for herself. "Fires," she breathed. "I apologize for my language, but if this is true, as it must be—*fires*. Levina...we are entirely compromised. We must leave Vose at once, and send messages to all of our critical contacts, instructing them to abandon their posts and to gather some place Owen would not have known about."

"What?" Captain Levina's face was etched with surprise and concern at Ciara's proclamation.

"We can't leave yet," Nyona protested. "Alia needs time to recover."

Mathis said nothing, allowing the growing cacophony of the others' questions to wash over him. What Ciara advocated would set the rebellion back years—if it didn't destroy it altogether. *That's just what the Conclave would want,* he thought, and his suspicion grew. Owen had been just fine until Ciara showed up. And he had seemed unsurprised when Mathis told him Ciara had been present for the execution of not only Mathis's parents, but Owen's parents, too. He stared at the former Master, wondering what other secrets she held close.

"Stop!" Kelda shouted over the din, using the tone of voice she'd often used to corral unruly students as Morell's Director of Education. "Ciara's right," she said after the other women had quieted. "If you all will stay calm for a few minutes, I can explain."

Just then, Captain Jana strode into the room. She stopped short with a quizzical look. "What did I miss?"

"Kelda was just going to explain to us why she and Ciara think we should vacate the island immediately," said Captain Levina. She crossed her arms in front of her chest and leaned against the front of a bookshelf.

"What? Why?"

Captain Levina gestured toward the table. "Kelda. Read the passage again. Then explain."

Hearing it a second time didn't help Mathis's understanding one bit. The language was archaic and unintelligible, as far as he was concerned. How could anyone think this passage meant they had to flee?

Kelda placed the book on the table and held it open with one hand. "I found this near sections describing Generation. I reexamined the surrounding context, and it's clear to me now that the males they speak of are not the fathers of Adepts, as I'd first thought, but the *sons.* And the 'minutia' is some aspect of Ability that enables a son—properly trained, of course—to communicate with any Adept who reaches out to him. It doesn't seem to be quite the same as what former Adepts can do—upon losing our Ability, we can still communicate with Adepts almost as well as we could before, though the Adept must initiate the contact. Sons, however, must be specially trained as children for this, and even so, they can only receive messages from Adepts at first—that's what the passage means by 'acquiring conveyance.' Assuming a son learns how to receive messages as a child, he can learn to *respond* to an Adept's message as an adult, as well."

"Fires," Captain Jana said after a few moments of baffled silence. "All sons of Adepts can learn to do this?"

Kelda shrugged. "The passage suggests that sons can't learn to respond to messages if they weren't first trained as children to receive them. We should assume that every son of an Adept under the Conclave's influence has received this training."

"That's why we must leave at once," pleaded Ciara, "and why we must assume most of our outposts are compromised. Owen worked alongside you for years, Jana. And if he only recently developed the ability to *send* messages back to the Conclave, that would explain everything that's happened in the past year: the attacks on villages near where rebels were active, the assault on Morell, the murders in Aldham, and now—this."

"Wait a minute," interrupted Nyona. "Are you saying Owen is— was—a former Adept's child?"

"Yes," Ciara replied.

Nyona blinked several times. "That is—astonishing."

Astonishing wasn't the word Mathis would have selected. Fantastical, insane, ludicrous—those were only a few of the words that jumped to his mind. It was mad to believe Owen's actions were the result of secret communications with the Conclave, and madder still to think his mother had been an Adept. Mathis had known Owen's mother, and his father, too. They had died alongside his own parents at the Conclave's hand. Owen was no Adept's child. Ciara clearly was trying to pull something over on the others.

"I wish I had understood this passage when I first read it," Kelda said, clasping her hands behind her neck with her elbows bent forward. "It seems so obvious to me now. And truly, it explains so much."

"Don't blame yourself, Kelda," Ciara said. "You didn't know anything about this. I didn't, either. It also would never have occurred to me as an Adept that I could use my Ability to communicate with someone who wasn't an Adept or Master."

"Nor I," Kelda said, and Nyona nodded in apparent agreement.

"The Masters who work in Generation probably know all about this, but they were always a strange lot who kept to themselves," Ciara continued. "Had any of us known, we would have taken precautions over the years. But we didn't—and, well, this is where we are now." She turned back toward the Captains. "Jana, Levina, truly—we must leave immediately. There is no time to waste."

When the Captains nodded their agreement, Mathis could no longer remain silent. "You believe this nonsense?" he demanded, not caring that his words, dripping with incredulity, sounded more like something Sonya would say than him. He could never truly influence the Captains' decisions, but he had to try. They were about to make a mistake based on Ciara's lie.

The women all stared at Mathis as if he'd lost his mind. Perhaps he had, but so had they if they thought Owen had been aligned with the Conclave all this time. "Captain Jana, I knew Owen his entire life, and you probably knew him just as long. You knew who his parents were, just as you knew mine, and you know the Conclave executed them all for being part of the rebellion. So you should well know it's damned *impossible* for Owen to be one of them. There must be another reason for why he did what he did. One that isn't based on a random passage in a book that makes no sense at all and Ciara's word."

Mathis's rapid breathing was painfully audible in the silence that followed his outburst, and he could feel his face flushing with anger. He had expected an immediate response. Instead, Kelda avoided his eyes while Captain Jana and Ciara turned and consulted silently with each other. Nyona scratched at the side of her head, one eyebrow ticked up, and Tovi, seated on a short stool in the corner, only stared at him with wide eyes.

The corner of Captain Levina's mouth twitched up and her eyes crinkled in bemusement, yet the silence stretched out to the point of discomfort before she spoke. "Well, I suppose there's no reason to keep this close any longer, don't you think?" she asked no one in particular. "And really, it's about damned time."

"For what?" Mathis asked, confused by their odd reactions. Ciara had gone pale at the Captain's words; paler than she'd been when she'd confessed the details about her involvement in the murder of his parents. *What could be worse than that?* His stomach tightened and his pulse increased. He regretted opening his mouth.

"I agree," Captain Jana said. She stood straight, her frame lean and strong. "So here it is: we have always known Owen's mother was once an Adept."

"But his parents were part of the rebellion!" Mathis yelled. The moment the words left his mouth, a possibility startled him in its obviousness. "Wait—was his mother someone like Nyona?" She'd always seemed more worldly and educated than the other women in their village. And if Nyona could have a child outside the Conclave, others probably could, too.

"No," said Kelda, shattering his newly found rationale. "The people you considered to be his parents were actually his foster parents. The Conclave always fosters out their male children. They certainly can't stay in Corval!" She tittered before growing serious. "Nonetheless, they had to have trained him to communicate with Adepts when he was young. Otherwise, according to this passage, he would have lost the capacity to do so completely."

"Is it possible they were not truly part of our cause?" Captain Jana asked, tapping her fingers against her upper arm. "They never once mentioned any sort of special training."

"They likely didn't realize what the training was for. I can't imagine the Conclave would divulge such a secret to mere fosters when not even all Masters know of it," Kelda said.

"Perhaps. Still, I would have thought it would have come up at some point if this training is as ubiquitous as you say. Mathis's foster parents also said nothing of it, despite telling us plenty else about the Conclave's intentions for these boys."

Nyona gaped at Mathis. A sensation of dread crept up from his stomach toward his throat. "My—what?" he asked, his voice sounding strangely high-pitched to his own ears.

The room quieted once more as a flush bloomed in Captain Jana's cheeks. "I did not mean to—well." Her shoulders slumped.

Captain Levina smiled, her teeth bright against her tanned skin.

"Like I said, it's about damned time, and I wasn't just talking about Owen." She sat down in a wooden chair, propped her feet up on the table, and crossed her ankles. Pieces of dirt flaked off the bottom of her boots, and the stack of books leaned dangerously to one side. "You're not stupid, Mathis. We don't need to spell it out for you—do we?"

Mathis's mind raced around thought after swirling thought. His parents had loved him as only true parents could, and he'd never, ever, *ever* heard them say anything about the Conclave that wasn't laced with contempt.

I can't be a child of an Adept. I just can't.

✿

Chapter 22

Alia

A LONE PINE tree's elongated, curved boughs quivered in the wind. Beyond the tree, minerals embedded in the ancient, gray stone of the wall that surrounded the outpost sparkled in the moonlight. When she'd first awakened from unconsciousness a week ago, Alia had found the view haunting yet beautiful. Now, it bored her. She wanted to get out of bed, out of this room, and out of this house altogether—but they wouldn't let her. Hasso had argued she needed complete rest to recover from her injuries, and the Captains had acquiesced to his demands. She took a deep breath, intending to sigh away her frustration, but stopped short at a sharp jolt of pain.

Reflexively, she reached for the bandage wrapped around her chest. Its scratchy weave and tight compression irritated the tender skin under her armpits. Hasso claimed it was all he could do for her fractured rib, and that time would take care of the rest. She endured the discomfort the best she could, but at times, she wished she were a child allowed to scream in displeasure. For the most part, she remembered to keep her breathing even and shallow, and when she forgot, her body quickly called attention to her error.

As much as she hated the bandage, she didn't dare unwrap it because it also held in place a bulky pad that covered the jagged knife wound two inches to the right of her spine. The pain of that injury was a constant, dull throb, yet it only really bothered her when she lay flat on her back. Once a day, Hasso cleaned the wound and replaced the pad with a fresh dressing. So far, there'd been no sign of infection, though he reported the skin around his stitching was puckering as it healed.

She didn't care about that. Scars mattered little compared to being alive. She remembered how it had felt when Owen plunged his knife into her back, and how she'd thought she was dying when the world grew black around her.

The rebels claimed that Owen had acted at the Conclave's behest, though no one had explained how that could be when she'd asked. Even Nyona refused to provide an answer, citing the Captains' orders. She did assure Alia that Owen was alone in his plot, but Alia didn't see how they could be so certain. As far as she could tell, Owen had shown no signs in advance of his murderous ways. Maybe his fellow conspirators also hid in plain sight.

It was only a matter of time before someone else succeeded where Owen had failed. Were the Masters truly that afraid of what she might be? What if they were wrong and she was not Sempiternal after all? What if everything that had happened over the last seven months had been based on a false premise?

Alia chewed on self-pity as she lay in bed in the shadows, propped up on a mound of pillows. Outside, the pine tree shuddered as one small, dark bird, then two, then three, four, five, and then too many more to count burst into the air from where they'd hidden within the tree's limbs.

Watching the flock coordinate their flight, Alia became aware of her selfishness. The danger she feared was not hers alone. Poor Tovi had also been a target of Owen's perfidy, and others in the rebellion —and other, truly innocent citizens, as well—had been brutally attacked countless times by the Conclave's Guard.

Besides, once she left the island, she'd have no time for self-pity. Sonya and Captain Jana had departed five days ago with nearly two-thirds of the outpost's contingent. The rest would follow soon, and it would take all of Alia's attention to manage the anticipated quick pace. Even at this late hour, the murmured voices of those preparing to leave carried into her room from the Captains' study.

She didn't know where they were headed, though she cared little. Anywhere on the mainland was closer to Corval—and to Sarabie— than where they were now. The Captains hadn't agreed to Alia's plan to rescue Sarabie, but Alia refused to concede. Once they were underway, she'd try again to convince them that helping Sarabie would help the rebellion. *There must be a way.*

Someone tapped at her door. Alia touched the lamp at her bed- side, illuminating the room—originally Captain Jana's—in a soft, yellow glow. She pulled up the blankets to cover the bodice of her nightshift. "Yes?"

The door opened partway, and Kelda poked her head around its edge. Shadows played under her eyes, and her gray hair, normally pulled back neatly in a bun, was loose and disheveled. "I hope we didn't wake you. Might we come in?"

"Of course. I wasn't asleep."

Kelda pushed the door open the rest of the way, revealing that Hasso accompanied her. He carried across his torso the black satchel that contained his medical supplies. "Why is he here?" Alia asked. "I feel fine, truly."

"I doubt that's *quite* the case, but Hasso has reported you've made fine progress. In fact, he's cleared you for travel, so long as we keep an eye on you." Kelda grinned, yet Hasso remained silent and brooding.

"Okay," Alia said slowly, puzzled by his presence. *He obviously doesn't want to be here.* "Then why does he have his kit?"

Kelda's face lit up in a broad smile, erasing all signs of weariness in that instant. "Assuming all goes well, he's here to remove your implant."

Alia stopped breathing for a moment before elation welled within her. *I will be whole!* Yet with that thought, anxiety surged, displacing her excitement. It had been a long time since she had even tried to reach for her Ability; she'd found the frustration of failure too much to bear. What if Ciara was wrong, and her Ability had already left her for good?

"Why now?" Alia asked, hoping her face did not reveal her warring emotions.

"It took a bit of doing, but Levina has finally agreed we can no longer afford to continue wasting your talents. As someone who has used Ability for a long time, there are things you should be able to do that Tovi cannot. Things that will prove most helpful—dare I say critical—in the future. So. We are going to remove your implant tonight, before we leave the island on the morrow."

"Let's not get ahead of ourselves, Kelda," Hasso said without humor. Something in his eyes suggested he was not agreeable to this plan. Although he'd treated Alia's injuries with competence and diligence, it was plain he still distrusted her. And as much as Alia wanted her implant removed, she did not want him operating on her if he disagreed with Captain Levina's order. She imagined it would be easy to make murder look like an honest surgical mistake. Alia pulled the blanket tighter around her at the thought.

Kelda shot Hasso a disapproving look. "I'm not. I'm certain there will be no problem."

"Let's see what the girl says first."

"What do you want me to talk about?" Alia asked. She'd say whatever they wanted her to say if doing so meant Hasso would finally feel comfortable enough to remove that...*thing* he'd put in her neck.

"He's talking about me, not you, silly," piped a child's voice. At the door, Tovi stood in front of Nyona, making the resemblance between mother and daughter quite striking. More than just their brown, curly hair and identical noses, the two shared something that defied physical description.

Kelda greeted the newcomers before turning back to Alia. "There is one little thing we need to do before we can remove your implant. On Levina's orders, Tovi will perform a truth assessment on you. I don't think it's necessary, of course, but *some* people have insisted on it." Her side-eye toward Hasso left no doubt as to whom she referenced.

Apprehension fluttered in Alia's belly. "So she changed her mind about allowing Tovi to do that, too?" She'd been eternally grateful that, up to this point, they'd refused to allow Tovi to try truth assessments. If they'd allowed her to do one on Alia when they'd first met, they'd not be having a discussion now about removing her implant. *I'd be long dead, and not by Owen's hand.*

"Tovi will still mask her use of Ability, of course—no reason to send out a shining beacon that we're still on the island! And actually, she's had quite a bit of practice of late. There should be no leakage at all."

"Is this a problem?" Hasso asked, his pale blue eyes warning of what would come if she refused.

"No—no. Not at all," Alia lied. "I'm just surprised, that's all. I guess I've been surprised by a lot of things lately." She forced a smile. "Let's do it, then, shall we?"

Her mind raced as her guests repositioned themselves to allow Tovi to reach her bedside. It was true that no Master had asked her to spy for the Conclave, but she'd intended to do so all the same after her abduction. And while she had changed her mind soon after coming to Vose, it was only after she'd learned about how badly the Masters had used her—and of her probable fate if she were to return to them—that she'd decided to remain with the rebels.

Tovi's truth assessment would reveal all of that, exposing Alia for the liar she was. But she couldn't change her memories; she could only hope that Tovi would explain to the others how she'd had a change of heart. *I have no other choice if I want to be made whole.*

She reached for Tovi's small hands to ease the child's efforts and reduce the amount of Ability she'd need to expend. Tovi closed her eyes and breathed deeply, settling into the trance. Alia did the same, blocking out the others' intrusive stares.

She felt a nudge at the edge of her consciousness. Instinctively, she started to defend against what her mind perceived as an attack before forcing herself to relax. As she did so, an impression of Tovi slid between her emotions and waded through her consciousness. Alia idly wondered if Tovi would understand even half of what she saw stored within Alia's mind. The things one learned from a lifetime in the Conclave would be foreign to most adults, let alone a six-year-old child.

The pretense from her mind lifted, and she opened her eyes. Seconds later, Tovi did the same with a small gasp. The girl breathed in and out slowly several times, never taking her eyes from Alia's. Her trepidation blossomed anew. *Did she see? What will she say?*

"When you're ready, love, tell us what you learned," Nyona said, edging closer to the bed. "Is Alia true to our cause?"

Hasso hovered over them. Waiting. Watching.

Tovi glanced at Alia, then smiled, exposing the gap between her two front baby teeth. "She is. She will not betray us."

She knows, Alia thought, *but she will keep my secret safe.* She grasped Tovi's hand again and squeezed it quickly in gratitude.

Kelda whooped with joy. "See, I *told* you, Hasso. A hundred times."

The medic seemed unimpressed. "What else did you learn?" he demanded.

"It's the only thing I learned that matters," Tovi quipped.

"Tovi!" Nyona said, seemingly scandalized by her daughter's attitude. "Apologize!"

"Oh, come now," Kelda said, laughing. "The child has the right of it. That *is* all that matters. It's time."

Hasso flipped his braid out of the way and lifted his satchel over his shoulder and head. "All right," he said in monotone, his expression unreadable. "Let's get some more light in here."

Kelda move around the room, activating additional lamps. "There's already some water for you in the basin over here," she said. "Alia, are you ready to proceed? I dare say, your lack of hair will make this easier for us. It won't take long at all."

With Kelda's presence, Alia's misgivings about having Hasso perform the operation flew out the window. "I am," she replied, hoping she truly was. She'd been unconscious when they'd implanted the device and didn't know what would be involved to take it out.

Hasso rooted around in his satchel. "Here." He deposited a brownish-green disc into her hand. "Place this under your tongue and let it dissolve completely."

"What is it?"

"Something to sedate you," he said, turning back to his satchel. "I can't give you maypop because we're leaving in less than twelve hours. This will start to work quickly, but its pain-eliminating effects won't last very long."

Alia popped the disc under her tongue, and it softened with her saliva. Flavors of valerian, feverfew, and something earthy and bitter she could not identify flooded her mouth.

Hasso unrolled a bundle of fabric onto the table next to the bed. Metal implements, held in place with a leather band, glinted in the lamplight. An assortment of small glass bottles and a stack of white cloths followed. Some of the bottles contained liquid and one contained what looked like thick sewing thread, but others were empty.

"Time to go, love." Nyona placed her hands on Tovi's shoulders, steering her toward the door. "We'll come visit Alia later."

"I'll talk to you soon," Tovi promised with a little wave.

Alia lifted her hand limply in farewell. She already felt rather woozy.

Hasso walked over to the basin and washed his hands. "Kelda—are you ready?"

"I am. Alia?"

Alia turned her head toward Kelda's voice. "Hmm?"

"Did that hurt?"

Alia blinked. "What?"

"She's ready, too," Kelda said, wiping away a small dot of red from Alia's arm with one of the white cloths before placing a pointy metal tool back on the table. "Let's get you on your side." Alia allowed Kelda to roll her toward the wall. For once, her rib didn't protest against the movement.

Glass clinked, and a hand pressed against the side of her head, holding it to the pillow. "You're going to feel some pressure, but no pain," said the medic.

Alia closed her eyes. At first, it didn't seem like Hasso was doing anything at all, and she wondered if he'd changed his mind. Then, as she seemed to float in her own bed, there was an odd tugging sensation at her neck, as if someone were trying to gently pry away one of the bones in her spine. Sucking sounds came from behind her, and the tugging sensation ceased.

Slowly, Alia realized that someone else had connected to her mind without her being aware of it. The presence was familiar, but it took her a few long moments to understand the import of it. She reached for her Ability, and tears of relief and ecstasy welled in her eyes as she found and embraced it.

Can you hear me? Tovi asked.

Yes. Yes, I can!

Chapter 23

Sarabie

Sarabie lifted her eyes from her book as the bars of the door rattled. The locking mechanism, once silent, had grown noisier over the months with repeated use. Calio thanked the unseen Guardsman posted just outside and then entered their suite, a covered wooden tray in his hands. The door closed, and the bars of her prison scraped and thudded back into position.

As Calio moved toward where Sarabie lounged, the polished silver clasps on his black uniform reflected light from the overhead lamps. It pleased her to see him in the proper garb of a Conclave servant once again. He seemed to stand taller, and the bright accents helped to counter the starkness of the fabric's color against his pale skin and hair. At first, they'd denied him the same freedom as they did her, so he'd dressed simply, wearing black leggings and an unadorned black housecoat that belted across his waist like a robe. These days, however, Calio wore his uniform more often than not.

"I've brought a treat for you," he announced with a grin before using his tattooed hand to pull the cover off the tray with a flourish. Clumps of green and purple grapes, huge and dotted with moisture, filled a bowl.

Sarabie clapped her hands in delight. She scooted awkwardly toward the edge of the chaise and reached over her abdomen, now well swollen after nearly six months of pregnancy, to pluck away several purple fruits. "Grapes? However did you find these?" She bit down on one and nearly swooned in pleasure at its sweet juice.

"A friend of mine came across them in the market yesterday. He bought extra, thinking I might like them."

"Oh, I'm so glad he thought of you! I wish you could thank him for me. Try them, they are simply wonderful!"

He folded into a cross-legged position on the floor and took a small bunch of green grapes from the bowl. After one bite, his light-blond eyebrows shot up his forehead. "It's tart!" he exclaimed past his mouthful of food.

"The purple ones are sweet. Try those next."

"These are very good, actually. I just didn't expect it."

They continued to sample the fruit until Sarabie's patience waned. "Aren't you going to tell me if you heard anything good today? You can't distract me forever with treats," she said.

After four months of captivity, Sarabie craved news from the outside more than anything. For the first three months, they'd lived in near-isolation. The tutors who came every third day refused to discuss anything other than the subjects they taught, and the servants who brought them food and supplies wouldn't talk at all.

Yet a month ago, the Masters began allowing Calio to leave their suite at least once a day. She suspected they simply no longer wanted to waste the efforts of a second servant on tasks Calio could do himself. He couldn't leave the servants' areas of the Seclusion wing, and he was not to speak of whom he served. Nonetheless, it was better than nothing, and his freedom had brought color back into her life.

"I did overhear something unusual," Calio said, tossing three grapes into his mouth at once. His cheek bulged as he chewed slowly.

"Stop it, Calio. You know I can't stand the suspense," she pleaded, pleased by the anticipation that welled up inside of her despite her admonition to the contrary.

He swallowed and wiped at the corner of his mouth with his index finger. "I know, dear Sarabie. And as you have been ever so patient, I shall tell you." He settled his hands on his thighs. "It would seem that not everyone has accepted the story of you being dismissed because you refused to repeat Generation."

"Truly? Who?"

"I can't say for certain. Two servants were discussing some sort of meeting where a few of the younger Masters questioned Master Gersemi about you and your friend, Alia. Specifically, they pressed her for more details concerning both of your dismissals. It sounded to me like they're seeking to disprove that you were dismissed for cause and that Alia left on her own."

"My goodness. Someone challenged the Headmaster—out loud?" Sarabie couldn't even imagine who would dare do such a thing. "I suppose some people might have been surprised to hear about me, but I'd always assumed most people accepted what they'd heard about Alia. She was a known miscreant and she constantly tested the Masters, ever since we were young. She got in trouble a lot." A smile came to her face as she thought back on her friend's wayward antics. "A *lot*."

"I see. Because of how she'd behaved in the past, others might find it easy to accept she'd abandoned the Conclave?"

"Yes. But if they now are questioning even that, then something must have changed. I can't think of what, though."

Calio cupped his knees with his hands. The red tattoo that marked him as a servant of the Conclave crawled down his right hand from his wrist to the knuckles of each finger. "They were definitely newer Masters. If so, they'd know you and that you would not refuse to do as you were told without good reason. That could lead them to question the truth of what they've been told about her, as well."

Sarabie nodded. "Perhaps. The Masters do lie an awful lot for no apparent reason. Like with you—why would they tell us that young men fought for the honor to become our servants if it weren't true? Until you told me, I had no idea that none of you had chosen to be here." She stared at her hands, still ashamed at her prior ignorance.

"It served the purpose of the Conclave for you to believe as you did. Would you have rather known we were all conscripted as boys and cut young? Would you have treated us any differently?"

Sarabie's cheeks flushed. "No." She met his blue eyes. "I apologize for that. None of you deserved what they did to you."

He looked away and shrugged. "No apologies are necessary. My life is what it is."

As is mine, she thought. There was nothing she could do to change her fate, though that acceptance had come slowly. Back when she was first imprisoned, she'd thought of nothing but escape —to the point where she'd even imagined an Adept had promised to rescue her! Weeks passed before she'd finally admitted to herself that the one-time "contact" had been nothing more than a dream brought on by the stress of her unexpected circumstances.

No longer interested in the fruit, Sarabie leaned back against the cushions of the chaise and rested her hands on the swell of her belly. In the last few weeks, her abdomen had become rigid as the child within her grew. Her new robes accommodated her expanding waistline, but remained the same ugly brown color. Unfortunately, Calio's newfound freedom did not extend to fashion.

"Wait a minute," she said, pulling her thoughts away from yet another descent into self-pity. "Those younger Masters who questioned Master Gersemi? Did you hear any names?"

"They said something about Marta, but I don't know if she was one of those asking questions."

That surprised her, though it shouldn't have. Her friend had been the first of their Initiate to head to Generation, and she'd been pregnant with twin Adepts the last time Sarabie saw her. She quickly ran the numbers through her head. Marta would have certainly birthed her children by now and moved into the role of Master. And the last time they'd spoken, Marta was already questioning the Masters' motives—at least when it came to Generation.

"I wish I knew who else was involved," Sarabie said, scratching at her nose. "Maybe when you go up later tonight, you could find out?"

"I can try, but please don't get your hopes up. If I am too inquisitive, the Masters might revoke my privileges, and then you'll get no news at all. Or fruit," he finished with a small smile. He collected the tray from the end of the chaise and carried it to a table near the entrance.

"True." She pulled away the leather band holding her long, black hair in a tail, allowing the tresses to fall freely. "I am glad *some* people are questioning what happened to us, though it won't make a difference. Nothing will change unless everyone pushes back, and that's not going to happen."

"Can you blame them? To reject the lies would be to reject their lives. You Adepts are kept in the dark about so much, for if you were not, the Masters wouldn't be able to retain their control over your Ability. So, yes, once a new Master is made, it is in her best interest to continue propagating those lies. The only other choice is to leave the Conclave in disgrace."

His astute observation proved how well he understood the reality of life in the Conclave. "You're right," she admitted, rubbing her abdomen. "That is the only other choice. And it is the choice I made."

"Why?"

His simple question caught her off-guard. "Why?" she repeated.

"Yes, why did you choose to leave? In all this time, you've never spoken of your decision. You said yourself that you always followed the rules. So why did you choose to break them now, when it meant you'd be forced to leave your entire life behind?"

She pursed her lips together, suddenly nervous. Calio was a friend now. Over the months, she'd considered telling him about what had happened to her, but she'd never had the strength to do it. With his direct inquiry, now was the time. He deserved to know why he, too, was a prisoner.

"When they told me I was carrying a male child, they said I needed to end this pregnancy and repeat Generation," she began. "If I didn't agree, then I would be banished from the Conclave. In the end, the decision was easy to make, as the first option was untenable to me."

"I see. You wanted to continue this pregnancy, then?"

"No, it wasn't that. I'd known from a young age that after my Ability faded, my duty was to bear a future Adept. We call it our 'gift' to the Conclave, and every Adept looks forward to it. Well, almost every Adept—Alia never had much enthusiasm for the idea. Anyway, I would have done whatever was necessary to provide my gift, and happily, if only—" she hesitated. She trusted him, but he still was a creature of the Conclave, and male besides. He wouldn't believe her. "It's hard to explain. You wouldn't understand."

He cocked his head to one side. "I would not understand that you'd been abused during your Generation, and you didn't want to repeat that experience?"

"How did you…?" Her mind raced. "Were you there?"

"No, no. I was not party to your ceremony. But I know how they work, and I know that not all of the men involved are gentle." He sighed. "And remember, I was assigned to serve you immediately after, when the bruises around your neck were fresh. You did not hide them as well as you thought."

Tears spilled from her eyes. She had been so excited for Generation and to finally meet the partner the Masters had selected especially for her. Her anticipation for that day, and for giving birth to an Adept and becoming a Master, had helped ease the loss she'd felt when her Ability had faded.

The day before Sarabie advanced to Generation, Marta had warned her that she would have more than one partner, but Sarabie had dismissed the warning out of hand because it went against everything she knew to be true. *I was such a fool.*

She'd never know for certain exactly how many men had visited her during her ceremony, but she remembered at least five. And her memories of the last man would forever haunt her dreams. He'd choked and hit her while he—did what he did—and she'd been unable to resist him. It horrified her to think that the child she carried might very well be his. A sob escaped from her lips.

Calio rushed to her side and pulled her into a comforting embrace. "I'm so sorry. I should not have made you think of such things right now."

Sarabie cried into his chest. Her tears were of loss and of sorrow, but also of relief. When she'd told the Masters what had happened, they'd claimed she was delusional. A small part of her wondered if it had truly been as bad as she remembered, despite her bruises, and if her decision based on those memories had been sound. Calio's immediate belief validated her choice.

After she settled and pulled away from him, he handed her a handkerchief. "You do not need to talk of it now, nor ever," he said.

"Thank you." Sarabie used the soft cloth to blot her eyes and cheeks. "So that's why I refused to do as the Masters wanted."

"I understand."

"And I accept my decision, and what's to come. I do. I just—" She raised her hands helplessly. "I wish more of the Masters would question what happened to me. If they did, maybe they could advocate for some other alternative. Something other than birthing this child and being cast out, my memories erased, and my entire life as an Adept forgotten."

"What if there is?"

His tone pricked goosebumps all along her arms. "Whatever do you mean?" she asked carefully.

"What if there is another option for you? Would you consider it?"

Her heart skipped a beat. "There were only two options present- ed to me, and I chose disgrace," she whispered, glancing around the room, worried that someone might be listening.

"We can speak freely here, Sarabie. The Guardsman outside is a friend, and the Masters long stopped having Adepts spy on us. Why should they waste the effort when, as you say, you've accepted your decision?"

"What do you mean, then, that there's another option?" His words were mad, but the hope they brought was too tantalizing to dismiss.

"Do you remember the message you received from an Adept when we first arrived in these rooms?"

She gaped at him for a moment, then managed to collect her wits. "How could you possibly know about that?" she said in a voice pitched far higher than usual. He couldn't have heard anything that day. *It was only a dream.*

"Because I received the same message not long ago. Alia is coming for you, just as she promised."

CHAPTER 24

NYONA

THROUGH THE SUN'S haze, the snow-capped peaks far to the south seemed almost blue. Nyona squinted, shading her eyes with one hand. Somewhere nestled within those mountains were the ruins of Brome—*and most likely Guards who are looking for us as well,* she thought. It defied common sense to think the rebels would return to the place where the Conclave had destroyed them once before, but common sense had never stopped the Masters.

She grimaced as a rock jabbed between her toes, reminding her to pay attention to the ground before her. After a little more than three months of travel, mostly on foot, Nyona had gone through two pairs of boots already. When they reached their next rendezvous point near Eads, she'd look for someone with an extra pair in her size.

"Mama, do you want to ride?"

Nyona looked up at Tovi, who sat astride the packhorse Nyona led by the reins. "No, love. We'll probably be stopping soon."

Tovi nodded and returned to surveying the hills that surrounded their group. Even though Tovi no longer used her Ability much—Alia had taken over that responsibility—she remained attuned to the general mood of the thirty or so rebels around her. Her perception of her mother seemed the most acute, but her awareness of Mathis and Alia was nearly as keen.

Mathis walked off to the side a few feet behind them, avoiding the dust the packhorse's hooves kicked up. The corners of his mouth curled up ever so slightly when he noticed her watching him. His smile warmed her. Since their escape from Vose, his dedication toward keeping Tovi safe had been steady and constant. It was a far cry from his distant behavior at the time around Owen's attack.

Sometimes, Nyona even thought she might be falling in love with Mathis, though she still hadn't sorted out whether she cared for him more as a brother than as a potential partner. What she felt for him was deeper and different than anything she'd ever felt for Brien, but the label she chose for her feelings was of no consequence. All that mattered was that she could depend on him as she could on no one else.

And as much as she hated to admit it—even to herself—she needed someone like that right now.

Time had helped ease the constant anxiety she'd felt since Owen tried to kill Tovi, but it hadn't eradicated her fears altogether. While they'd escaped from Vose before the Conclave's Guard arrived to render the island uninhabitable, and had suffered no attacks since then, that didn't mean their luck would hold forever. Other rebel groups had not been as fortunate.

It does no good to think of such things. Captain Jana and Captain Levina were smart and would not invite trouble with a careless decision. She had to trust them to get her and Tovi safely to their new home—wherever that might be.

"Nyona!" Sonya yelled from the front of the group. "The Captains need you."

"I'll be right there," Nyona called back. She motioned for Mathis to come closer, then handed him the horse's reins.

"Hopping to her commands now, are we?" Mathis asked with a smirk.

She ignored his remark. The passage of time had *not* diminished Mathis's disdain for the woman he'd once thought of as his sister, and Nyona's patience was wearing thin at his intransigence. If *she* had finally forgiven Sonya for killing Brien a year ago, then Mathis should be able to forgive Sonya for a decision she'd made well over a decade ago. Instead, he held tight to the sense of betrayal he'd nursed since he and Sonya were teenagers.

Two weeks after they'd left Vose, Nyona had finally gotten the story out of him.

It had been late, when most everyone else, including Tovi, was asleep. The fire had nearly died out, and in the blue-black sky, stars scattered in familiar patterns. As Nyona and Mathis chatted quietly, she'd made an innocent comment about how it seemed Sonya had matured since the events on the island.

"Think what you want," Mathis said, his voice tight. "Sonya's still got her own agenda, and it may not be the same as ours. I'm sure we'll find out the hard way, as usual."

"Mathis, please. You really need to get over this hostility you have toward her. It makes no sense. I had good reason to despise Sonya for her actions, yet I've been able to forgive her. But for you…it's been nearly twenty years since your parents died, and what, fifteen since she took up with Hasso?"

"Thirteen."

"Fine; thirteen. She was still young and didn't know anything more about the situation than you did. Why do you continue to waste so much energy being mad at her? They were her true parents, after all, and she obviously wasn't bothered by whatever it is you think Hasso did concerning their deaths."

That had been the wrong thing to say, and she regretted it almost immediately.

"Are you suggesting I should feel differently because they weren't *my* true parents?" Mathis hissed through clenched teeth. "They were the only parents I knew. They were true to me. And they died because of Hasso, and Sonya *knew* that, but chose to train with him anyway when he showed up. Then she ignored me, the only family she had left, so she could make friends with the powers that be. She didn't want to be associated with her lowly older brother. So don't take her behavior now as anything more than a plan to worm her way up even higher in the ranks."

She raised her eyebrows at his vehement cascade of words, skeptical of his claims. "Please. We're in a fight for our lives, and you think she's manipulating the system for a stupid rank? You're out of your mind."

"You don't understand," he huffed.

"Then help me understand. Tell me how Sonya could have possibly known that Hasso was somehow responsible for your parents' deaths back when she was a teenager."

"He told us."

This admission shocked Nyona. "He did?" Hasso never struck her as someone willing to volunteer much of anything, let alone details of his exploits as a creature of the Conclave.

"He came to us, right after he joined, and apologized for it. He confessed that our parents died because he told the Conclave where to find them."

"How'd he know that? Was he in a Guard unit near your home?" Wherever that had been; Mathis spoke little of his life before the rebellion.

"No. He was an Extir." Venom laced his words.

Nyona gasped, then remembered to keep her voice down lest she wake someone. "How? That order was dissolved before I was born."

"I don't know. Maybe they don't make any new ones—or maybe the Conclave lied to you about it, like they lied to you about most everything else. In any case, he was *definitely* an Extir."

"But your parents were executed, not assassinated. Why would an Extir be involved at all?"

"They'd sent him to investigate an accusation that my parents had become involved with the rebellion. After spying on them for months, he turned over what he learned to the Masters. He was directly responsible for their deaths."

She resisted pointing out that unless Hasso actually performed their executions, he was not *directly* responsible. Her snark would not help Mathis see past his uncompromising position, however. "But now you know the Conclave's interest in your parents wasn't random because the Masters gave you into their keeping," she said. "So at some point, they would have figured out that your parents had switched sides—if not from Hasso, then from someone else."

"Doesn't matter; it wasn't someone else. And Sonya didn't know then about—what they say I am." He still refused to acknowledge the truth that he was a child of an Adept, despite the Captains telling him they'd known it all along.

A glaring inconsistency jumped out at her, and she seized it. "What about Ciara?" she asked. "You said she was somehow involved in your parents' execution, too, but you don't have a problem working with her now."

"That's different."

"*Fires*, Mathis," Nyona said, exasperated. "Stop being so stubborn. If she was involved, it's not different at all."

"Yes, it is. Hasso would have seen Sonya and me dead along with our parents. Ciara let us live."

"Is that what she told you?" Other than oblique references, Mathis had not spoken of the conversation he'd had with Ciara the day she'd arrived on Vose. "Tell me what she said. All of it. Maybe then I will understand."

At first, he didn't respond to her quiet request. Dying embers snapped, drawing their attention to the remnants of the fire. Waiting for him to say something tested her patience, but she knew he'd talk when he was ready—or else he'd divert the conversation to a topic far less personal, as he often did.

That night, he chose to speak. "Ciara was a Master newly made, and Hasso's liaison with the Conclave. She passed on the information he gave her about my parents to the other Masters. They then sent her out to oversee the execution of all four of us." He half-heartedly tossed a pebble toward the fire's remaining embers. "As Ciara tells it, when she saw me, she couldn't give the final order. I guess she had some crisis of conscience. She let us go and ordered Hasso not to go after us."

Nyona lifted one eyebrow. "I'm surprised they didn't find themselves on the execution list for that."

"Well, when she got back to Corval, she claimed we'd run away before she arrived and that Hasso had been unable to locate us. The Masters believed her, so their punishment was the isolated post in Aldham instead of death. In the end, she was the one with courage, while he only did as she asked. And that's why Ciara's situation is different." He leaned back against his knapsack and crossed his arms behind his head.

She chewed on her lip, thinking. Something didn't sit quite right with Ciara's story, but Nyona didn't want to distract Mathis from his own tale by chasing a thread she wasn't even sure led anywhere. "Maybe the execution of your entire family was meant to be an example of what happens to people who fail to live up to their contracts with the Conclave," she said instead.

"Maybe." His tone indicated that his willingness to discuss the matter was coming to an end.

Nyona pulled her feet closer to her bottom and wrapped her arms around her shins to keep her knees close to her chest. "How long after that did it take for Ciara and Hasso to join the rebellion?"

"Five, six years? Ciara claims the situation with my parents left her disturbed, and that while she lived in Aldham, she saw how the rebels did more for the citizens than the Conclave ever had. Then, a few years into their post, Hasso came back from some assignment with Captain Levina in tow—this was before she was a Captain, of course. She and Ciara became close, and the rest is history."

Nyona mulled over all he'd said. "So Ciara and Hasso ultimately turned away from the lives they knew. Why is Hasso's conversion unacceptable to you, while Ciara's—and mine, for that matter—aren't?"

"Some things are unforgivable. I can't explain it any better than that."

With that, he'd crossed his arms on his chest and closed his eyes, signaling that the conversation was over.

Nyona brought her thoughts back to the present as she neared the front of the line of horses. What Mathis had said that night months ago was true—some things *were* unforgivable, such as Owen's attempt on Tovi's life. Sonya's decision as a teenager to train with Hasso was not. Mathis needed to let go of his grudge—as Nyona had let go of hers.

Sonya still annoyed Nyona more often than not, but she no longer blamed Sonya for what had happened back at the farmhouse. It had taken an entire year—and, truth be told, Sonya's quick actions that had saved Tovi's life—but Nyona had come to accept that Brien's death was the result of many misunderstandings, including the rebels' understandable belief that she and Tovi were of the Conclave. And the hard truth was that if Brien had not charged wildly toward Sonya with his sword, she wouldn't have thrown her knives at him in self-defense.

Captain Levina spotted her. "Here she is." Gray and blonde hairs stuck to her forehead, and dust had mixed with the perspiration on her neck. It was just as well they'd abandoned the trappings of a Guard unit when they'd escaped from Vose. Their simple outfits in shades of light brown, common amongst itinerant communities, didn't show as much dirt.

Sonya and Captain Jana parted so Nyona could pass between them. She stepped over a small mound of stubby, yellowed grass. "You needed me?"

"Yes," said Captain Levina. "We wanted to get your input on a little something we're putting together."

Delight infused Nyona; it had been some time since they'd asked for her opinion on any matter of strategy. "How can I help?" she asked, acting as if she'd expected this all along.

Captain Levina brushed away the sweat from her forehead with the sleeve of her shirt. "Well, there's been a change of plans. After we meet back up with Hasso at the next rendezvous point, we're not going to head south after all."

"We're not?" Nyona said, surprised. "What about Renai? Is she not returning with him?" Her former roommate had grown increasingly unstable on the road, so Hasso had taken her with him when he'd left them seven weeks ago on some assignment the Captains held close. It had been nice to not have a constant reminder hanging around of a time when Nyona had been so trusting and naive.

"She is, but Captain Keya's agreed to take her on. They're still going south."

"So where are we going, if not south?" It had always been the plan to turn south at Eads, and she'd heard no rumors suggesting that route was no longer safe.

"We're continuing east," said Captain Levina, her eyes twinkling in the sun. "To Quental."

Nyona shook her head once, convinced she'd misheard. "Are you sure you meant Quental? That's right across the strait from Corval—and the Conclave."

Captain Levina's smile displayed a mixture of predation and amusement. "Exactly. That's where you come in."

⚜

CHAPTER 25

MATHIS

TWO MEN AND two women consolidated their gear next to Hasso's tent. On the Captains' order, Sonya had chosen the team from the other groups who'd joined their rendezvous near Eads. It seemed the main criteria for selection was an utter lack of self-preservation. Mathis spit off to the side. With Sonya and Hasso at the helm, he wished them luck in their mad plan. They'd need it.

A flash of white-blonde hair near the Captains' tent caught his eye, despite the deepening shadows of twilight. Alia disappeared inside her tent. While he'd once found the Adept's baldness disturbing, he'd never get used to her new appearance. The fakery of the wig she wore—not to mention her painted-on eyebrows—seemed obvious to him. He didn't see much chance in her disguise holding up if the Conclave found them.

"Are you just gonna stand there all night?" Avrey asked. "We all have things to do, you know."

Mathis glanced over to the flat boulder that served as a makeshift gaming table. The cards were dealt, but neither Avrey nor Tobin had yet made a play. "I'm coming," he said.

"Well, hurry it up," Avrey grumbled, scratching behind his ear. The boy had shorn his hair nearly to his scalp again, as he did at every rendezvous. The uneven, red stubble gave him a worn look that belied his fourteen years. A faded vest, stitched together from miscellaneous scraps of brushed leather, added to the perception that the cook's assistant was down on his luck. "We only have time for one round before Virin yells at me."

"Oh, we have more time than that," said Tobin. "There aren't many people left—what, fifty? It won't take you long to prep the meal." The older Guardsman from Captain Keya's group peered at the cards he held close to his scruffy face. He often refused to wear his glasses, claiming they made his head hurt, but Mathis knew he put them on when he thought no one was looking.

"Doesn't matter how many there are," Avrey grumbled. "I'm sure Virin's got something up his sleeve for this last meal that will be more complicated than it needs to be."

"He hasn't called for you yet, boy, so quit your whining and enjoy the game." Tobin pointed to the stool, then snapped his fingers toward Mathis. "Sit."

Mathis straddled one of the tripod campstools and picked up the last pile of facedown cards. He kept his expression blank as he used his thumb to sort through the abysmal hand Avrey had dealt him. With these cards, his part in the game wouldn't last long. It was just as well; he still had a lot to do before they left in the morning for Quental.

He looked up to see Avrey focused on something behind him. "Do you think they'll make it?" the youth asked in a low voice. "The Captains should have fought to have only ours go. Can we really trust them? No offense, Tobin."

The older man shook his head. "None taken. Some of us *are* untrustworthy. That's why they didn't pick me," he said with a wink to Mathis. "But it's meant to be a group effort. This way, everyone can claim a piece of the success, rather than your Captains keeping all the glory for themselves."

Mathis snickered. "Glory? I think you're confusing this mission with one that isn't completely insane."

"That's what I'm saying!" the boy said earnestly. "You know they're asking for some serious trouble on this one, especially with Alia going, so why invite strangers into the mix?"

Mathis looked up from his cards, dubious. "Alia's going? Where'd you hear that?"

"Hasso was talking to one of the other men last night. Something about needing her for messages."

"You must've heard wrong," said Tobin. He pulled a single card from the ones in his hands and squinted at it. "No way they'd let her go. Maybe they were talking about her sending messages to the team."

"I heard what I heard." Avrey set his jaw in a way that signaled there was no changing his mind. "And that wouldn't make sense, anyway. Who on the team could Alia send messages to? They'd probably need to send them back as well, and Alia and Tovi are the only ones who can do that. And they're not gonna send Tovi."

"Huh. I suppose. Still, color me skeptical. Now come on, play your card. You're the one that's in such a damned hurry."

Mathis pretended to analyze his cards as his mind churned through unanswered questions. Tobin was right. Why would the Captains risk Alia, when an alternative was staring them right in the face?

Not many people knew Mathis was—what he was. The Captains hadn't advertised it, and he'd even denied it at first. How could his mother not be the woman he'd grown up with and loved? The woman whose memory he'd cherished and honored since the day she died? It was a ridiculous notion, no matter what the Captains or Kelda—or Ciara—said. He'd refused to accept that his true mother was one of *them*, and even worse, that she might still be alive somewhere within the Conclave.

But after about a month on the road, a strange, low buzzing sound had begun in his ears. It wasn't constant, so he dismissed it as the onset of a summer cold. Then the buzzing abruptly stopped right as Tovi asked him a question. He turned around, yet the child was nowhere in sight. Alia pounced, gleeful he'd responded to their contrived test to send him a message using their Ability. Only then did he admit he'd heard a voice in his head once before, back in Morell, when a frightened Tovi had spoken of something she'd overheard. At the time, he'd blamed his imagination.

Kelda later concluded his parents must have provided him with the necessary training to communicate with Adepts at some point during his childhood. Because he remembered no such thing, she surmised they had discontinued the training once they'd decided to keep him from the Conclave, never imagining the rebellion would someday have an Adept—or two—of their own. According to her, without at least some guidance as a child, he wouldn't have been able to hear Tovi's mental question as an adult.

Scouring his memories, Mathis now wondered if things he'd thought nothing of as a child had meant something more. Flashes of puzzles and games that he'd assumed were normal childhood trappings now took on a taint of suspicion. In particular, he re-membered games of hide-and-seek where he would sit quietly with his eyes closed, inhaling and exhaling between each silent count, concentrating hard on listening for clues to find his mother. She'd taught him how to harness that focus, and the only times he'd failed were when Sonya, still a toddler and incapable of playing such games, would wander by and disturb him. With a sour twist in his gut, he realized that Owen had been the only other child he knew of to play the game without rushing through the count aloud.

Had his mother truly once intended to turn him over to the Conclave for their use one day? He struggled to reconcile this possibility with all he'd ever known of his parents. Yet the fact remained that he could indeed communicate with Adepts now—so his parents must have had such a plan in mind at some point.

Heaving a sigh, he brought himself back to the game and set down a card. Avrey immediately slapped one down on the boulder next to Mathis's. "Ha! Try to beat that, Tobin."

The grizzled Guardsman scratched at his gray-and-black beard. "You're not as clever as you think, kid." He carefully placed two cards in a straight line above Avrey's, and the boy groaned. "Now it's Mathis's turn to avoid defeat," Tobin said with a self-satisfied grin.

Mathis laid a card on top of one of Tobin's two, keeping him in the game for a little while longer even though his mind remained preoccupied. A few weeks ago, Mathis had finally figured out that if he pictured Alia in his mind and focused hard enough, he could transmit a brief message back to her. He'd assumed she had reported that success to the Captains. Why, then, would the Captains still send Alia to Corval?

The upcoming mission was clearly suicidal, and it involved both Sonya *and* Hasso. Mathis was crazy for even thinking about volunteering for it. Yet it was plainly obvious he should take Alia's place. At the end of the day, he was just a Guardsman, no matter his parentage. The rebellion had plenty of those, and messengers, too. But Alia—she was Sempi…some kind of everlasting Adept with powers he couldn't even comprehend. She was irreplaceable.

"Come on, Mathis," Avrey grouched. "We haven't got all night."

"Sorry," Mathis said. He chose a card at random and set it on the rock.

Tobin threw the rest of his cards down in disgust. "Are you even trying?"

Mathis looked down and snorted. If they'd been betting money, he'd have lost everything for playing a final card so early. "I didn't mean to. My mind was somewhere else."

"Obviously." Tobin gathered the cards into a pile. "Do you want to play another round?"

"No—I need to take care of something. You two carry on if you want. Sorry." He apologized again as he nearly jumped from the stool. With his mind made up, there was no time to waste.

Fewer than twenty steps brought him to the Captains' tent. He scratched at the flap covering the entrance. "It's Mathis."

"Come in."

He pulled the flap aside and ducked under it. The tent was sparsely furnished with two cots, a folding table, and three campstools. Captain Jana and Captain Levina occupied two of them, and a bunch of papers covered the table.

Captain Levina looked up as he entered, then frowned. "Is there a problem?"

"You can't send Alia to Corval," he declared without preamble.

"What are you talking about?"

"Avrey overheard Hasso saying Alia was going to Corval. So she could send messages back and forth."

"That is ridiculous," scoffed Captain Jana. "We are risking enough as it is for her to travel with us to Quental. By rights she should head south with the others. She is certainly not going to Corval."

Mathis felt stupid for listening to Avrey. "So the team is on its own then, once they leave?" *If so, they're doomed for sure.* He was glad he'd not volunteered outright.

The corner of Captain Levina's mouth twitched up, as it often did when she found something amusing. "Oh, they won't be on their own."

"I don't understand. If I'm not going, and Alia's not going..."

Captain Jana's eyes narrowed as she sat up straight. "You do not need to understand our orders, Mathis. Only follow them."

Mathis's cheeks burned from the reprimand. He knew he had no right to demand the details of their plans, but what they said made no sense.

"Oh, come now, Jana," Captain Levina said. "It's not like he's a stranger to all this. Honestly, I'm surprised neither Alia nor Nyona told him about it. I guess keeping secrets is part of an Adept's training." She chuckled at her own joke.

"Fine. You tell him, then," Captain Jana said with a scowl. "You are the one who agreed to it in the first place."

"That I did; that I did. Oh, don't glare so, Jana. All will be well." Captain Levina leaned forward on the table, resting her chin in one hand. "You see, Mathis, we don't need to send someone with the team to transmit messages because once we get to Quental, Alia will make contact with those already in Corval who can."

His continued confusion over the Captains' plan overshadowed his displeasure of learning that Nyona had kept him in the dark. He'd thought they'd grown much closer over the last few months, but he must have guessed wrong. "I still don't get it," he said with some annoyance.

"We have people inside the Conclave."

"How?" he asked, astonished. "Who?"

"Who they are isn't important, and the how, even less so. What matters is that Alia's been in contact with them for the past month to set our plans in motion, so she doesn't need to physically be there for messages to get to the team."

Masters, Mathis decided. Their contacts had to be active Masters who supported the rebellion, like Ciara once had been. "Okay," he said. "So then are these people going to bring Alia's friend—out?"

"That's the plan, basically," said Captain Levina. She shifted back away from the table.

"What if something goes wrong and someone from the team needs to go inside?"

Captain Jana shrugged. "One of the men will dress as a servant."

Mathis's mind raced, but he wasn't certain where it was headed. "Isn't that a little too—easy? He's not going to be able to waltz in and escort the girl out of the Conclave on his own. Things could change at any moment while he's in there, and without a way to communicate with Alia, he'd be completely in the dark. It would be suicidal."

Captain Levina crossed her arms and considered him. "What are you suggesting, Mathis?"

His heart beat rapidly. "Send me."

"Absolutely not," Captain Jana said. The inner corners of her eyebrows dove toward her nose in another scowl, accentuating the scar that crawled up her cheek. "We cannot risk you any more than we can risk Alia."

"It's not a bad idea, though," mused Captain Levina. "Obviously, he has the look, though he's more muscular than any of them would be. Cut his hair and give him a fake tattoo, and I think he'd pass."

"I do not care how much he looks like them. I still do not like it, Levina. We already lost Owen. Are you willing to lose Mathis, too? We have made too many plans for that to happen."

"I know, but it's true he could keep in contact through Alia, and we had considered it once before..."

Mathis stood silent as the Captains argued, almost seeming to forget he was there. As the minutes dragged on, he wished he'd never offered to go to Corval. *What was I thinking?* Yet their debate ended soon after that thought crossed his mind, and Captain Levina's broad grin of victory revealed that it was, in fact, too late to take back his offer.

CHAPTER 26

ALIA

SHARP SCENTS OF brine and kelp wafted by in the near-constant breeze. A path of weathered wooden planks followed the shoreline and clumps of tall sea grass abutted the path on both sides, keeping the threat of encroaching sand at bay. Across the strait, the buildings of Corval glittered with light. And in the middle, taller than anything else, rose the yellow-and-amber stone towers of the Conclave. Beacons lit the topmost layers, making them seem as if they were swathed in permanent sunset.

It was strange to see the city from this perspective. Alia had never spent much time in Quental; the town was merely the place she passed through on her way to assignments elsewhere in Corinas. Since they'd arrived, she'd seen a few young Adepts doing the same. Mathis was worried that someone would notice her, but she'd waved off his concern. No one would expect her to come so close to Corval, and no Adept had bothered to even glance in her direction so far. Why would they? In her merchant's garb, she was far beneath their notice, and even if they did, with her wig and makeup, no one would recognize her as the rogue Adept Alia.

Muffled shouts and signal bells carried across the water from the harbor of Corinas's capital city. On this side of the strait, the docks were silent, the workers having gone home for the night long ago. Quental was a sleepy coastal town that attracted those who wanted to live close to the seat of power but not in it. The population of Corval, on the other hand, was evenly divided between sycophants to the Conclave and people who had no choice but to remain. The latter included those who were too poor to move from their ancestral homes and those who lived within the Conclave itself.

As a young girl, she'd known that the Conclave controlled her future, but unlike her fellow Adepts, she'd chafed at that reality. Her decision to remain with the rebels had been the first decision she'd made about her life that was truly her own, and it had empowered her, despite the danger. Between that and her Ability humming just beneath her consciousness—the Ability she was in no danger of losing—she finally felt in control of her own life.

Kelda and Ciara were convinced now of her Sempiternal status, and Alia believed them. Certainly, she was older than any other Adept in generations, and her power seemed to be getting stronger. Between that and the help from the book the rebels had found, she could manipulate more energy with her Ability than she'd ever thought possible. Sometimes, she felt like she could take over the world—if she wanted to.

No wonder the Conclave fears me so.

Pebbles crunched behind her, and Alia turned her head to find Ciara walking along the path. Ciara pulled her coat closer around her chest as her blonde hair whipped about in the wind. She sat on the bench next to Alia and attempted to corral her hair behind her ears several times before giving up the fight.

"Why are you still out here?" Ciara asked. "The sun set long ago."

Alia gazed back across the water toward Corval. "I like watching the city. It seems so much smaller from here. And look at how the light doesn't illuminate much of the Conclave beyond its towers, even though it's so bright. I wonder why that is. Have you seen anything in the book describing it?"

"No. It probably is described somewhere—the light is clearly infused with Ability—but understanding the mechanics of the Conclave's outdoor lighting system hasn't been the focus of our inquiries," she finished in a bemused tone.

Alia grinned. "Of course not. I was just curious."

Waves lapped against the sandy shoreline, and a lone seagull cried from somewhere over the water. As they sat together in silence, Alia considered whether to ask Ciara a question that had been at the back of her mind for months—ever since she'd learned that the eunuchs who served in the Conclave were also sons of Adepts, like Mathis.

After another moment's pause, she spoke. "Why didn't Mathis become a eunuch? Or Owen, for that matter?"

Ciara looked sideways at Alia. "That's an odd question out of nowhere. Why do you ask?"

"Well, if all sons of Adepts are fostered until they can be useful to the Conclave, why weren't Mathis and Owen returned when they were old enough to be made eunuchs? I figure they had other plans for Owen, and that's why he was spared. But why Mathis? His foster parents didn't turn to the rebellion until it would have been too late for him to become a servant, had that been the plan. Did the Masters intend for him to be a spy, too? Or did his foster parents simply refuse to return him? Is that why they were executed?"

"No. That had nothing to do with it. I also don't think Owen was truly destined to be a spy, either—I think it just ended up that way."

"Then why weren't they returned like Calio and Stefan and all the others? They should have all received the same training by that point to receive messages from Adepts, so they would have all been equally useful."

Ciara leaned against the back of the bench with a pained expression. "Let's just say that not all sons of Adepts are meant to become eunuchs, and leave it at that."

As if Alia would let the subject go after such a response! Ciara clearly wanted to tell Alia what she knew, or else she would have simply denied any knowledge whatsoever about the subject. "What else can they become?" Alia pushed.

A hint of a sigh escaped Ciara's lips. "I will tell you, but you must keep it close. Levina and Jana don't want us to speak of it just yet. It will raise too many questions."

"I will. I promise," Alia said eagerly. For Ciara to cave so quickly, Alia's suspicion must have been correct. The former Master wanted her to know.

Ciara kept her gaze fixed toward Corval. When she spoke again, her voice was barely audible over the sound of the wind. "If they aren't returned to be made into servants of Adepts, they're allowed to grow up to become fathers of Adepts."

For a moment, it was difficult to breathe, and not just because of the residual effects Alia felt from her still-healing broken rib. "Are you saying that my father, and yours, and Nyona's...are all born of Adepts themselves?"

"Yes. You can't make a new Adept from an Adept alone. Her residual Ability must be paired with a small amount of the inaccessible Ability that was passed on to a male child. Only when the two are combined will a new Adept be made."

Alia consciously closed her jaw. If what Ciara said was true, then it made what Sarabie had experienced that much worse. The man who abused her was not some stranger to the Conclave. "Is this something all Masters know?"

"No. I suspect few Masters have the presence of mind to ask, nor would they likely get a truthful answer if they did. Most continue to believe, as we all were taught, that it is impossible for an Adept to produce a male child in the first place. But the reality is that some women are selected in advance to give birth to boys, but when those women become pregnant, they aren't told the truth. In the end, they think they have given birth to an Adept like everyone else."

"But—how can the Conclave possibly control the sex of a child?" Alia asked.

"I'm not sure they can. It's easy enough to make the claim, but much harder to see it through in practice. Look at Sarabie, and look at all the eunuchs in the Conclave. Were they all truly planned? Probably not. Certainly, if we tried to do it ourselves, the results would be left to fate." Ciara stood from the bench. "Shall we go inside? I'm cold, and they should be finished by now. Remember, not a word of this to anyone, especially not to Nyona."

Alia nodded. She certainly wouldn't be the one to tell Nyona that Tovi's father had been more than some random trouper.

They made their way along the pebbled, dimly lit path to the beach house that belonged to a wealthy merchant with familial ties to the rebellion. A mixture of wood and stone, with extra windows on the side facing the water, the home was large yet unassuming. With their host and her household traveling on business, there was more than enough room for Alia's small group. None of the neighbors questioned their presence, either, because the owner frequently rented out her home to other merchants when she was away.

Alia followed Ciara inside the house. In the cozy living room with windows facing the strait, Nyona sat in a plush, overstuffed chair. She read from a thin leather-bound book while Tovi slept nearby on the sofa, curled up on her side. A multicolored quilt covered the child.

Ciara tilted her head to peer down the hall, then moved to look up the stairs. All was quiet. "They're not done yet?" she asked with a hint of annoyance.

"No," Nyona said in a hushed voice, glancing at Tovi. "The Captains are still talking to Mathis, and Sonya and Hasso haven't yet returned from delivering her orders to those at the inn. Kelda's in the kitchen with Avrey. Alia, there's probably some food left over if you want something to eat before it's your turn."

"I'm fine," Alia replied. She didn't want to eat anything while her stomach protested against the anxiety that had built up over the last few hours. Tonight, she would relay the final instructions to their friends in the Conclave. If any of the Masters caught wind of what they planned, it would be over before they started. Alia had to do everything she could to ensure everyone got back from Corval alive.

Levina thumped rapidly down the stairs. "Okay," she said, clapping her hands together. Tovi jerked awake. "Sorry, Tovi. But it's time, anyway."

Nyona set her book down and reached over to smooth Tovi's curly hair away from her forehead. "Are you ready, love?"

Tovi stifled a yawn, then sat up. "Yes, Mama."

"You ready, too?" Levina asked Alia.

Alia forced her anxiety aside. "Yes. Let's do this."

"All right, then. You know what to do. Don't take any unnecessary risks, and don't dawdle. Get in, and get out."

"I will," Alia said, nonplussed at the reminder. As if she would risk their lives by doing something she shouldn't! She understood the responsibility she bore for their safety, and she would not let them down. "Please: everyone be quiet, and it will be done."

Tovi pulled her feet and the blanket closer to one side of the sofa. Alia sat in the now-vacant space and grasped Tovi's hands. She didn't truly need the child's help, but she'd agreed to let Tovi assist her efforts. If necessary, the child would ensure that no hint of Ability leaked through to signal their location—or even worse, the location of those helping them inside the Conclave.

Alia closed her eyes and entered a trance with her first inhalation. Her mind turned to Corval, and then to the Conclave itself. Even at this late hour, a familiar cacophony of Ability bombarded her. She kept a pinpoint focus, and as she dodged this way and that, she concentrated on where she expected Calio to be. Soon, she brushed against his mind, and quickly relayed the Captains' timetable to him. Upon his assent and understanding, she allowed the contact to ebb away so as not to cause an inadvertent surge of Ability.

Her first task complete, Alia directed her attention to the area of the Conclave where the Masters lived. Here, she had to be especially wary. All of the Masters were on high alert, and Master Gersemi even had her own pet Adepts searching for Alia and Tovi.

Fortunately, it didn't take long to find whom she sought. *Can you talk?* she murmured to the consciousness of her old friend.

Yes. I'm alone. An image of Marta's full, blonde curls and serious eyes came into Alia's mind. *Is it nearly time?*

It is, Alia said through the delicate thread of Ability linking her to Marta. *We are in Quental. Sonya and the others will cross over to Corval tomorrow morning. Mathis will deliver a written message to Stefan. It will read: "The fruit will be ready for pickup at three o'clock," or whatever time they ultimately decide. That will tell you when you must be at the door.*

Anticipation emanated from Marta. *I understand. Once he receives the message, Stefan will inform Calio of the time. They've worked out how to get Sarabie out of her rooms, and once she's in the Conclave proper, I will join them. We shouldn't run into anyone, but I must warn you: if we do, I don't see how we'll avoid raising an alarm.*

I will be with you the entire time, monitoring, Alia reassured her. *I also think I've found a way to turn someone aside if they show too much interest.* She didn't mention that the method was untested from afar, nor what would likely happen if the method failed. It was best for Marta to believe Alia and the other rebels had everything under control.

Marta accepted her statement without question. *That is good to know. Who will be meeting us at the door?*

Mathis. He will come bearing fruit. Alia felt a tug at the edge of her consciousness from Tovi, warning her that her allotted time was nearly over. *Marta, I must go. But first—are you sure you're ready for this?*

Yes, Marta responded without hesitation. *I cannot remain here any longer. I am ready to join you all.*

◆━━━━━━━━━❧❧━━━━━━━━━◆

CHAPTER 27

MATHIS

MATHIS TRAILED A few steps behind Sonya, who strode toward the gate with purpose. Her dark green robe swirled around her ankles, exposing her polished black boots. She hadn't tripped once, as he thought she might. As he'd *hoped* she might.

With the amber and yellow stone of the Conclave's towers growing ever closer, he wished that he'd found some way to foreclose Sonya's plan. He'd prepared for his role in this game; she now made up the rules as she went. But as it always was when she was in charge, his opinion meant nothing.

Earlier that day, Mathis had completed the opening salvo of their original plan, and it had gone without a hitch. Dressed in the servant's uniform Kelda had made for him, he'd walked right up to the side gate and casually lifted his right hand to show the dye that mimicked the tattoo all eunuchs bore. A Guardsman at the gate had waved him through without even asking his name. The red-headed eunuch, Stefan, had met him at the servant's entrance, and

Mathis had given him the note indicating the time he'd return. He had an answer ready in case the Guards asked why he was leaving again so soon, but it seemed no one really cared about the comings and goings of the Conclave's servants.

He'd returned to the merchant's city apartment via a circuitous route, though the extra precaution had been unnecessary. No one had followed him. At that point, they were to wait until it was time for the rescue attempt to begin, and then they'd all go to the center of the island. Mathis would pass through the Conclave's walls using a rarely used door, and Sonya and the others would take up positions in nearby streets while Hasso remained at the merchant docks with the boat to ensure a quick getaway.

At least, that is what was *supposed* to have happened.

Shortly before they were to leave for the Conclave, Alia had reached out to him to say the plan had changed. Instead of meeting Alia's friends in the storeroom near the garden, he'd now have to enter through the same gate he'd used that morning and help break Sarabie out of her room in the first place. Even more, Alia wouldn't be able to keep in contact with him as she'd planned. He'd be on his own until he met up with Marta.

"Fires. What happened?" Sonya had asked right after Mathis relayed Alia's message.

"Something about Marta being worried. I didn't ask more; I focused on keeping the new orders straight."

"Well, that's it, then," Sonya said. "The rest of you will take up your positions as planned, but I'm going inside with Mathis."

"You can't," Mathis protested. "I look like them. You don't. Or did you think you could pass for a Master?" he scoffed.

"I'll go as a merchant," she said, opening and rifling through their host's closet. "They meet with people in the Conclave all the time, right? I can pass for one of them." She pulled a dark green robe with a bright blue sash from the wardrobe. "Besides, if something else goes wrong, you'll be glad to have me with you." Mathis had argued with her some more, but in the end, she'd pulled rank, and there was nothing more he could do.

So here they were, an hour later, at the same gate he'd passed through that morning. Two Guards, including the one who'd been there that morning, stepped from their darkened alcoves.

"State your business," said the new one with the air of someone whose job was boring and routine. He held a thin canvas-bound book in his hand.

"I am Merchant Sonya. I have a meeting with Master Gersemi to discuss—well, that is none of your business." Her tone held all of the barely contained impatience one would expect of the merchant class, but Mathis found himself fighting to keep his anger hidden. How stupid was she to use those names? Did she ever *think* before she opened her fool mouth? *This is what happens when she's in charge. Every. Single. Time.*

The Guardsman flipped open his book to a page marked with a ribbon. "I don't see your name on the list."

Sonya shrugged. "I don't know what to tell you. This one came to get me not long ago." She waved dismissively toward Mathis. "If my name's not on the list, the fault is his."

Acting. You're acting, he thought as his fury grew. He bowed his head. "My apologies, Merchant Sonya," he said in a voice pitched much higher than normal. He then addressed the first Guardsman, who'd seen him through that morning. "You. I've been coming and going all day," he fibbed. "I'm sure you know that I'd not bring someone to see the Headmaster if she were not invited."

"He's got the truth of it," the first Guard told the second, nodding.

The second looked up at Mathis's face, then down at his "tattooed" hand. The bluff had worked that morning, perhaps because no one in his right mind would *pretend* to be a eunuch. Fortunately, this time seemed to be no different.

"All right," said the second Guard. "You may proceed, but next time, make sure your guest is on the list!"

As Mathis and Sonya passed through the gate, he almost felt sorry for the two Guards; he had no doubt that once the day was over, they'd no longer be amongst the living.

From the gate, Mathis and Sonya crossed a small courtyard decorated with potted topiaries. When they reached the side entrance of the building itself, he hesitated. This is where he'd met Stefan that morning, but he hadn't gone inside. It was one thing to pass muster with Guardsmen who had never themselves set foot inside the Conclave. Those who lived within were more likely to see through his fraud.

"Go on," Sonya urged in a harsh whisper. "They'll wonder why we're just standing here."

For once, Sonya spoke true. There was no turning back now. He pushed down on the latch and opened the door inward. They entered a large foyer with halls that fanned out in several directions. Servants moved through the room, but none gave them much more than a brief glance. Mathis sighed silently in relief. There must be enough eunuchs in residence that the sight of one not known personally raised no alarm. Sonya's presence seemed to cause no concern, either.

Sonya poked him in the side. "Follow me," he said, for the benefit of anyone who might be listening. "I shall take you to your meeting."

"Proceed," she said. "I haven't got all day."

Mathis clenched his jaw, but followed her order. With Alia's directions firmly in mind, he led Sonya down the third hallway from the left. At the fourth intersection, he turned left without hesitation. *One...two...three...*and another left. As they continued, they passed fewer and fewer servants. *One...two...*This time, he chose the passage to the right. Finally, they were alone.

Halfway down the corridor, Mathis stopped and spun around, towering over Sonya. She backed up a step. "Why did you use your name—and even worse, *her* name?" he hissed, releasing his pent-up anger in a rush.

Sonya raised an eyebrow at his onslaught. "Why? Because they wouldn't dare hold up someone saying they had a meeting with the Headmaster."

"You think it's that simple? That it won't get back to her that a stranger named *Sonya* came to meet her, but never did? You don't think Master Gersemi knows perfectly well who you are and what you look like on account of Owen? *Fires.*" He turned his back to

Sonya, not wanting to hear any excuses, and continued on. After a moment, her boots tapped behind him.

The door Mathis sought was near the end of the hall. He removed a slender tool from his pocket and squatted to pick the lock. It clicked, and when he pulled the door open, he grimaced as the hinges squealed.

Not far beyond the threshold of the door, a staircase led down. They each activated a tiny, cylindrical glow lamp before Sonya shut the door. The light cast by the devices did not carry far, but it was sufficient to get them down the stairs without breaking anything.

At the bottom of the staircase, Sonya spoke. "Look. I had to say something. I doubt those Guards are going to report a thing. Why would they? We're fine. In fact, this place seems to have hardly any security at all. If it's this easy to bypass what they've got, then we should have raided them a long time ago." Her voice contained a mixture of disdain and defensiveness.

It was the closest she'd ever come to an apology. "It's one thing to sneak in a couple of people, and another thing to attack them head on," he said.

"Oh, please. We'd just bring in more people before they knew anything of it. In fact, that's precisely what we should do the next time. Bring more people in, then attack."

"Maybe today was different. Maybe there are usually more people. In any case, we need to finish this mission first before you start dreaming up new ones."

"Fine. Though at this rate, we'll be out of here in no time."

As they walked away from the stairs, puffs of dust rose from the ground, creating a hazy nimbus around Mathis's lamp. The corridor narrowed until there was less than a forearm's length of space between his shoulders and the stone walls on either side of him. As claustrophobia crept up, he increased his pace.

"Wait," Sonya commanded. "Something's not right."

Mathis stopped abruptly. "These are the directions Alia gave me."

"Of course they are. You were right, what you said back there. Today *is* different, but it's because they know we're here." She glared up at him. "I'm a damned fool, and so are you. It shouldn't have been this easy for us to get this far, unless someone tipped them off. Unless *Alia* tipped them off."

"Alia's one of us now. You know that." He'd not been completely convinced of it himself, even after Tovi's truth assessment, until he started working with Alia through her Ability. He'd seen enough of her mind now to know her affiliation was true. "We got in the building because I apparently look like a damned eunuch, thank you very much, and now—we're obviously somewhere no one's been in years."

"*Trapped* somewhere no one's been in years, you mean. There's only one way in and out."

"If Alia's goal was to betray us, she didn't need to change the plan at the last minute. She could have told them what we originally planned," he argued.

Sonya looked behind her, then peered around him into the darkness. "Maybe. But we should prepare for a trap anyway. We'll show them that we aren't to be trivialized." She thrust her glow lamp into his hand and yanked her robe over her head. Underneath, she wore her usual close-fitting black leathers. She shoved the wad of fabric against the seam where the stone wall met the floor. Light gleamed from the blades of her knives as she loosened them from their sheaths.

"You'll need that to get out of here," he said, gesturing with one of the lamps toward the discarded robe.

"If what I suspect is true, we're not getting out. But I want to be free to fight, whatever happens."

He handed Sonya back her glow lamp, then bent down to scoop up the robe. "Why don't I hang on to this for you, just in case?" Mathis didn't want to waste any more time, and carrying the robe himself was easier than fighting with her about whether or not to keep it. He threw the robe over his shoulder and continued down the corridor.

A crack of light appeared in the near distance. "Marta should be on the other side of that door," he said in a low voice.

"Walk carefully. Don't make any noise. I want to listen to what's on the other side before we go through." Sonya squeezed around him to take the lead, and they covered the last fifty feet slowly and silently. She put her ear to the door.

"Are the berries in season?"

Sonya flinched from the door, but at the expected words, Mathis released a bit of the tension he held in his shoulders. "Picked fresh this morning," he said.

The door clicked and slid into the wall, and Mathis blinked in the light. A woman in a gray robe with a single band of silver around one sleeve stood before them in a small, rectangular chamber. Each of the other three walls contained a door, and an iron lamp hung from the middle of the ceiling. The woman's long, blonde hair fell in ringlets beyond her shoulders. She smiled in a way that seemed familiar, but her expression changed to one of astonishment as Sonya pushed past Mathis into the room.

In one swift motion, Sonya pulled Marta to her so the woman's back was to Sonya's chest and pressed a knife to her throat. "Who are you? Tell us now, or die instead," Sonya hissed.

The Master froze, her eyes full of fury. "I am Marta. Let me go this instant!"

"Sonya, what are you doing?" Mathis nearly yelled. "She said the right words."

"Words *Alia* told her to say, right?" Sonya's arm tightened around Marta's shoulders, drawing the knife closer.

"Yes, but—" Mathis paused. His mind chased a memory of something Kelda had said, months ago, when he'd been summoned to the Captains' tent after Ciara arrived in Vose. Sonya had been there, too. It was a question-and-answer code that women of the Conclave—or formerly of the Conclave—used to acknowledge their involvement in the rebellion. Something about jewelry, or gems, he thought...*Ah!*

"With what were you crowned?" he asked, hoping his instinct was correct. If not, then there was no telling what Sonya would do.

The corner of Marta's mouth twitched. "I was crowned with nothing but lies," she said.

Sonya held Marta a moment longer, then pushed her away. "Alia could have told her that, too," she grumbled.

"She didn't," Marta said, rubbing at her throat with her thumb and first two fingers. "You are Sonya? Why are you here? You are supposed to be waiting outside the walls. How did you get past the guards?"

Sonya shrugged. "Plans change. Don't they?" Her eyes narrowed again with suspicion.

"Yes—I suppose they do." Marta looked up at Mathis. "And for that I apologize. One of the other Masters was pushing to know my schedule today, and I got—well, paranoid. I thought it best to alter the route we'd originally planned, just in case, but then I realized I'd need help." She smiled apologetically.

Her expression again reminded Mathis of someone. After a moment, he was able to put his finger on it. With her hair and coloring, she looked a lot like Ciara. Perhaps Adepts shared similarities with one another, like the eunuchs.

Marta caught him staring and returned her own quizzical look. "Is something wrong?" she asked.

"Nah. I'd just realized that you remind me a bit of Ciara."

"I should hope so. She's my mother, after all." Marta chuckled at the shocked silence that followed. "Oh. Did she not tell you?"

Chapter 28

Sarabie

A THUD SOUNDED from outside her chambers. Sarabie twisted her head toward the entrance. "What was that?"

Calio had already darted to the door. He pressed his ear against the polished wood. His chest rose and fell as he listened.

"What's going on?" she whispered. Calio waved her off with a short, choppy motion of his hand. Her heartbeat quickened, and she pushed herself inelegantly from the chaise. *Is it time?*

They waited as several long moments passed. Just as Sarabie was ready to dismiss the noise as a false alarm, the bars to her prison rattled and scraped. Calio hopped backward and stumbled over the rug. The door opened, and a tall eunuch Sarabie didn't recognize rushed inside. A woman dressed in a black tunic and leggings followed, and behind her, a blonde-haired Master wearing a robe with a single silver band embroidered around the upper portion of one sleeve.

"Marta!" Sarabie cried. "Then it *is* true!"

Marta hurried to Sarabie's side. Her friend embraced her and then held her at arm's length, eyeing her protruding midsection. "Sarabie, Sarabie, my poor dear—look at you! Yes, it's true. I am going with you. I so wish I could explain everything to you now, but there's no time."

"And even less time than we had a few minutes ago," the woman in black said. "Do what you need to do, and let's go."

"All right. Sarabie, Calio: this is Sonya and Mathis. They're with Alia."

"Alia is with *us*," Sonya retorted as she surveyed the room.

"In any case," Marta continued with a small roll of her eyes at the black-clad woman's words, "they're here to help us get out. Calio, do you have the supplies?" Calio nodded and dashed into the bedroom.

Sonya remained near the door with her hands resting on the hilts of two knives sheathed at her waist. The woman fixed her eyes on the antechamber where usually a Guardsman kept post, her slim yet muscular body tensed and her expression stern. With trepidation, Sarabie wondered if all rebel women were like her.

At least the eunuch would be familiar. He prodded at the side of his leg, then fiddled with his belt. He raised his eyebrows when he caught Sarabie looking at him. "What?" he asked, in a voice much deeper than she expected.

"How is it that you came to live outside?"

"Huh?"

"Outside the Conclave," she clarified. "As a eunuch, how did you manage to escape?"

Mathis scowled as Sonya snorted with laughter. "I'm not a eunuch."

"But you look like—"

"I'm *not*," he huffed.

"Want to check?" Sonya smirked, shaking her head. "I'm sure he wouldn't mind. You could tuck your hand right down—"

"Shut up, Sonya," Mathis said, his cheeks flushed.

"He's not a eunuch, Sarabie," Marta said, grinning. "But it's good for us that you thought he was."

"But...he looks like...and the tattoo—?"

"It's a clever disguise. Nothing more," Marta confirmed.

Calio's return saved Sarabie from further embarrassment. He dropped two leather satchels on the table, then shook out a gray Master's robe that had been draped over his arm. Light glinted from the intricate silver patterns along the robe's sleeves, neckline, and hem. *The robe of a senior Master.* A seed of doubt began to germinate inside of Sarabie. *Whose is it? Does she know it is missing?*

"That's what she's going to wear?" Sonya said. "Won't it be rather obvious she's not a Master, given her condition?"

"It's larger than she needs," Calio said, "and all the design work will draw eyes away from her midsection. I'm certain it will keep her pregnancy hidden from casual observers." The corners of his mouth turned down as he evaluated Sonya. "I don't know what we're going to do with you, though. You can't go outside dressed like that."

Mathis pointed to a swath of green fabric draped over the back of a chair. "She wore that coming in. She can wear it going out."

"A merchant's robe? I suppose that will work."

Sonya wrinkled her nose and brow. "Of course it will. People see what they want to see. Wearing that, the idiot Guardsmen at the gate didn't even question my claim of a meeting with Master Gersemi," she scoffed. "They sent us straight through."

"What?" Marta exclaimed. Her face had gone pale, and Calio looked as if he might be sick. Anxiety surged through Sarabie at their response, though Alia's friends seemed not to notice.

"She told the Guards she was a merchant here to meet Master Gersemi," Mathis said. "She even used her own name. Pure ego, this one."

"It worked, as I told you it would, and here we—"

"Silence, you fool!" Marta thundered. The two rebels looked at her with bewilderment. "Do you know what you've done? With the high alert in place, Master Gersemi gets a report every hour during the day of all visitors who pass through the gates. That is why only Mathis was to come; eunuchs aren't visitors. I assumed you had somehow avoided the Guards altogether to get in."

Marta's eyes darted around the room, searching until she spotted the clock. "The next report will be delivered to her in twenty minutes! Calio—help Sarabie change. And you," she said, pointing to Sonya, "get back into your merchant's garb. If we're to have any hope at all, we must flee at once."

Sonya pulled the green robe over her head as Calio ran to Sarabie's side. He helped her unfasten her brown robe, and it fell to the ground around her ankles. She turned around and reached one arm behind her to receive the robe from Calio. Mathis gawked at her as she dressed, his cheeks flushed. *How odd*, she thought. *Why would he stare? I'm merely changing clothes.*

"Let's go—oh!" Marta cocked her head to the side. "It's Alia." She closed her eyes.

Despite the imminent danger, Sarabie felt a twinge of jealousy that Alia had reached out to Marta instead of her. Yet it was no matter. Soon enough, she would talk to her friend in the flesh.

But first we must get out of here. Sarabie watched the clock as they waited for Marta to finish her communication, growing more and more fearful with each second that passed before Marta's eyes fluttered open.

"We're clear to leave," Marta reported. "Alia detects no Ability directed here or along our path."

"Let's move out," Sonya said. Without waiting for any acknowledgment from the others, she sprinted out the door.

"Wait!" Marta said, grabbing one of the satchels from the table. "You don't know the way..." Her voice faded as she chased after Sonya.

Mathis gestured to Sarabie and Calio. "Go, go! Follow them. I'll be right behind you."

"What about Stefan?" Sarabie asked. "Needn't we wait for him?"

"He'll meet us along the way," Calio said. He removed a small glow lamp from the remaining satchel and held it out to her. Sarabie's hand trembled as she took the device. Calio smiled encouragingly. "Hurry now, my dear. We've not much time." He ushered her before him into the antechamber.

Exhilaration coursed through Sarabie as she stepped over the wood-and-metal threshold. *This is happening.* She could hardly believe she would soon be truly free.

A red tapestry to the right of the door quivered against the wall. Calio activated his glow lamp with his thumb and pushed the tapestry to the side with his other hand, revealing a dark, narrow corridor. Sarabie hurried after the bobbing weave of lamplights before her. Behind them, the bars of her former prison clanked as they moved back into place.

Mathis soon caught up to her and Calio, and the three of them rejoined Marta and Sonya at the end of the corridor. A door blocked their way. Marta pushed against the side of the wall with the heel of her hand, seemingly at nothing, and the door slid open.

Light from their five glow lamps merged to dimly illuminate a small room with three doors. They passed under an unlit iron lamp to the opposite wall. Marta activated another hidden mechanism to open the far door. Once they had all passed through, she pushed against that side of the wall. The door slid shut.

The group continued down a narrow, dust-filled corridor. Sarabie closed her eyes and stifled a sneeze. She had no idea if they were anywhere near where residents of the Conclave might be, but she feared making any unnecessary noise. If she were the reason their escape attempt failed—no. *Don't think like that.* They would not fail. She had waited too long for this chance, and Marta and Alia would not let her down.

Sarabie's confidence lagged when she noticed the steep staircase at the end of the hall. Her back and legs already ached from their hurried pace. Sonya flew up the stairs, taking two at a time, and Marta was nearly as quick. Sarabie's heart sank. How was she to get up all those steps?

Calio squeezed next to her and put one arm around her back. "I'm right here."

With his help, Sarabie managed about a third of the way up before she had to stop. Her breath chafed her lungs, and her face burned. "I...can't..."

Her feet suddenly lifted from the ground, and if she'd had the breath to do so, she would have cried out. Mathis cradled her in his arms and carried her to the top of the steps. He set her gently on her feet near where Sonya and Marta waited in front of yet another door. "Thank you," Sarabie whispered in a ragged voice.

Marta brushed stray hairs away from Sarabie's forehead. "Breathe. We're going to be outside soon, and you must appear calm." She pulled a key from her robe and unlocked the door. Calio opened it and poked his head outside, then quickly pulled back and nodded once.

"Go!" hissed Marta, shoving the door open the rest of the way with her shoulder.

Sarabie bumped into the others in her haste to follow. They went to the right and through an unlocked door set against the left-hand wall. Stacks of crates and baskets took up most of the large room, and a workbench laden with pots and garden tools stood next to a door set with four small frosted-glass panes. A eunuch with bright-red hair jumped up from where he sat on a crate.

Marta hastened forward and clasped the eunuch's hands. "Stefan! We must get out before Master Gersemi receives her next ledger of visitors. I don't think we have that much time left."

"We can move quickly, but we can't run." He lifted his chin toward Sonya. "Who's that?"

"That's Sonya. She came with Mathis."

"Another rebel?" One of his eyebrows twitched.

"Yes. I'll explain later. She will walk with you and me. Let's go."

Stefan opened the windowed door, and Sarabie stepped outside. The brilliant azure sky nearly took her breath away, and she shaded her eyes from the bright sunlight. *How much life have I missed, locked away as I've been?* She breathed in deeply, filling her nose with scents of earth and fertilizer. Songbirds called to one another, and a bee buzzed by her head.

Mathis maintained his position behind her as she walked next to Calio through a vegetable garden at an aggravating, sedate pace. They passed a few eunuchs toiling to harvest the summer's bounty, but none looked her way. Even if they had, they were not house servants, and would not know her on sight—especially as she appeared now, garbed in the robe of a Master.

"It's down this way," Calio murmured over his shoulder as they approached the outer wall of amber and yellow stones.

"You're certain no one else will be there?" Mathis asked.

"Yes. It's not often used because only a few eunuchs have the key. And none of them besides Stefan are in residence this week."

"I still don't see why we couldn't have come in that way, like we planned," Mathis groused.

Calio shrugged. "Here it is." He pushed aside a thick cascade of ivy.

BONG...BONG...BONG...

Sarabie's heart skipped a beat and bile rose in her throat. Marta, Sonya, and Stefan sprinted toward them, the women's robes tangling around their legs.

"What is that?" Mathis asked.

"It's an alarm," Calio whispered, his face drained of color. "Come down here. The ivy may hide us." Sarabie allowed Calio to lead her down a few steps to a short metal door. Her heart pounded, louder to her own ears than the bells that signaled her doom.

BONG...BONG...BONG...

Stefan jumped down the steps and fumbled with a large key. Calio snatched it from his fingers and deftly inserted it into the lock. "There's still time. They may not know where we've gone yet." The mechanism clicked, and he pushed open the door. "Go!"

BONG...BONG...BONG...

Sonya ran through the door first. Sarabie clung to Calio's words, and the hope they provided, as she trotted after the green-robed woman. Despite the danger, she couldn't help but feel giddy at being outside the walls of the Conclave for the first time in over a year. *I am free!*

BONG...BONG...BONG...

A shout and clash of metal caused Sarabie to look back over her shoulder. Calio was dragging Marta away from Mathis and... *Stefan?*...who were fighting each other with short swords.

What?

Sarabie didn't know what to do. Calio and Marta ran down the street bordering the wall, but she'd have to pass the fighting to follow them. Should she go down the street closest to her and hope Mathis came her way? Or follow Sonya? She didn't move, frozen with indecision.

BONG...BONG...BONG...

A flash of motion passed by in her peripheral vision. Ahead, Sonya ducked down and yelled something she couldn't hear. A sharp pain blossomed under Sarabie's left armpit. Sonya ran back toward her, but then lurched backward and crumpled to the ground. Blood flowed from a tangle of skin and muscle at the woman's throat. The large bolt that had punctured clear through her neck skittered against the cobbles.

BONG...BONG...BONG...

Sarabie's scream was cut short by a thrust to her lower back. Gasping, she fell to her hands and knees not far from Sonya's unmoving body.

Sarabie? Sarabie! The intrusion into her mind was faint, yet persistent. Sarabie somehow managed to push back with her right arm to sit on her ankles. Confusion and pain clouded her thoughts.

I...an enormous surge...couldn't get through...

BONG...BONG...BONG...

Sarabie clenched her eyes against the agony coursing through her body. What had gone wrong? Only minutes before, she had felt such elation—and now...*Don't give up*, she told herself. *Move. Get away.* A quick breeze brushed past the side of her face, and then another.

BONG...BO—

CHAPTER 29

ALIA

A CRUSHING AGONY enveloped Alia as she felt Sarabie's life slip away. She squeezed her eyes tight against what she could not see as tears flowed. Her breathing increased in pace until it became a pant. A child's wail grew in volume, competing with shouts and the increasing pressure in Alia's mind and heart.

Someone pushed her torso forward so her head fell between her knees. "Breathe, dammit," a woman ordered. Alia tried to acquiesce to the command, but her lungs had a mind of their own. A din of agitated conversation surrounded her, and her ragged breaths turned into lurching sobs. She wrapped her arms under her thighs and succumbed to pain and sorrow.

Alia's abdominal muscles were sore and weak by the time she regained control of her emotions. The rushing noise in her ears cleared, and she lifted her head. Nyona sat in the upholstered chair next to the sofa, cradling Tovi on her lap. She stroked the child's dark curls as Tovi sniffed away her tears. Tovi's face was red and splotchy, and her lower lip trembled. Ciara and Kelda stood next to the chair, gripping each other's hands. Their eyes, full of fear, were fixed on Alia.

Levina sat next to her on the sofa. "Have we lost them all?" she asked quietly.

Alia pushed against her knees to slowly sit upright. "I don't—I don't know. I only know that—" She took a deep breath to steady herself. Once she spoke the words, it would be real. "Sarabie is dead. I think Sonya is, too. I don't know about the others."

Kelda covered her mouth with her hand. Tovi whimpered, and tears filled Nyona's eyes. Ciara hugged herself around her waist, her face pale and drawn. "What happened?" Ciara asked in a tremulous voice. "Tovi couldn't explain."

"I don't know that I can, either. It happened so fast." Her fingers brushed against the hair of her wig as she rubbed at her temples. They'd been so careful, even changing the plan at the last minute when Marta expressed concern about being watched. No one knew of their plan who should not; the barrier Alia maintained around her Ability when she reached out to Marta and the others had been impenetrable.

Then how?

Levina shook Alia's shoulder gently to get her attention. "Tell us what you can. I need to figure out how bad things are for us."

Alia tried to focus past her sorrow to report on what she'd observed through her Ability. "I detected no Ability directed along their path, so I thought they were safe. In fact, there was very little Ability being used anywhere within the Conclave's walls at the time..." *Idiot. That was your first clue, and you ignored it.*

She swallowed before continuing. "I passed on that information to Marta, and she said they were leaving. After that, I didn't want to reach out to her again until enough time had passed for them to get outside the walls. I didn't detect any Ability for some time after that, so I thought all was well."

Her voice dropped to a near whisper. "But then came an intense surge out of nowhere—it felt like I was being bombarded from all sides all at once. Tovi tried to help, adding her Ability to mine, but

I couldn't break through. I tried to warn Sarabie—I-I tried..." she trailed off as grief threatened to overcome her once again.

Levina patted and rubbed her back. "We know you did. But—are you certain Sarabie is dead? And Sonya, too?"

Alia leaned her forehead on the hand of the arm she had propped against her knee. Her head pounded. "I—felt Sarabie die. And just before, I sensed some of what she saw, including some sort of fight and Sonya bleeding and unmoving on the ground." She gritted her teeth against the memory of Sarabie's final thoughts, which had been nothing more than a chaotic amalgamation of pain, regret, and confusion.

Levina sighed, raking both hands through her short, graying hair. "Well, we all knew this plan was a long shot. We rolled the dice and lost." She smacked her palms against her knees and stood up. "But we're not going to stick around to see what else they might have up their sleeves." She moved swiftly from the sofa to the back door, then slid the door open a fraction. Outside, the cheerful, summer sun mocked their plight. "Avrey! Go fetch Captain Jana from the docks right now. Now, I said!"

"A coordinated attack," Kelda mused as Levina closed the door and turned back to the room. "Quite unexpected. I should consult the book, to see if it speaks of this. I wonder if it is a specific technique meant to overwhelm—"

"There's no time for academic exploration, Kelda," Levina said. "We're leaving. We have to presume we're compromised here."

"But Alia didn't tell anyone where we were staying in Quental, did she?" asked Nyona, looking back and forth between Alia and Levina. "Shouldn't we wait a bit to see if the others return? Hasso might be bringing them back on the boat even now."

"Yes, please," Ciara said, wringing her hands. "We must wait. Alia only knows what happened to Sarabie and Sonya. The others might have survived."

"No," Levina said with finality. "We can't assume we're safe here, especially given that we don't know why things went as wrong as they did." She tilted her head slightly to the side. "I'm sorry, Ciara. If they are safe, they will find us—and quickly if they're with Hasso.

And if they are not safe—well, we will have lost *everything* if the Conclave gets to Alia and Tovi, too. We've time to throw together a few essentials, but once Jana and Avrey return, we're leaving."

"But what if something happened to Hasso and he wasn't waiting at the docks in Corval?" Ciara pressed, worry and concern etched into the lines of her face. "And what if Marta has been taken? Do we leave her behind?"

For some inexplicable reason, Ciara's focus on the fates of Hasso and Marta alone filled Alia with a sudden rage. "Aren't you forgetting a few people? Or are Mathis, Calio, and Stefan not that important to you? The others in the team might still be alive, too. Do you not care about their fate? Are you not bothered by Sonya's death? Or *Sarabie's*?" She was yelling by the end.

Ciara looked as if she might cry. "I do care about them. It's just that—well, I've known Hasso longer than the others, and Marta is my daughter. To lose her now that we're so close—"

"Like we lost Sarabie?" Alia shot back, her anger unassuaged. "Sarabie is dead. Dead! Because of us." *Because of me.*

"Alia—" Levina began.

"It's true!" Alia interrupted, seeking to deflect her own guilt. "We changed the plan at the last minute. Marta told us of her worry, but *we* decided to make a change." Alia opened her eyes wide as her anger found a new target. It seemed so obvious, now that the thought had crossed her mind. "Hasso's the one who came up with the new plan. He must have known what was going to happen. He betrayed us somehow."

"Impossible," Levina said, as Kelda and Ciara both shook their heads with vigor.

"Mathis told me what he once was. An *Extir*. They know nothing else but to lie. You all think you know him, but you don't. He and Owen were probably working together all along." Alia was babbling, but she couldn't stop now that it all seemed so clear. It wasn't her fault that Sarabie died; it was Hasso's.

"Hasso *saved* your life after Owen tried to kill you," said Kelda, a befuddled expression on her face. "Why would he do that if he were in league with the Conclave?"

"I don't—I'm sure there's some reason," Alia stammered. "Maybe he wanted to throw us off so we'd get closer to Corval. So the Masters could pluck me and Tovi right out of your grasp."

"Owen tried to kill Tovi, too," Levina reminded her. "Look, no one is pretending that losing Sarabie is not of consequence. And if any of the others are lost—including Sonya and those who joined us from the other units—it will be a crushing blow. But Hasso did *not* betray us."

Alia shook her head at Levina's words. "He did. I know he did."

"Get a hold of yourself," Levina said, her tone brooking no further dissent. "We've probably worked with Hasso for longer than you've been alive. We know him. You're simply wrong."

"Hasso would never betray me or my child," Ciara said.

"How can you be so certain?" Alia insisted.

"Because Hasso and I have been partners since shortly after I was assigned to be his liaison when I was newly a Master."

Nyona, her mouth agape, appeared to share Alia's surprise at Ciara's confession, but Levina and Kelda seemed unfazed by the news. Yet it did make a certain amount of sense, once Alia thought back to all she knew of Ciara and Hasso and how they interacted with each other. She'd assumed they merely were like Nyona and Mathis: the protected, and the protector. Even so, the only people aware of their plan were those supposedly dedicated to the rebellion's cause, and the four people inside the Conclave who wanted nothing more than to escape. *Who else could it have been?*

The back door slid open, slamming within the pocket where the door disappeared into the wall. Jana strode in, Avrey at her heels. "What in fires is going on, Levina? Avrey ran up as if a unit of Guards was at his heels, saying you had demanded my return." Her cheeks were flushed, and a thin sheen of sweat glistened on her brow. The boy breathed heavily next to her, his stringy red hair all disheveled.

"They were attacked," said Levina. "We lost Sarabie. We don't know about the others."

Jana's eyebrows shot up, raising the scar along the side of her cheek with them. "*Fires*," she said. "Sarabie's dead? For certain?"

"Yes," Alia said without emotion.

"Fires," Jana said again, looking around the room as if she needed further reassurance of Alia's truth. "I guess that explains Hasso's signal."

"His signal?" Levina and Ciara said simultaneously.

"About ten minutes ago, I spied Hasso through the dock's scope. He and some others were in a rowboat out in the strait, and he signaled that the mission had been aborted. I was about to head back to find out if you knew what was going on when Avrey showed up."

Ciara let out her breath. "Who else was with him?"

"Mathis—he was rowing, and then there were two others I didn't recognize. Thought one of them might be Sarabie, until I saw his signal. I checked the traffic in the strait, and didn't see the others. I'm guessing now that Sonya's taking extra precautions before heading back."

"She's not," Alia said. "She's dead, too."

Jana's scar stood out red and angry against the sudden paleness of her face. "Truly?"

"Yes," Alia said. "Sonya's dead. Sarabie's dead." How many times would she have to say it? Did they think that if she denied it, the truth would be different? *If only I had such power.* What good was it to be Sempiternal if she couldn't prevent harm to those closest to her? Today's events only proved the absurdity of believing that a single Adept, no matter how powerful, would ever be able to challenge the might of the entire Conclave.

It's hopeless.

Levina shook her head. "Alia doesn't know for certain, Jana, but it doesn't look good. If Sonya's not with Hasso and Mathis, we have to assume the worst."

Jana nodded. "Which means that we must flee. Again." Her face clouded with anger and disappointment.

"Yes. For now."

CHAPTER 30

NYONA

NYONA PAUSED TO kiss her daughter on top of her head as she passed behind her. Tovi sat at the end of the table near Kelda and Ciara, watching the women write in leather-bound books spread open before them. Lamps on both ends of the table illuminated their efforts. It had become a nightly routine; the former Masters would spend hours, until well past after everyone else had gone to bed, copying from both *A History of Corinas* and Kelda's notes detailing her study of the book. At least this safe house, where they'd spent the last two nights, had a proper table for their work.

The decision to duplicate the book and Kelda's notes should have been made long ago. Losing either would set the rebellion back years, and after the failed effort to rescue Sarabie, they couldn't afford any further losses.

Nyona still found it hard to believe how badly things had gone for them in Corval. What was to be a major coup had turned into an absolute disaster. While no one had expected it to be easy,

Nyona had been confident in their plan's ultimate success. Yet thanks to Marta's traitorous eunuch, Stefan, the Conclave had known they were coming. Sarabie and Sonya had died, as had those joining them from other rebel groups.

Now, here they were, three weeks later, running from the Conclave and trying to pick up the pieces once more.

Alia slumped across a bright blue armchair near the door to the kitchen. Her bald head rested against the chair's short, wide back while her legs dangled over one of the chair's arms. A blanket partially covered the young woman's body, and her white-blonde wig lay discarded on the floor beside the chair. Alia stared out a window as rain pattered against the glass pane. She continued to mourn deeply for the friend she'd lost.

It could have been far worse, Nyona thought. In those horrible moments when she hadn't known Mathis's fate, she'd realized how much he had come to mean to her. It was a feeling she'd denied for far too long, and the moment she saw him safe in Quental, she'd resolved to tell him.

She just hadn't found the right time yet.

As if her thoughts had been a beacon, the front door opened, and Mathis entered the small home that belonged to some many-removed relative of somebody affiliated with the rebellion. Mathis's brown hair was damp, and the fabric of his green shirt was mottled from the rain. He caught her eye and smiled briefly as he crossed the room, and then he disappeared into the bedroom he shared with Calio, Avrey, and Hasso.

Nyona bit at her lower lip, considering if now might be the time. Before she could change her mind, she walked to Mathis's door and tapped the wooden panel with two of her knuckles.

"Ya," came Mathis's muffled response.

Nyona opened the door, her stomach a bundle of nerves. Mathis sat on the edge of one of the lower bunks set against the bedroom's wall, rifling through his travel pack. "Are you busy?" she asked.

He flashed a half smile. "No. Come in." He shoved the pack against the wall.

Nyona closed the door behind her. She sat down on the empty

bunk across from him, uncertain how to begin. It wasn't as if she could come right out and say she loved him, out of nowhere. It was better to begin with safer topics. "Is Calio any better?" she asked.

"Not really." Mathis leaned forward to rest his elbows and fore-arms on his thighs, clasping his hands together. "If I didn't know any better, I'd say something had been going on between him and Sarabie. He acts as if he lost a partner."

"What would you know of such things?" Nyona teased, but then dropped her lilting tone at his affronted glare. "Well, he did care for her for a long time," she pivoted. "And he feels responsible for what happened. Marta, too. They blame themselves for not knowing Stefan's true intentions."

"They're not the only ones," he said, staring at his feet.

"You can't blame yourself; you didn't know Stefan at all. You hadn't even met him before that day. How could you possibly have known he was acting on behalf of the Conclave?"

Mathis glanced up at her. "That's not what I meant." He sighed —a short, soft sound—then looked down again. "I-I shouldn't have let her go." Sorrow tinged his words.

Nyona furrowed her brow. "Sarabie? Marta said she ran ahead —"

"Sonya."

Nyona could not have been more astonished. For as long as she'd known him, Mathis had been unrepentant in his disdain toward Sonya, refusing to let go of the stubborn grudge he'd held since they were teenagers. Before this moment, he'd not even seemed to mourn her passing. Indeed, this was the first time Nyona had heard him even speak Sonya's name since he'd acknowledged that he'd witnessed her death.

She crossed over to his bunk and sat next to him, taking his hands. His palms were rough and callused under the knuckles of each finger. "Talk to me," she said, hoping he would.

He remained silent for a few moments before he spoke again. "At first, I think I was in shock it had happened. Sonya'd always man-aged to survive things she had no business surviving. Deep down, I must have figured the same thing would happen in Corval, no matter how stupid she acted. I guess that's why I didn't fight back harder when she pulled rank and said she'd be going with me inside the Conclave, especially when the others agreed with her plan."

Mathis stared across the narrow room, avoiding Nyona's eyes. "I spent over a decade hating her for getting so close to Hasso. It didn't help that after she started training with him, she moved up in the ranks of the rebellion very fast and shoved it in my face, knowing I could never achieve the same as a man. I don't think she'd have been pleasant to be around even if I'd tried to mend things between us. But she was the last connection I had to my parents. Her being gone makes it seem like that part of my life never happened."

Nyona squeezed his hands, taken aback by his emotional honesty. "Your memories of your parents are true, no matter what. Sonya's passing can't diminish them."

Her words didn't seem to have much effect, though he nodded in an obligatory fashion. "I should have insisted that she stay behind, like she was supposed to," he said. "Or I should have gone after her and Sarabie instead of being so fixated on killing that damned eunuch. Maybe the both of them would have survived if I had."

"Mathis, that *anyone* survived was because the Masters didn't expect Sonya to be there and because they sorely underestimated you. You can't second-guess yourself now. Besides, if you hadn't continued to fight Stefan, there's no way Marta and Calio would have escaped. And if you'd gone after Sarabie and Sonya, then—" Her voice caught. "Out in the open like that, you probably would have died as well."

He brushed his thumb back and forth against her hand, then gazed down at her with emerald eyes gone dark. "Would that have saddened you?" he asked quietly.

Nyona swallowed around the lump in her throat. "Of course," she said. The barest hint of a smile appeared at his lips, and he lowered his head toward hers.

The door opened, and Nyona and Mathis broke apart from each other. Hasso stepped into the room, his face expressionless. "The Captains want to speak to everyone," he said, gesturing behind him. As he pivoted to walk away, his braid slipped from his shoulder to fall down his back. He didn't bother to close the door.

Nyona's heart raced. Hasso hadn't noticed what had almost happened. *What* did *almost happen?* As they stood from the bunk, she smiled uncertainly, not knowing if she'd imagined that Mathis had meant to kiss her. Yet when he pressed his hand gently against the small of her back to lead her before him, that simple contact confirmed she hadn't misread his intent.

Out in the main room, most everyone else had already gathered. Levina, Marta, and Jana had joined Ciara and Kelda at the table, though Jana stood, as there weren't enough chairs to go around. As they waited, Kelda chewed on a fingernail, and Levina propped her elbow on the table, resting her chin in her hand.

Nyona looked back at Mathis and motioned toward her daughter, who now sat on Alia's lap. Mathis nodded and remained by the door while she moved to stand near Tovi. She passed Hasso along the way. He leaned against the wall, his ankles crossed and his arms folded across his chest—and his attention focused on Ciara, as it often was.

Ciara whispered something to Marta. Next to each other, their resemblance was striking: they had the same blonde, curly hair; the same hazel eyes flecked with brilliant blue; and the same short, pert noses and full lips. Perhaps the obviousness of their relationship was one of the reasons the Conclave had kept Ciara so far away from Corval. No Adept was supposed to know who her mother was, just as no Master was supposed to know which Adept was her daughter —*or that she'd birthed a son*, Nyona thought, glancing toward Mathis. How Ciara and Marta had found out about each other— and had communicated secretly for years—still remained a mystery to her.

Calio and Avrey came in from the kitchen and stood near Nyona. Avrey wiped his hands on a towel tucked into his waistband. "This won't take long, will it?" the red-haired boy complained. "I just put something in the oven."

"You will stay for as long as I require," Jana said sharply.

"Yeah," Avrey said, his eyes cast down at the reprimand. "Just don't be getting mad, then, if something burns when I'm not in there to mind it," he muttered, low enough that Jana wouldn't hear.

Levina clasped her hands together on top of the table. "Now that we're all here, I'll get started. As you know, we'd hoped to have caught up to Captain Keya's group by now. That we haven't leads us to believe that the Conclave's knowledge of our plan ran deeper than we thought. It's too risky for us all to be in the same place right now. So, we're splitting up."

Her pronouncement left Nyona feeling uneasy. Where would they go? Whom would she go with?

Ciara voiced Nyona's questions. "How do you want us split up? I assume we will be headed to different destinations."

"Yes. We're just going to split into two groups. Some of us will continue south, toward Aldham. That group, led by me, will try to gather up what's left of our cause. Hopefully, we'll find not only Captain Keya, but also all the others who headed south after the last rendezvous at Eads. Everyone else, led by Jana, will head west to establish our new headquarters near Brome."

Nyona coughed to clear her throat. "Brome? Are you serious?"

"Yes," Jana said. "We will not go to Brome itself—there is nothing left standing there to shelter in, in any case—but there are plenty of other defensible locations in the mountains. Plus, the Conclave's Guards searched through there already, and with winter coming on, they will not return any time soon. We will have plenty of time to set up a strong—and hidden—post."

"When are we leaving?" Kelda asked. "Each group should take their own copy of the text and my notes. We're not quite done, but if Ciara and I hurry, I think we could complete our work sometime tomorrow."

"Write faster," Levina said. "We're leaving tonight, after we eat."

Kelda looked at Levina as if she were daft. "But-but—we must create an index of findings between the two, and copy that into—"

"There's no time for that," Levina interrupted. "I want to leave under the cover of darkness. If anyone's been following us, they won't expect us to travel at night. So finish up what you can in the next few hours. You're almost done copying the book, yes?"

Kelda opened and closed her mouth several times before she capitulated. "Yes; I only have a few pages left. I suppose the index can wait," she said glumly.

"Good girl," Levina said with a smile. "As for the groups: Kelda, Mathis, and Alia will come with me. Everyone else will go with Jana."

"What?" Nyona said with alarm.

"Tovi is my charge," Mathis protested. "I should stay with her."

"We can't have our two Adepts in the same group. And frankly, Alia needs you more than Tovi does," said Levina, cocking her head to the right.

"I agree," Kelda said, nodding. "I'm convinced that surge in Corval was specifically designed to disable a Sempiternal. Until I can find a way to defend against their new technique, Alia must be well protected. Mathis is our best fighter."

"Exactly," Levina said. "And in a small group, we'll be able to hide her more readily."

"You proved your mettle in Corval, Mathis," Jana said, adding her voice to the chorus of inevitability. "We need you to apply your efforts now to protect Alia. Tovi will be safe amongst the rest of us."

The Captains launched into a longer discussion of the logistics of their plan, but Nyona heard not a word of it. She was fixated on Mathis, wanting to remember everything she could about him. After tonight, she didn't know when—or if—she'd see him again.

"That's all," Levina concluded. "Pack up, everyone, and say your good-byes. We leave in two hours."

Mathis caught her gaze and lifted his chin toward the front door. "Tovi, love, go with Alia and make sure you're all packed up and ready to go," Nyona said. "I'll be there in a few minutes."

"Okay. Let's go, Alia," Tovi said as she hopped down from Alia's lap. The older Adept allowed the child to lead her to the room they shared with the other women.

Alia's expressionless demeanor drove home the wisdom of the Captains' decision, no matter how much Nyona disliked it. Since Corval, Alia had become more and more withdrawn, while Tovi had shown incredible strength. At the Captains' order, she'd even managed to perform covert truth assessments on the four who'd survived the raid on the Conclave. Alia had been useless at the time, and while Tovi had been distraught herself, she'd set her emotions aside to do what the Captains needed her to do. That day, Nyona had never been prouder of her daughter.

It was true; Alia *did* need Mathis more than Tovi did.

But what about what I need?

Nyona went outside and looked around for Mathis. The sun had dropped behind the hills to the west, and a black-and-blue sky moved in to displace the existing gray. Rain dripped from tree limbs, many still holding fast to autumn leaves in yellow, orange, and red. Mathis stood protected under the darkening shadows of the eaves of an outbuilding. She joined him under his shelter, moving in close.

"I take it they hadn't told you about this plan of theirs?" Mathis asked.

"No."

"By the time you even find a place to set up in the mountains, it'll be well into winter."

"It sounds like that's the idea—to buy more time before they come looking for us."

"They're already looking."

"I know."

They listened to the last remnants of the rain that had fallen all afternoon. The first part of their journey that night would be a damp, muddy mess. She shivered involuntarily.

Mathis put his arm around her shoulders. "Are you cold? Maybe it's best to stay inside while we can."

He'd misread the reason for her shiver, but she reveled in the contact, no matter the cause. "No. Once we go back inside, we'll have to get ready to leave. And I'm not ready for that just yet."

"You're strong, and a survivor. You'll get through this just fine."

"As will you," she said, wrapping her arm around his waist to pull him closer. Her heart beat faster as he settled against her side. *Now is the time,* she thought. It might be the last chance she'd have.

Her stomach fluttered with butterflies as she searched for the right words. She couldn't come right out and say it—she just couldn't. "Mathis…please be careful. I need you to return to me safely," she said.

He looked at her with hope and expectation. "As Tovi's protector —or something more?"

Her heart skipped in her chest. "Definitely something more."

Mathis turned toward her and pressed his lips against hers, hesitantly at first, but then with greater urgency as she leaned into him. A thrill of excitement coursed through her as the kiss shifted and grew deeper. Finally, she had to push herself away. Her skin felt flushed, and she wanted nothing more than to lead him someplace private—but they only had two hours, and she didn't want their first encounter to be rushed.

Instead, she canvassed his face, trying to memorize his features. There was a certain familiarity to him, as if she'd known him her whole life. *I wish I had. I wish we'd had more time.*

"We won't be apart forever," he said, as if he'd read her thoughts. "With luck, we'll find everyone we need to find quickly." He grinned. "And I'm feeling pretty lucky right now."

"Me too," she said, and reached toward him for another kiss.

Chapter 31

Master Gersemi

As she strode through the corridor, women looked down at the marble floor, up toward the silver-tiled ceiling, or anywhere else they could to avoid her eyes. Their deference was warranted as a matter of course, but especially so after today's meeting. *Fools. They're all such fools.* They acted as if their recent victory over the rebels meant the threat to the Conclave was over.

She knew better. The rebels were like those disgusting insects that resided in a hovel she'd once been subjected to on assignment as a young Adept. No matter what you did to get rid of them, they always came back.

The heels of her shoes clacked against the ground with each rapid step, and her robe, more silver than gray, swirled around her ankles. At the end of the corridor, two eunuchs dressed in black uniforms embroidered with silver stood before a double door carved with intricate patterns. As she approached, one scurried to grab the door's curved, silver handle.

"Master Gersemi," the servant said as he opened the door, his head bowed. She ignored his greeting and entered her private rooms. The heavy door shut behind her with a thud.

Inside, a fire burned brightly in the hearth, casting a comfortable warmth throughout her reception room. Overhead lamps illuminated paintings and the occasional red-and-silver tapestry. She paused in front of a rendering of the First Adept and pursed her lips. A thin layer of dust coated the painting's frame. It had been Stefan's job, back before she'd positioned him with Marta—her nose wrinkled in distaste at the thought of that traitorous child—to maintain the condition of her collection. Her current crop of servants were abject failures in comparison.

Ah, Stefan. You were not meant to be sacrificed so soon.

Mathis's skill in defending against Stefan's unique combat techniques had been—unexpected. And the presence of the rebel officer —a woman who had eluded them for years—had distracted the Guards. In the end, no one had reached Stefan in time, and all his training had been for naught.

To be fair, it was by pure, dumb luck they'd even learned of the rebels' ridiculous plan to "rescue" Sarabie. Stefan's assignment had been merely to monitor Marta's communications with Ciara. At the time, Gersemi never imagined that he'd end up uncovering a plot that extended well into the Conclave itself.

She walked across a large, dark-red rug to the massive wooden desk near the east-facing windows. Neat stacks of papers and books lay on the desktop. Some were reports of what was happening in Corinas in general—how the citizenry were getting along and the like—and a smaller stack contained the paltry, disappointing reports from her Guards out in the field.

There was still no sign of Mathis or the rebels who'd managed to get away with Marta. Even worse, they'd not found any other rebel groups since they'd destroyed that pathetic island enclave far to the west. The idiots around her thought that proved the rebels were finished. *Fools.*

Gersemi selected a report from the top of the stack and idly flipped through it. How could the rebels have just—*vanished?*

Before, even with stale news from Owen, she'd had *some* idea of what the rebels were up to. Allowing them the false belief that the Conclave was unaware of their activities—and locations—had actually helped to keep them in check. In fact, if the rebels hadn't come across Nyona, her child, and a copy of the rogue book, they'd still be under control today.

She pulled the leather chair away from the desk and sat down, perusing the piles of paper. One small stack was an updated report on Sempiternals—not that it did her much good now. She laughed to herself. Truly, what else could go wrong?

Her eighteen years as Headmaster had brought few regrets, but disassociating Alia from the Conclave was one of them. It had seemed a prudent use of resources at the time; the girl had always been difficult, and all agreed her usefulness as an Adept was rapidly coming to an end. She'd been designated for a male birth in any case, and the Masters in Generation had determined they could afford the loss.

Consequently, Gersemi had decided to use the girl as bait—calling her "Sempiternal," knowing the rebels would not be able to resist—in the hopes that once they took her in, Alia would work with Owen to scuttle the rebels' plans.

Anger flared up within her once again. *How could I have possibly known she actually* was *one?* There hadn't been a confirmed Sempiternal in nearly three hundred years. Gersemi clenched her hands into fists and tried to keep her breathing steady.

They'd had a scare nearly ten years ago, but they'd implanted the suspicious Adept just in case. The girl had been a notorious trouble-maker and deviant, worse than Alia'd ever been, and she was slated to be culled during Seclusion. Another Master had come up with the brilliant plan of implanting her during Ritual, in front of the other Adepts, as an object lesson. It had worked; the Adepts all believed the implant was due to the girl's well-known disciplinary issues, rather than because the Masters suspected her of a far greater taint.

After it was all over, and the girl cast out, further research con-firmed—so she'd been told at the time—that the Conclave had eradicated all lines linked to Sempiternals long ago. That false comfort likely was why she, and everyone else, had missed the true signs in Alia.

Someone knocked at her door. "Enter," she called.

The door opened and one of the eunuchs stepped inside, his eyes cast down. "Master Gersemi, Master Leyta is here. She says she brings the records you requested."

"Yes, yes. Send her in."

The servant bowed and removed himself from her sight. Leyta entered the room, carrying two thick tomes close to her chest. She hurried toward Gersemi and eased the books onto an empty spot at the corner of the desk's surface.

"Here they are. The original records from the past thirty years." Leyta brushed a lock of brown hair away from her face. "Her parents aren't listed."

"I'm sorry. I must have misheard you," Gersemi said. "You were just going to confirm what seemed to be an error in your working copies. You mean to tell me that the original record is *blank*? How is that possible?"

Leyta shrugged. "I have no idea. These records were curated long before I had access to them."

"Is there no one down there who had prior access?"

"No."

Leyta wisely left unspoken the fact that the Masters who led Generation when Alia was born had all perished during the plague. *Another regret.* Gersemi's scientists had promised her that having past or present Ability made one immune to the disease. She would have never allowed its dissemination into the wild otherwise. An outbreak of plague was meant to quell the uptick of interest in the rebellion's message, and in that, it had worked. The people of Corinas had turned their attention away from the group of upstarts and had focused instead on mere survival.

But the scientists had been wrong—or they'd lied. Either way, the end result was the same. The plague had killed a large number of Masters, and even worse, Adepts and former Adepts within Seclusion. The citizenry didn't know that, of course. They still believed the Conclave had remained untouched, and that belief helped strengthen the Conclave's power. If Ability could defy death itself, who could doubt the Conclave's right to rule?

She reached across the desk and pulled the top book toward her. "Is this it?" she asked, opening the book where it had been marked with a piece of rigid leather.

"Yes. That's the listing for all in her Initiate. See how those spaces are blank? It couldn't have been a mistake given that everyone else's are complete. That means the working copies are intentionally false."

Gersemi traced her finger down the page. Leyta was correct; nothing in Alia's record detailed the girl's true lineage. "Can't you piece it together based on the Seclusion records for the parent Initiate? Some sort of…process of elimination?"

"We're trying to do that now, but it's not obvious. Besides, even if we do figure out the mother, there's no way to learn who her father was."

Gersemi folded her fingers together on top of the open book and regarded Leyta. "And you're telling me that *no one* noticed this incomplete record before now?"

The younger Master held her gaze. "No one."

Gersemi squinted slightly, considering whether it would be worth the uproar she'd cause if she ordered truth assessments of every single Master in Generation. It was quite—*convenient*—that such an egregious lapse in record keeping had gone unnoticed until the moment it mattered the most. Gersemi suspected that someone had modified Alia's record once her impossible status became clear. After all, these were the same women who had assured her years ago that the Sempiternal lines had died out. It would be in their best interest to lie to her now.

Then again, the leadership of Generation had been under a great deal of stress for some time, so their distraction when it came to records might be plausible. Only three women of Alia's Initiate had successfully completed Generation thus far. Gersemi had already had to authorize more than two attempts for those who languished. It was a break from all protocol, but what else could she do? Ever since the plague, they'd had fewer and fewer Adepts born each year. She would do whatever she must to restore the Conclave's strength.

She hated to think about all the women they'd thrown out after failing Generation on the presumption that the plague had rendered them barren. Nyona had proven that theory incorrect. Who the father could be remained a mystery, however. All living sons of Adepts were purportedly accounted for, though in light of Alia's false record, Gersemi no longer trusted those reports.

I must have that child, Gersemi thought. Nyona's daughter belonged to the Conclave, no matter how she had been conceived.

She closed the book back on its mark. "Thank you for bringing these; I will examine them at my leisure."

"I wouldn't spend a lot of time on it; the records simply aren't there. And without knowing the identity of both parents, we won't be able to determine where there might be a lingering taint. I suppose we can take some solace in knowing that the father—whoever he was—is no longer here. All of the men in service now are well under thirty years old."

"True. Thank you, Master Leyta. You may go."

Once Leyta left and the door closed, Gersemi stood up from her desk. She walked to the fireplace and poked at the burning logs with a blackened metal tool that hung against the yellow stone wall. Embers drifted up into the chimney as fresh air circulated through the glowing debris.

Perhaps it was time to appoint new leadership. Leyta had proven a disappointment. In addition to this latest records failure, Gersemi still had not heard a satisfactory explanation for the sordid business with Sarabie. Leyta claimed they'd had no idea the new boy they'd used as part of Sarabie's ceremony would act the way he had, but the Masters in Generation were the ones who'd deemed him appropriate in the first place. How they had chittered with excitement after administering their tests! They'd thought he might be the one to turn things around, and she'd allowed them their delusion for the sake of morale.

At least he's no longer a source of trouble. That order had been easy to give.

In any case, he had not been the one they sought. The man destined to father the greatest Initiate of Adepts since the time of the Founding still remained infuriatingly outside the Conclave's control.

Gersemi crossed the room to stand before the arched window that faced west, toward the strait and the mainland of Corinas. The setting sun colored the clouds pink and orange and caused glints of light along the surface of the water. *You're out there somewhere. Where?* He couldn't have gone far, and her Guards were searching for him even now. He was to be returned to her, unharmed, as soon as possible.

No one would dare disobey her in that. She'd made herself quite clear.

She supposed she should thank Ciara for disobeying her own orders on that fateful day, long ago. Gersemi's predecessor had been hot tempered—and a fool. Why waste a child destined to father Adepts out of spite? Not long after the boy's foster parents were executed, the old Headmaster had died, and Gersemi had risen to take her place. Almost immediately, she'd rescinded the order and called off the Extirs. The decision had proven wise, as her later research pointed to him as being the key to the Conclave's restoration.

The corners of her lips turned up in a genuine smile. It made perfect sense, of course. Mathis was, after all, her own son.

Acknowledgments

Between work, school, and many other things, this book has been a long time coming. Thanks goes out to the following:

The participants of the 2005 South Bay NaNoWriMo write-ins, for encouraging my creativity and helping me avoid practicing for the law school entrance exam;

My readers at JukePop, for keeping me on task;

My team of editing and design professionals, for being fabulous and amazingly helpful;

My friends and family, for cheering me on;

My mother, Kathy, for teaching me how to read; and

My father, Leonard, for encouraging me to read stories worth the time.

Secrets
of the
Conclave